As You Wish

By Cathy Jackson

Edited by Jennifer Harshman, Harshman Services

Cover design by Desiree DeOrto

Acknowledgements

I want to thank GOD. Without Him, this story wouldn't be. I thank Him for teaching me and leading me every day.

Matthew Jackson, you are my heart and my life. Your encouragement has brought this book to life. Thank you for being my husband.

Connor, Ian, Jessa and Joseph, you are all my lights. I am so happy that each of you have been placed in my life. I love you all very much.

Jennifer Harshman of Harshman Services. I cannot express my gratitude of thankfulness. You took a chance on me. I hope that the chance you took pays off in spades!

Amy Miles and Danielle Bannister, you have inspired me to keep writing when I wanted to give up. You ladies are the BEST!

Desiree DeOrto at Desi's Art Designs, you are one of the most gifted women I know. Your talent with pictures is truly amazing! I am so thankful for friendship.

Jamie Taylor, Stacy Schuster, and Sharon Martin, you were my first beta readers. Your encouragements and ability to correct my errors make you my first choice for my next book!

Authors and Bloggers, your acceptance of who I am and what I write make you all golden in my book. I truly am thankful for each and every one of you.

Reader, this book has been a labor of love that I hope will encourage and inspire you. You are the ones who will make this book more than what I could ever make of it myself.

For Mom…

As You Wish

Chapter One

Daniel quietly descended the stairs, then slipped on his shoes and jacket. He pulled on a hat and a pair of large reflective sunglasses. Moving out his back door, he cut across his neighbor's yard and moved onto the quiet street of the town.

At 3 A.M. there was hardly any traffic out and it was the perfect time to think and clear his head. It was quiet and he could see the traffic lights change color as if there were cars moving along the road.

He walked for a while, not really noting where he was going. This was Gen's town, her hometown where she had grown up. He was from another country, another setting, but this was his life now and had become his dad's, too, after Daniel's mother died. Daniel knew this town— though not all of it—just where he and Gen had gone.

Gen and he had done a lot of things in this town and for the most part the locals were very good about their privacy and keeping the family hidden from the media. He was grateful for their thoughtfulness.

Sitting down on a bench, he watched as it began to rain softly. It was a very light rain— more of a heavy mist—and he huddled into his long coat. It wasn't a cold rain like it would have been in his own country. He gazed at the road as the water slowly began to collect into a small puddle.

He didn't see the woman as she made her way down, appearing out of the mist like a ghost. He didn't see that she wasn't really looking where she was going but just wandering.

Looking up, Elizabeth saw a bench and sat down on it. She had on a short jacket and a wide-brimmed hat, both of which kept the rain from her, not that she noticed it had started raining.

She was lost in memory: the memory of her husband and their life together. They had five wonderful children when he was taken from her. His life insurance covered the mortgage on their American home with a considerable amount left over.

The idea to move to a different country had been appealing. So after she lost her husband, she and her children pulled out a map and decided where their new home would be. They had not lived in their American home long and had not really made it theirs.

After they had picked a country, the youngest of her children closed his eyes and picked a town. They sold the house, got passports and visas, packed up, and started a new life. Everyone was excited when the youngest picked the place they were moving.

Elizabeth and each child had a large suitcase and a small carry-on as they left the house that was just a place to live. She had left a large amount in the bank to accrue interest while they were away. They were ready to begin again.

They had checked their bags at the airport and each had their carry-on as they boarded the plane. They had been nervous and excited as they took their seats. She had tried to reassure her children and had told them what to expect as they made their way there.

The kids were happy to be taking this trip. They knew that moving to a different country would be both exhilarating and new.

When the plane landed after the long flight, they exited, staying very close to one another. They hadn't been familiar with the customs, although she and her oldest son had done as much homework as they could, and they tried to understand what was going on around them.

She had been looking at a map of the terminal when she bumped into a man wearing a trench coat and mirrored sunglasses. Immediately she dropped the map and felt his hands steady her.

"Are you alright?" She had heard the man say. She hadn't known why, but his accent and voice sounded really familiar. She shrugged it off, not taking the time to think about it.

"Yes." She stepped back from him, blushing. "We are just in from America and my family and I have never been here before. We were looking for the luggage carousel and," she had leaned forward, whispering quietly, "I got lost." She moved her eyes to her children, and smiling brightly, she leaned back away from him.

She saw him pick up her map and hand it back to her. He'd glanced around and then leaned over the map. Placing his finger on the map, he pointed out an area. His hand had a light feathering of hair at the top.

"You take a left here and then a right there." He looked up at her to see if she followed. When she'd nodded her head, he continued. "This symbol here," he pointed to it, "is what you are looking for. Got it?" She nodded her head again. "Good. Any other questions?" He didn't really have time to answer any, but she was new, as he had been once, and he would answer anything else she asked about.

"No, thank you." He hadn't introduced himself, but as she scrutinized his features, half covered by the ball cap and mirrored sunglasses, she thought he looked familiar.

"Right. Welcome to Great Britain!" He smiled and she thought she had seen that smile before. Her own lips answered his and she watched him move away from her.

She turned to her kids. "Lost, huh, Mom?" Her second child looked at her and then the man's retreating back. "Looks like we know where we are going now, thanks to that guy." He snickered and she blushed again. She looked again to the man who had helped her and she shrugged. Maybe he was an angel. One really didn't know. She knew angels were real. Maybe she had just met one.

"Alright, guys. Let's grab our stuff." They made their way to the luggage carousel and retrieved their things.

They hailed a cab outside and it took them to the small bed-and-breakfast where she had rented rooms. She had seen the pictures online and read the reviews hoping that everything she read was true.

It was a big house and the rooms that she had put the money down on were spacious.

Meals were served at the same times each day and there were plenty of sights for the kids to see.

They made their way to the place and noted it was exactly as described. She checked in with the children and met Mabel, the woman who ran the house. She was a nice lady with a wonderful husband. She showed them to their rooms, which adjoined, and they settled their things in, ready to rest after such a long flight. Soon after, they found a church and explored the town a bit.

Now, as she sat on the bench in the rain, she wondered if the kids were ready to move on again. She felt restless herself, and was ready to move on. She had already lost so much: her husband, her mother, her father, and her only brother. All had died in less than five years. She hoped disaster didn't follow her. She needed a time of peace.

But tomorrow was Sunday, her favorite day of the week, and she would take the kids to the small church they had been attending since they had arrived in the town.

The pastor was an older gentleman who was very good with her kids. He had three grandchildren of his own and she wondered where the mother and father to those children were, but she never asked him. She knew the children were good and loved him, especially the youngest, who seemed to clutch onto her grandfather.

The church was small and the pastor gave an excellent sermon every Sunday morning and night. She wished there were evening services one night a week and had mentioned it to him. He had told her that right now was not a good time, as he was helping to raise his grandchildren, but if he could, he would try to work that in.

She thought she should go home. She really wasn't sure what time it was and she was tired, but her body couldn't rest. She shifted in the seat.

Daniel looked up then and noticed there was a woman sitting beside him. Her hat was wide-brimmed with a red lace ribbon around it. Her short black coat was thin and her long white dress (or was that a skirt to a nightgown?)Shone under it. It was thin, too.

What she was wearing appeared to be in good shape, so he thought her not to be a person without a home. But what was she doing out in the early morning hours, dressed like such and sitting all alone on a bench? She should be home, as should he, he realized.

He thought to talk to her, but what if she was someone who was waiting for him, to take more photos of him and his family? He thought to move away from her and began to do so.

Stupid tears, she thought. Grief closed over her and she felt the tears slide down her face. She sniffed and felt her nose run. That's just great. Here she was on a bench in the middle of the night, losing it. Awesome! Why did it have to be now?

When he heard the woman next to him sniffle, he stopped. Was something wrong with her? Did she need medical attention? He thought to move over to her now but decided against it. Instead, he opened his mouth to speak.

"Are you alright?" He looked to her now and saw her shoulders stand up. Her eyes found his.

"What did you say?" She had heard that voice before but didn't know where. It was elusive, like a dream.

"I asked if you were alright." He said the words again and noticed the tears falling down her face. She was crying, but what was wrong?

She was unsure how to answer that. Should she tell him yes and leave or be truthful with him? "No."

"Are you hurt, injured?" He looked her over but because of the dim light and because she was covered up, he didn't see anything physically wrong with her.

She shook her head and looked down again. "My heart hurts," she said quietly. The words that fell from her lips felt like a punch in his chest. His heart hurt, too, because he was missing his wife. "Why does your heart hurt, Miss..."

She looked at him. "My husband is dead and I am all alone. I mean, I have five children and I love them with everything that I have, but it's not the same as having a spouse."

She started crying again. She didn't mean to unload on him, but the words wouldn't stop falling from her mouth.

His wife was gone, too, and he knew how it felt trying to carry on day after day, making a life for his children without his wife beside him. He could see it was hard on her as well.

He gentled his voice before he began speaking to her. "Is that why you are walking around in the dark in your shift in the rain?"

She looked up. It was raining? She hadn't noticed that. As she did, she felt her clothes were soaked, but she couldn't seem to bring herself to care.

"I don't know why you care." She crossed her arms, her grief turning to anger. "It's not like you understand the loss of a spouse you have children with." She flounced and turned from him, shivering a little. The arrogance of some people.

He looked over at her. Now she was angry. At him? For what? "I don't care," he said, affecting a stance much like hers. "I just thought you might want to get some dry clothes on if you were going to be out in this weather."

And yes, he did understand losing a spouse, thank you very much. That is why he was out in the rain in the early morning.

She turned to him and moved closer to him, hands on her hips. "I tell you what, if you don't care, that is fine. I am doing just fine on my own and I don't need anyone. And if I want to sit out in the rain and freeze before I make my way back to my children so we can go to church, that is my business and not yours." She crossed her arms again. "Some people!" She looked out at the light as it changed from red to green.

He couldn't believe she had just spoken to him like that. People were mean and rude. He crossed his arms, too. "Do what you want, then." He looked out into the rain and across the town.

Her rage began to settle and she looked at him. She wanted to apologize but didn't know how. The rain had turned colder and she could feel it through her coat now.

"Look, mister, I'm sorry. Sometimes I just..." She shivered. "That was mean and uncalled for. I didn't..." She paused, hoping this was coming out right. "Look. I'm just sorry, okay?"

He nodded his head. A slow smile crossed his face. "It felt nice to yell at someone, didn't it?" He heard her laugh then.

Yes, yes it did." She laughed louder now. "Sometimes it just gets overwhelming, you know. I love him with all that I've got and now I've got no one to give that love to. I love my children, but it's not the same. I just wish sometimes..." She smiled, shivering again. "I don't know what I wish for."

"How long were the two of you married?" He knew the woman—the stranger in front of him—was hurting and wanted to make her feel better.

"Eighteen years."

"Yikes!" He gestured wildly. "That's a whole lifetime!" He knew he was overacting, but she was so sad.

She laughed. "I know! I lived it." She smiled again. "Every single day of my life was about this man and our family." She looked into the puddle on the street, which was bigger now, and she shivered again. "He had red hair and was tall—over six foot. He was kind and sweet and loving." Loving, really? She had just said "loving" to a total stranger whose voice sounded familiar to her? She gave up placing it.

"He sounds like a great man. I know why you love him."

"Yes, he was. The best husband I could ever ask for."

She sniffled again, shivering.

"Sounds like you were very blessed." His words were honest, pure.

"I was. I will always be grateful for the times I had with him." She smiled again.

"Why don't you head home, Missus…?" He didn't know her name. She looked out over the street, feeling the rain press harder now.

"I would."

He watched her and she made no motion to move, just looked out into the rain. He moved up to her now and nudged her. "Will you be going home soon?"

She looked down to her hands. "I would if I had a home."

Had a home? "Where are your kids? Are you all out on the street?"

"No, we have rooms at the bed and breakfast in town. The kids were sleeping and my oldest knew I was taking a walk. He was watching over the other kids when I left."

"Then you all have somewhere to sleep?" He was relieved to hear that. He would have invited her and her children to his house for the night and then helped them in the morning.

"Yes." At least the kids slept, she thought as she stared at the rain. He saw her shiver again.

"Is the bed and breakfast far from here?" He tried to remember where one would be in the town, but it eluded him right now.

She looked around herself. She didn't know where she was. "Oh, no!" She stood now, trying to get her bearings. All of the water that had collected on her hat fell from her head down her back, and she shivered again. "I don't…" she looked around again. "I mean…" She spun around to the man she was talking to. "I'm think I'm lost." She walked around in a circle, moving to try to acclimate herself.

He watched her, shivering now from the cold. "I don't want you to take this wrong,

Missus…," he paused; he didn't even know her name.

"Elizabeth. Elizabeth Seraphim. Like the angel," she blushed. She always introduced herself that way. She didn't know why.

"Elizabeth Seraphim. Alright." He moved next to her, not introducing himself. "I hope this doesn't seem forward, but if you want, you are more than welcome to come back to my place." He saw her look to him, frightened now. He held up his hands and looked her over. "I just want to offer you a cup of tea and dry clothes. My dad is more familiar with this town than I am and I bet he could help you find your way back to your children."

What was he doing? Inviting a total stranger into his house. She looked him over and nodded her head. "Don't do anything funny. I know stuff that could hurt you."

Chapter Two

He stifled a chuckle. He wondered if she could hurt anyone. He began walking her to his house.

"My dad lives at my home and takes care of my children when I have to be away. They are all asleep at my house," he said.

She looked at him again. "That is very thoughtful of your father. You are truly blessed, too." She had softened her voice. "Your wife? Is she away on business," she held up her hand, "or are you married? Not that I am asking…" What was she doing?

"My wife is… away." He stopped talking and unlocked the back door of his house, ushering her through. He shut the door behind her.

"I bet you miss her, then. My husband had to leave occasionally and I was so happy when he came home." She stood, dripping water on the rug inside the door.

"May I take your hat?" he asked quietly.

She took it off and felt her wet hair slide down her back. She handed it to him. "Thanks.

It's pretty wet, though."

Taking off his own jacket, he hung it on the tree by the door. "Your coat?"

"Yeah." She moved to take it off and remembered she had on her long white gown. It had a lace panel at the front that fell to her navel. It was her husband's favorite. "Then again, maybe not."

She wrapped the coat back around herself. As she did, the coldness settled over her again and she shivered.

"If you think that I would do anything wrong, please don't." Had he done something to offend her?

"That's not it." She blushed, although she knew he didn't see it. "This was my husband's favorite gown, you see, and it…" She didn't want to tell him. "Well," she swallowed, "It's a little transparent."

He got it now. The coat covered the necessities but when she took it off… He cleared his throat. "Oh, yes, I see."

He led her toward the kitchen and then had a thought. He looked to her. It was still dark and he couldn't see her any better in here than he could outside.

"You must be cold," he said. "Would you like a hot shower while I wake my dad? You can lock the door with the bolt so you wouldn't have to worry about me coming in."

Her face burned again. She was cold and the shower sounded nice. "Could you show me where your father's room is first? I want to see him with my own eyes and then I might take you up on that shower."

He turned and led her toward the stairs and moved to his father's door. He knew his father had a sermon in the morning and needed rest. Daniel opened the door just a little and moved back so she could see his father.

"See? Sleeping." He turned to her. "Would you like a shower and dry clothes now, or talk to him?"

She eyed him again in the dim light. He still had on the mirrored sunglasses and ball cap.

"Do you always wear the glasses and hat?"

He nodded his head. This was his protection from the outside world. "Yes."

"Why?" She stepped up to him. She wondered what his eyes looked like under the glasses, what color his hair was. It had to be dark.

"Privacy."

"You're not a serial killer or rapist, are you? Is that why I am here in your house? So you could do what you want with me?" She wondered if that was the reason for the disguise. So no one would recognize him as he went about his nefarious business.

He laughed out loud and then covered his mouth. "No."

He led her to his room and then through it to his bathroom. Probably best not to have his dad or his children see a strange woman showering in his house. She needed to get in and out as soon as she could.

"There are towels in the bath and my wife is about your size so I am pretty sure her clothes would fit you if you want them."

He saw her consider it and then nod her head. He hadn't moved to turn on a light and other than the streetlight filtering through the window, there was no other light in the spacious bathroom.

"I can knock on the door when I find a set and put them down by the door. You can get them when you are ready."

"Thank you. I don't know why you are doing this for me, but thanks." She smiled at him.

"All I ask is that when I am in the room, you don't turn on a light. I prefer you didn't know who I am." His voice was soft.

She leaned forward to him again, trying to be close enough to him to see him. She winked. "Your secret is safe with me, Bruce Wayne—or are you Peter Parker?" She regarded him for a moment. "You look nothing like Obi Wan Kenobi, so that's out." She laughed and so did he.

"There should be everything you need in the tub and under the sink. My wife kept everything she needed there. Let me know if there is anything else you need."

"Okay, thanks."

She shut the door and threw the bolt just in case. She flipped on a light now and saw that the bathroom was nice. There was a large garden tub, a double sink, and a large stand-up shower. Bottles and containers littered the sink and around the tub were scents and candles. The bath was done in blues and greys.

She slipped off her coat and laid it in the tub. Next she did the same with her gown. She turned on the shower to the right setting and stepped in.

The feel of the warm water cascading over her skin was lovely. She felt the heat slowly begin to seep into her bones, warming her. She heard a soft knock at the door and then it was quiet. She washed her hair and then her body.

Elizabeth turned off the water, found a thick towel, and wrapped it around herself. Opening the door, she saw the clothes on the floor and pulled them to her, throwing the bolt on the door again. A soft sweater, pants, and undergarments were in the pile. She forwent the undergarments and slipped on the sweater and pants. They were each a little snug on her, but the overall fit was nice. And the clothes were so soft.

She towel-dried her hair and ran her fingers through the long blonde tresses. She slipped on the socks and checked herself again. She didn't want to touch any of the things on the counter, so she didn't use anything else. Feeling much better, she threw the bolt and came face-to-face with a man.

When he heard the door to the bath shut, Daniel rummaged through his wife's things until he found a set of clothes for the woman. He wasn't sure about undergarments and put those in the pile, too, along with a soft pair of his wife's socks. He didn't know what else to get her so he knocked on the door and went in search of his dad.

He hated bothering him again, but he honestly didn't know where a bed and breakfast was in this town and if anyone knew, it was his father. Walking up to the bed, he shook his father carefully, quietly. "Dad, I need your help."

"What is it, Son?" He sat up now, trying to wake so he could help his only child.

"Could you come with me?" He picked up his father's robe and handed it to him. He didn't know how to explain to him what he needed.

"Sure, Son." He pulled on his robe, tying it as they walked out of the room. Following Daniel into his room, they walked over to the door of Daniel's bath. As they did, the door opened.

Chapter Three

A big smile crossed the woman's face as she recognized the older man. "Reverend Templeman!"

Out of the corner of her eye, she noted the other man moving to the shadows. As he did, she saw brown hair peeking out of his ball cap and a long jaw coming down almost to a point at his chin. His mouth was small and set into a line. She had seen all of that together before. She looked back to the older man as she felt for and turned off the light to the bath. The man stayed where he was, though.

"Reverend, what are you doing here?"

John Templeman beheld the woman in front of him. "Elizabeth Seraphim, what are you doing in my son's home?" He looked around himself. "In my son's room." The old man hoped it wasn't what it looked like.

"Your son found me wandering on the street, sir. In the cold and in the dark. He brought me in from the cold and offered me a shower and warm clothes." She looked to the man now. "I am very grateful to your son." She turned her eyes back to the Reverend.

"Indeed." He looked to his son, too. He knew his son had a big heart. "Let's go to the kitchen and have a cup." He began to walk out and felt her follow him.

The one who brought her to the house did, too. She felt better knowing the Reverend was this man's father.

When they made it to the kitchen, the Reverend gestured to the chair. "Why don't you sit down, my dear? My son has already warmed you on the outside with the shower and clothes. Let me make you a cup and warm you on the inside before you go home." He moved to make the tea and then turned to sit down across from her. "What were you doing out so late?"

She glanced at the man who still stood inside the doorway, not coming into the kitchen. "I was… thinking, sir. I guess I lost track of time and location. Because I found myself on a bench and I began talking to your son," she glanced at him and then back to the Reverend. "Your son was kind enough to help me and then said you could help me find my way back to my children." She blushed. "Being new in town, I am not quite sure where everything is. Your son assured me you would know."

She heard the tea kettle whistle and saw the old man get up. He poured her, him, and the other man a cup of tea. He gave her a cup and then took one to his son who was still standing in the shadows in the doorway. The Reverend sat down now and took a sip of his tea.

"I can indeed, my dear. But first let's have a cup." He took a sip of his and watched her do the same. He waited for her to set her cup down. "What's on your mind this early in the morning?"

"I was thinking about my husband, Reverend. I was missing him; that's how I got lost. I guess," she toyed with her cup, "I just began to wander around town until your son found me."

"It was good it was my son. No telling what kind of riff-raff is on the streets when it gets dark." He looked to his son and smiled.

She took a drink of her tea, feeling the heat settle into her bones. "Yes, sir. Only problem is, I don't know my way back— to the bed-and-breakfast—and I was hoping you could help me." She glanced outside and noted that it had stopped raining. "I can probably navigate my way home if you point the way and give me directions."

John stifled a laugh. Elizabeth would get lost in the church. Letting her go out into the streets of the town before dawn, alone, was probably not a good idea. He did have a good idea that came to him then.

"I tell you what, Elizabeth, let me go and write down the directions for my son and he will drive you home." He let out a loud yawn. "I have got to get ready for service in the morning and I know my son can help you more than I can. I am just an old man." He smiled on the inside at what this would mean for the two of them.

She heard the man at the door frown. She had never heard anyone frown before, but she made out the upside-down smile on his face. He wasn't happy about it but wouldn't say anything to his father.

John ignored his son's pout. "Besides, it has stopped raining and a drive would do you both good."

"I've got…" Elizabeth heard the man clear his throat, "plans in the morning, father." His voice was one of annoyance.

"Oh pish–posh, it won't take that long, Son." He was already planning the longest route back to the bed-and-breakfast. As soon as the door shut behind the two, he was going to have Mabel check on the children at the B&B. He knew Mabel would guard those children with her life!

"Now, let me go write down directions for my son." He stood, taking his cup with him, and looked to the other man. "Why don't you sit with Mrs. Elizabeth while she finishes her cup? I'll be back in a moment, Son." He patted the other man on the back and walked out of the room.

He stood there for a moment and then brought his cup over to the table and sat down. He looked over to the woman— Elizabeth—and his breath caught. She had pulled her long blonde hair over her shoulder and had begun braiding it. He wondered if that was a fidgeting movement but didn't ask. He watched her from behind his glasses until she was done. He wanted to ask if she wanted something to tie it off with, but then she began unbraiding her hair. Her hair slid over her fingers, which were making the motions as if she had done this a thousand times before.

She looked out the window and then took a drink from her cup. She looked to him again and he saw her hair shift with her. "Reverend Templeman is an excellent Pastor. You should be very proud of him."

He nodded his head. He was proud of his father, just like he knew his father was proud of him. He knew there were things he had done in his career that his father had not approved of, but his father loved him still. "I am."

She took another sip of her tea. "Tayler, Olivia, and Raven—they are your children?"

He nodded his head again. "Yes."

"They are beautiful! Tayler has the best personality and is funny! Olivia is beautiful. I bet she looks a lot like her mom. And Raven is such a cutie. You should be a very proud father." She took another sip of her tea and noted it was just about gone.

"I am." He did love his children and he was very proud of them.

"So what do you do, Mr. Templeman? You must lead a very secretive life. You won't take off the ball cap and I have yet to see you without the glasses."

She was teasing him now. He hadn't introduced himself and he would have let her know that Reverend Templeman was his father if he had known it would help put her mind at ease.

"I would rather not talk about it." At home he was always husband, dad, and son. He wasn't who he was in the outside world.

She finished her tea and sat back. "Do you have a tragic story, is that why you hide behind your hat and glasses? Are you scarred and afraid I would faint from fright?" She thought for a moment. "Is that why I see your children but not you at your father's church?"

"You attend my father's chapel?" That thought didn't so much surprise him as it did intrigue him.

"Every Sunday morning and evening. Your father is an excellent speaker and delivers a powerful sermon. My children are blessed to hear the Word of God from that man's lips. Not that I think he is without flaws, but he definitely delivers a beautiful message."

He couldn't really remember the last time he listened to one of his father's sermons. He knew that when he last did, he felt what his father called conviction in his heart. So he stopped listening. "My father does many things well, Mrs. Seraphim."

"Elizabeth, please, call me Elizabeth." She laughed. "Mrs. Seraphim makes me sound holy and I can assure you that I am not holy." She laughed. "Far from it."

His left eyebrow went up at that and he smiled. "So I am not the only one being secretive, Elizabeth." He leaned across the table, careful to stay in the shadows. "Do you have some tragic mystery in your past, or is it the present, that you dare not tell?"

She leaned forward, too. "I cannot tell you, Mr. Templeman. For if I did, I would have to kill you." She leaned back and laughed, knowing she was being dramatic.

They laughed together now, each of them looking at the other, not that Elizabeth knew it. He had slanted his head down toward his cup, but he wasn't looking at it. Elizabeth noted her cup was empty now. She looked up, wondering where Reverend Templeman was.

"Your father has been gone a while now. Do you think he is alright?"

The Reverend walked into the kitchen, waving a piece of paper in his hands. "I have them, Son." He handed the paper to his son. "Take my car." His eyes moved to Elizabeth. "It needs to be warmed up for the children, anyway." He looked back to his son. "Now follow those directions. If you don't, you could get lost again and I know," his eyes slid to Elizabeth again and then back to his son, "you have plans for today."

The younger Mr. Templeman stood now and so did Elizabeth. She walked over to the Reverend. "Thank you for helping me. I will see you this morning for service."

He smiled back at her. "I know you will. Tell your children I will be waiting at the door for them like I always do."

"I will." She turned and moved next to the younger Mr. Templeman. As they neared the door, she heard the Reverend say, "Give her a coat, Son. It may be cold outside."

He turned to his father.

"Just let her have your spare jacket. You can have mine. I have another one in my room I can wear." Reverend Templeman was still smiling at her.

"I'll bring it to," she looked to Mr. Templeman, "chapel and give it back to your father."

He nodded his head. He had a feeling his father had something up his sleeve. He pulled his jacket from the tree and slid it on her shoulders. He pulled his father's on and then opened the door.

"Remember, Son, follow the directions, even if it looks like you can find a short cut. Follow the directions." He looked after the two at the door.

"I will, Father." He guided Elizabeth out the door and shut it behind him.

The Reverend laughed softly as he saw the lights of the car pulling out of his drive. He had written down the longest route to the B&B that he could think of. He had already called Mabel and she had checked on the children. They were fast asleep. Elizabeth was wearing his daughter-in-law's clothes and had been drinking tea in the kitchen at the time.

He knew they were both lonely. She had already come to him and told him all about her situation. They had discussed it and he had helped her through some big decisions in her life. His son was needing someone, too. He filled his time with work and children, but the Reverend knew that wasn't enough. They both needed each other, they just didn't know it yet.

As he made his way back to bed, he had a thought. He may invite the Seraphims back to his house for Sunday dinner. It wasn't unusual for the Reverend to do just that, but today he would make sure his son could be there. It was time Daniel told Elizabeth who he really was. She was going to find out sometime and today just might as well be the day.

When they were in the car, the sun was lightening the sky and she could feel an urgency in the driver. He glanced at the note often, not looking at her. He muttered at times because it seemed like the note had him looping back on himself. She saw him look out the window and then back to the street.

"You're not going to burst into flames, are you?" She held back a laugh when his head swiveled around to her and then back to the road. His mouth was set into a line again. "I mean, if you are a vampire and you're racing against the sun so you don't die, I understand. Let me out of here. Hand me the directions and I'll hoof it from here so you can climb back into your coffin."

"What?!" He swerved as he looked over to her and then the road again.

"I get that you don't want me to see you and that it seems you want to get rid of me so you can go back home, but you remind me of a vampire in a movie." She sighed dramatically. "Racing against the sun so you don't burst into flames." She laughed. "Hurry!"

He avoided looking at her again. It's not that he was racing the sun, but he didn't want her to know who he was. Besides, he reasoned, he had a radio spot to do and the car that would pick him up would be there soon.

"I just have a busy morning ahead of me, Elizabeth. That's all." He knew his voice came out impatiently. The directions kept having him loop around in circles and he was irritated.

"Stop the car." Her voice was quiet, controlled.

He did look at her now. Something was wrong. "What?" She looked at him. She was tired of not seeing him and she was ready to be back at the Bed & Breakfast. "I said, stop the car. I want out."

He kept driving, doing another loop. The town was not that big! "Why?"

"Because you're insane, that's why." She took a deep breath. "Stop the car, Mr. Templeman. Now!" She concentrated on him now, ready to leave the car.

He signaled and pulled over to the side of the road. He saw her begin to unbuckle her seat belt. "What's wrong?!"

She kept pulling on the buckle. "Oh, you would ask, wouldn't you?" She pulled on the buckle. "First you talk to me on a bench in the middle of the night in the rain and then, then you take me home and I find out your father is the pastor of my church." She yanked on the seat belt. "And then you help me and your father is kind to me." She let go of the seat belt and felt tears running down her face. "Now I am an inconvenience to you because you have a life." She glared at him.

The sky had lightened up considerably and she could see his face. Granted, he still had on the sunglasses and ball cap, but he looked so familiar to her. She had seen that face before, but she didn't know where.

"So," she reached over and grabbed the paper out of his hands, tearing it in half. Of course she got the half she didn't need. "I am leaving this car now." She flung the paper on the floor as she pulled on the seat belt again. The stupid thing would not release. She took her palms and wiped at the tears that fell down her face.

She flounced back in the seat and looked at him. "I don't care who you are. You could be John

Lennon or Darth Vader, so cut the 'You can't know who I am' act, okay?" She sighed. "I just need to be back with my children, alright?" She looked out the window.

He gaped at her in shock. He cleared his throat and signaled again, looking at the torn directions in his hand. "I didn't mean to come off as insensitive. I thought I was trying to help you." He sighed. "I just have to be somewhere this morning. I haven't seen my kids in a month. You haven't been an inconvenience, Elizabeth." The car pulled up in front of the B&B. "You are here." He turned to her and unbuckled her seat belt.

It had a trick to getting it unbuckled. His dad would never get the thing fixed. He wondered why, but his dad had always laughed and his mother had blushed.

"Have a good day, Elizabeth," he said, softly. "It really was nice talking to you."

Elizabeth opened the car door as the first rays of the sun peeked over the hill. "Thank you again, Mr. Templeman." She got out and smiled at him. She walked into the B&B.

Daniel sighed. There it went—his favorite jacket. He would miss it. He thought about the woman, too, as he began to retrace the car's motion, minus the loops, back to his home. She was different, he thought as he pulled into the drive. She was stubborn and strong-willed. He wasn't sure what to think about her. He would also have to talk to his dad. These directions he gave him were too long and convoluted. He wondered if his dad had done that on purpose.

Chapter Four

The church service ran about 40 people as Elizabeth and her children walked up to the doors. Reverend Templeman was there greeting people as they entered. His smile was big as his gaze held the family. "Good morning, Elizabeth," he said, shaking her hand.

"Good morning, Reverend." She smiled as the Reverend shook her hand and then dropped it.

"How are you and the children today?"

The kids smiled at him, except for her youngest, who was sleeping on her shoulder. David was four now and he was a handful.

"Fine, Reverend," her oldest son, Paul, replied to the man who was the leader of the chapel.

"Good. Good." He looked over each of them. His eyes stopped, resting on Elizabeth.

"Please see me after service, Elizabeth. I have something I wish to discuss with you."

"Of course, Reverend." There was a line forming so she ushered the children into the chapel.

Her youngest son, David, named after her husband, continued sleeping and woke up about halfway through the service. Her fourth child, April, colored as she listened to the Reverend's sermon. Her third child, Ben, and her second child, Lily, followed along with the passages while the Reverend preached. The sermon was good, filled with strong points and relevant life lessons.

Reverend Templeman was an excellent orator who could keep a congregation's attention. He was wild and flamboyant.

When the service was over she had her children gather their things and head toward the doors. Lunch would be served at the B&B promptly at 1:00 P.M. and Mabel didn't like anyone to be late to the table.

Living there was like being at home. Mabel always made enough food for everyone and no one left hungry, even Paul, her teenaged son. Mabel was sweet and kind, an older lady whom Elizabeth had offered to help more than once.

They made their way toward the doors, seemingly always the last ones to leave. Her children all beelined over to the Reverend's grandchildren. Tayler, Olivia, and Raven always waited patiently for John to greet people as they exited. Her children always talked quietly with them for a moment before they left the chapel. Elizabeth waited until the last person left and then made her way over to the Reverend.

"That was a fine sermon you gave today, Reverend. Thank you." She smiled at him, remembering what he had said.

"Thank you, Mrs. Elizabeth." She smiled back at her. "I was wondering, do you have plans for lunch?"

"The B&B serves some really good food, Reverend. That is where our lunch would be today. Why?"

"I thought you would want to come over and keep me and the children company today." I stopped over at The Mill on the way here and they are going to have a feast ready for us to take home. What do you say?"

Elizabeth smiled. "We would love to, sir."

"Good! Good." He smiled at her again, wider. "I am going to go round up the kids and we will meet you there. I hope you don't mind, but I asked Deacon Wayne to drive you and the kids. He should be at the B&B around twelve thirty. Is that alright?"

Elizabeth nodded her head. "That sounds fine. Thank you." She made her way to the children and ushered them out the door. It was only a short walk to the B&B.

Once they made it back, the children all relaxed for the brief time they had before Deacon Wayne came to pick them up. Elizabeth found the jacket she had worn and placed it in a paper sack from one of the local boutique stores, along with a thank you card.

A little while later, there was a knock on her door. Opening it, she saw the Deacon. "Hi, Mrs. Seraphim."

Deacon Wayne was a nice man in his mid-thirties around the same age as Elizabeth. He had never been married and was a perfect gentleman. He seemed to be good with her kids and made her laugh.

"Hello, Wayne. The kids and I are ready to go." She picked up the bag and the kids moved out the door toward Wayne's van. It was a larger van that Wayne had once said he kept just in case he married and had a large family. Preparing for rain, he said laughingly. "Thank you for driving us today."

"No problem, Mrs. Seraphim."

"Elizabeth, please." She laughed and so did he. They all climbed into the van and began to make their way to the Reverend's house. A few minutes later, they were pulling up in the drive and piling out of the van.

"Thanks again for the ride, Wayne."

Wayne stayed in the van and watched Elizabeth and the kids all climb out. He liked Elizabeth and knew she had been widowed. He didn't mind that she was a little older than he.

She came with a big family and, as nice as she was, the family was an added bonus for him.

"Anytime, Mrs. Seraphim."

He couldn't bring himself to call her Elizabeth like she had asked. It seemed too familiar to him to do that.

Elizabeth turned and they all filed up to the front door of the house. She rang the doorbell and waited for the Reverend to answer the door.

The Reverend was on the phone as he heard the doorbell ring. "Stuck in traffic, huh? Do you know how much longer you are going to be?"

Daniel looked around himself. It didn't look like it was going to move anytime soon. What did everyone do, decide to wait until today to get out and run errands?

"No, Dad. Please just tell the kids I am trying." The radio spot had run longer today than he thought it would and that meant he was going to hit the after-church traffic. He wanted to be home with his children. He just wished the traffic would move.

Miraculously, as he had that thought, the traffic began moving at a pretty fast pace. He accelerated and switched lanes. At this rate he would be home in less than twenty minutes. That was great.

Elizabeth heard the front door open and saw a big smile on the Reverend's face. He said, "Welcome! Come in!" He waited for everyone to enter and shut the door behind them."The kids are all in the backyard. Wouldn't you know it, lunch is going to run," he glanced at the clock, "about thirty minutes late. But it gives the kids time to visit and play." He had ushered them to the back yard and he saw the younger children begin to play.

The ground was dry despite the rain the night before. That was good because the back yard looked like a city park. There were all kinds of ladders and climbing toys, things to ride on and in, things to climb on. There were more than enough things to keep the children occupied.

"Tea, Elizabeth?" He was almost giddy. He had hit a snag, but he was sure that would be remedied soon.

"Yes, please." She smiled at him as he gestured to a large outdoor dining set. The table had twelve chairs set around it with a large umbrella over the top. It was done in the same colors as the bath.

They walked over to the table where two large pitchers of sun tea waited for them.

"If I may," she said, staying his hand as he started to pour hers. She picked up a glass and made it for the Reverend and then one for herself. She lifted the glass to her lips and drank. It was sweet and warm.

"Hmmm... Peppermint?" She guessed, turning to the Reverend.

He watched as she tried it. The flavor was not his favorite, but he wouldn't tell her that.

"Yes. Do you like it?"

Elizabeth wrinkled her nose a little. "Not my favorite, to be honest, but it's not bad."

John laughed. "Then let's dump this out and try the other."

Elizabeth leaned over and smiled at him. "What's in the other one?"

"Peach." He gestured toward it and she saw the peaches floating toward the top. "That's my favorite."

She saw him dump the peppermint tea into a planter and reach over to do the same with hers. She laughed as he dumped it and took the glasses into the house. As he did that she made two more glasses. She handed him his and they tried that flavor.

"Very nice." This one was good.

"Special recipe, that one. My favorite." His smile faded a little. "It was my wife's, too. Although there were days that she liked the peppermint." His smile picked back up.

Elizabeth made her way over to a chair and sat to watch the children playing and laughing. "What was your wife's name, Reverend?"

He looked at her. "John. When I am at home, I am John."

"Alright. What was your wife's name, John? Tell me all about her." She took another sip of her tea and sat it off to the side, turning her full attention to John and his description of his wife.

Daniel could not be happier to be home! Traffic had cleared and he had made it home in record time. He couldn't wait to see his children.

This was one of the things about being an actor he disliked: he had to be so long away from his children. But one often had to make sacrifices and this was his.

He pulled his car into the garage and as the garage door hit the floor, so did his feet. He wound his way through the house, looking for his children along the way. He didn't see them in the kitchen with his father like he thought they would be, so he made his way to the back yard.

He saw his children playing and a big smile came across his face.

Opening the door, he stepped outside to hear the sound of a woman's laughter. As he did, he turned to the side. It was Elizabeth.

He ducked back into the house before she could see him. But not before he heard her talking to his father again, and laughing as his dad did. It had been so long since he heard his father laugh that the sound made him smile.

Taking his mobile out of his pocket, he dialed his home phone. Daniel watched his father rise as he heard the sound of the ring. Reverend Templeman looked back at Elizabeth, curled up in Gen's chaise, and smiled at her as he said something to her. He laughed again. Turning, he looked into the house and stopped for just a moment, seeing his son.

He stepped into the house, closing the door behind him. He smiled at his son. "Hello, Son. How was the spot?"

"It went fine, Dad, but what are Elizabeth and her children doing here?" He looked out the door and saw five additional children running around his back yard.

"New program at the chapel. I have decided to adopt a family for a month. This month is the Seraphim family." He looked proud of himself as he looked to his son. "There are so many families out there now without fathers and I think that there needs to be a strong male influence in these children's lives." He nodded to the children as they played outside, having a good time.

"I understand that, Dad." His father was always coming up with one thing or another to help the congregation of his church. This one was very convenient and the timing seemed too perfect. "But this is my home."

"And this is your hometown, Son. If members of your own community can't see you in your own hometown helping those less fortunate, what would they think?"

His dad had a point. But in his house? "Couldn't you do this at the church?"

"I wanted to show this family what it would be like to have a family that cared for them, someone who loved them. And I intend to be that person and I intend to show your children what it is like to be a part of their community." He laid a hand on his son's shoulder. "You can't shelter them their whole lives. They have to learn to be a part of something greater than themselves."

"By integrating themselves into that family?" He flung his hand out. "Who knows whether or not they are even going to stay in the community, Dad?

They are living at a B&B, Dad. They could leave tomorrow."

"Yes, they could leave tomorrow, Son, and if they do, I want them to remember this community cared about them, loved them." Reverend Templeman was mad and felt himself shake. "If you can't find it in your heart to make this family a part of your life for a little while, Son, you need to leave. Because I intend to have lunch with them and visit with them this afternoon."

"Oh, I will." He started to the door. The kids were all having a good time. He hated to bother them, but he wanted to see his children. He looked out over them, waiting for them to see him, but they were too busy having a good time. He looked back to his father. "Does it have to be this family, Dad?"

He looked to Elizabeth then and saw her rise. She went to push Raven on the swing. She smiled as she pushed his daughter and talked with Olivia. Tayler and the teenager were laughing together and playing. They all looked so happy.

"Yes, Son. It has to be this family. At least for a little while." He knew his son's home was a sanctuary for him. He also knew his son valued his privacy. John knew there was nothing Elizabeth and her family would do to take that from him. But Daniel had hidden out so long from prying eyes that it was instinct to keep himself hidden. "Can't you try, Son? Try to help this family."

Daniel looked out over the children again. He saw Olivia fall and moved forward to help her. Elizabeth and two girls he did not recognize moved to comfort his daughter. He wanted to go to her, but at the same time he was angry at what was happening. He turned to his father. "This once. This once I will allow you to have them here but then you all meet at the church. I made sure it had everything it needed for families of all sizes. Next Sunday you meet there."

John shook his head. "No, Son, this is my home, too. They will meet here. And they will continue to." He laid his hand on his son's shoulder again. "Please reconsider."

Daniel put his hands on his slim hips. "No, Dad. I've got phone calls to make for tomorrow."

"Aren't you going to have lunch with us? I ordered plenty for everyone." He saw his son retreating back into his shell. "You're going to miss lunch with your children."

"Are Elizabeth and her children going to be here for dinner, too?"

"No, they will have their meal at the B&B, I suppose."

"I will have dinner with my children then." He turned and made his way back to his room. Shutting the door behind himself, he became angrier. This was his home. The one place he didn't have to be Danny Tensley the actor, he could be Daniel Templeman the father. And now that was taken away. If he went downstairs now he would have to become someone else and he didn't want to have to do that in his own home.

It was a little later, when he was reading through scripts that had been sent to him, that he heard children running on the stairs, laughing. It had been a long while since he had heard happy children in his home. They were giggling and joyous.

"No, no," he heard his father say, "Girls wash your hands in one bath and boys in the other. And I'm going to check them!"

Daniel smiled. His dad had always said that to him. He did, too. Not that he ever sent Daniel back to the bath to rewash. Daniel did it right the first time because he wanted to please his father.

He heard his father laugh again and heard the sound of female laughter. Elizabeth was upstairs with his father. In his home.

He made his way to the door and then stopped. If they saw him they would be ecstatic that they were in his home. They would probably ask to take pictures. Outside of his home, yes, but not in. He made his way back to the bed and sat back down.

"Good." There was a pause. "Good." Another pause. "Good." He knew his father was inspecting hands and approving of them. "Time for some lunch, what do you say?" A resounding cheer went up from all the kids and his father and Elizabeth laughed. Daniel heard everyone descending the stairs. Soon all was quiet upstairs again. He missed the sound of everyone.

The sound of a vehicle pulling into his drive brought him to the window. As he watched, his children—and he supposed Elizabeth's—all climbed into the van. He squinted, trying to see who the driver was.

Deacon Wayne. Of course it was. Deacon Wayne was the youngest Deacon in his father's church. He had a huge van that would more than adequately seat all nine children, his father, Elizabeth, and himself.

He knew Wayne wanted a large family one day and Elizabeth's family fit the bill. She was smart and funny. She knew pop culture and had a smile that would make Wayne smile, too. She was perfect for him. Maybe he would talk his dad into meeting at Wayne's house next Sunday.

He watched his father walk out of his house now. He reached over and held Elizabeth's hand for a moment. As Daniel watched, he saw her wipe away a tear. It was a quick movement, one he was sure her children missed as they situated themselves in Wayne's van. He saw her hug his father and give him a watery smile that seemed to light up her whole face.

John turned to lock the front door and as he did, he looked up and locked eyes with Daniel. There were times, like now, that his father's gaze seemed to pierce him. John eyed his son for a moment and then smiled at him, nodding his head.

Daniel saw his father turn then and stroll toward Wayne's van. It was Wayne who had his attention now. His father had offered Elizabeth the front seat of the van and he had opened her door. He saw her sit in the seat and immediately Wayne smiled and turned his head toward her. He saw her smile at him, but it wasn't the same smile she gave his father. Wayne laughed and adjusted his mirror. He saw Elizabeth move to the side, a little out of his reach. Didn't the woman know Wayne liked her? And she had exactly what he wanted: a large family, and he was nice enough. She should be happy Deacon Wayne liked her.

The van pulled out of the drive and was gone. It looked like he was going to spend the evening alone. He usually did when he was home on Sunday nights. He rarely went to his father's chapel. When he did, every sermon seemed aimed at him, preaching to him about his life and how he should turn it around. But he didn't want to. His life was exactly like he wanted it. He wasn't changing anything for anybody.

He made his way to his bath and decided to soak before the kids came home from church. He had already read through some scripts, only a few catching his interest, and he was ready for a break.

He went to turn on the water and noticed the jacket in his tub. He picked it up, dry now, and decided to wash it before he gave it back to Elizabeth.

But it was the gown that drew his attention. He remembered from last night that it was long and white and as he held it up he realized why she hadn't wanted to take her coat off in front of him. The entire front was lace and a thin ribbon snaked up the front to hold the entire top together. Unlace the ribbon and the entire front would open and fall, as there were no shoulders to it.

He swallowed. If someone who was up to no good found her, it would have been nothing for them to remove what stood between her and them.

A part of him was angry at her foolishness. She should have known better than to wander around alone in the dark wearing nothing but a little bit of lace and satin under a coat that barely covered her midsection.

Her lace hat with the matching red ribbon around the brim was dry, too. She had lain it flat so it wouldn't curl. The woman had to have common sense, she just didn't show it last night.

He went to pick up the gown and it slid through his fingers, soft even though it had been soaked by the rain. He remembered her standing just inside the door last night, dripping on the carpet. She must have been freezing, but she never told him that.

Deacon Wayne would be a good person to help take care of her. He would make sure she never wandered around in the rain half naked and freezing. He would make sure she was at home under the covers, with him. He would keep her warm and she would never have to wander around again.

Yes, the sooner Mrs. Seraphim settled down, or better yet, left town, the better off he would be. The better off his family would be.

He folded the gown carefully and placed the hat on top of it. He would see that his father got the articles back to Elizabeth. She said the gown was her late husband's favorite. He could see why. That gown left very little to the imagination.

As he turned on the water, an idea formed in his head. As it happened, he found himself on a break for about a month before filming began on his next movie. It was time he had planned to spend with his children and father, but now it looked like he would be taking on a different role: one of matchmaker between Deacon Wayne and Elizabeth Seraphim.

Chapter Five

Church was good that evening for Elizabeth Seraphim and her family. They had a good day with Reverend Templeman and the kids had fun playing with Mr. Templeman's children. Everyone was exhausted and happy as they made their way back to the B&B. As tired as they were, they still stopped and made time for ice cream.

They sat outside under the big hard-topped shell table and laughed as the ice cream dripped on their clothes as it melted. They each had something different and tried each of the others' orders. They had forgone dinner at the B&B for ice cream and they all thought the treat was amazing.

Reverend Templeman was sitting at home when the phone rang.

"I got it, Dad." He heard his son shout from the kitchen. It was already in John's hand.

"No, it's alright. I have it, Son." He pulled the receiver to his ear. "The Seraphim family is at The Dip. Just thought you wanted to know," the voice at the other end of the line said.

"Oh, alright. Thanks." He hung up the phone and looked at the clock. Eight-thirty, not too late. "Son! I'm going for some ice cream!"

He heard Tayler, Olivia, and Raven squeal. He smiled. That is exactly the response he wanted from them. Next he heard footsteps on the stairs as six little feet moved down them. The kids had not dressed for bed yet and none of them had dessert after they had eaten dinner.

"Ice cream?" Daniel had some papers in his hand as he exited the kitchen. "Now?"

"Yes, now," John said as he slipped on his shoes. He saw the kids doing the same. He made no move to stop them.

"But the children should be in bed soon, Dad." He looked to his children, who were already putting on their jackets.

"Oh, come on, Son. It would be a welcome change for the kids. No paparazzi outside at night. And as warm as it is we can catch the cream before it drips. What do you say, kids?"

Daniel looked down his nose at his dad. "Alright, just for tonight." He heard his kids cheer as he slipped on his own shoes. "And I'm driving."

"Whatever you say, Son." He half smiled as he followed his grandchildren and son out the door.

"Where are we getting the ice cream?" He helped his children into the car, buckling as he went.

"Oh, oh, The Dip. I thought we could go to The Dip."

The kids cheered again and Daniel smiled. "Alright, The Dip it is." He turned on the car and pulled it out of the driveway. Crazy thing to do, get cream in the night, but that is what his father wanted.

A few minutes later, they pulled into The Dip and the kids got out of the car. "April! Lily!" They all turned and Raven saw what her sister did and smiled, too. "David!" Her sisters had yelled; she thought maybe she should, too. The girls all ran over and hugged. Daniel turned around and saw Elizabeth with her back to him, getting napkins.

"Dad." He looked to his father. He had to have somehow known they would be here. He looked around. There were no other patrons here and the lot was deserted except for his car.

"What, Son?" He looked to the menu. He really didn't have to. It hadn't changed as long as the stand had been there.

"Did you know they would be here?" He had turned from them.

"Me? No. Just wanted some ice cream." He glanced to his son and then back to the menu.

"Think I will have me a plain cone. Small. What about you, Son?"

Daniel looked at his father and then glanced over at the family. The kids were all talking a mile a minute and Elizabeth was helping his daughters as they perused the menu. She was sitting on her knees now, her face the same level as Olivia's and Raven's. She wasn't reading off the menu to them or looking down at them, she was on their level talking and smiling at them. He saw her move a piece of hair out of Olivia's eyes and pull back his daughter's hair. His daughter smiled at Elizabeth and she responded to the little girl's smile.

"Dad, tell me, did you know they were here?"

He looked his father in the eyes. His dad avoided his gaze. "Sometimes, Son, ice cream is just ice cream. It may not be what you want, but it will always be what you need." He smiled. "Definitely a plain cone. Small." He waved at Elizabeth. "Hey, hey!" He began to walk over to her and the children.

Daniel laid his keys on top of the car and began to walk home. He knew his father could make it home with his children. He needed to get some air to clear his head.

David was on the other side of Elizabeth. She saw him touch his stomach and wince. She opened her mouth to ask him about it.

Raven looked from Mrs. Elizabeth to her daddy. "Where is my daddy going, Mrs. Elizabeth?"

Elizabeth watched Mr. Templeman walk off away from everyone. He was in shadow again and his head was down. "Maybe he forgot something, Raven. Now he just needs to remember." She watched him walk off from them. "Sometimes walking around for a bit helps me, too." She looked back to the little girl. "Now, what kind of ice cream do you want?" Daniel walked a little way from them and watched them. He really didn't know why he had walked off, only that he had to move away from the people, so he did. His father smiled and laughed with all the children and with Elizabeth. She seemed to gravitate toward his father and Daniel watched as she slipped her arm into his father's. He watched his father sigh and lay his head against Elizabeth's. He smiled and closed his eyes for a moment. He picked up his head and pointed to the girls enjoying their cones.

Daniel really needed to shake off what was bothering him. He turned and walked down the road. His home wasn't really that far away, but he didn't want his father and children to walk in the dark. This way they would have the car to drive home in.

"John," she didn't look to Mr. Templeman as he walked off. "Why didn't your son stay?"

John looked to where his son was walking and watched as he turned a street corner. "Sometimes we have to lose ourselves, my dear, to find out who we truly are."

"Is your son lost, John?" He didn't look lost. He seemed to know exactly where he was going.

"My son has been lost for a couple of years now, Elizabeth." But now I think he has found something. And that is going to make him better."

Elizabeth looked into the old man's eyes. "What has he found, John, that is going to make him better?" She waited to hear what it was.

He laughed as he looked at where his son had gone. "That I can't tell you, my dear. It would spoil where he is going."

Elizabeth looked to where his son had been. "Isn't he going home?"

John laughed out loud. "Yes, Elizabeth, he is going to find his home. He just doesn't know it yet." He looked at her and then his grandchildren. He slipped his arm out of hers and went to the kids.

It was later that Daniel heard his children and father come through the door. He went to the stairs to help them, but they were already making their way up them and to their rooms.

His dad stopped in front of him. "You missed it, Son."

"I've seen my children eat ice cream before, Dad. I know what they like and what they don't."

"I'm not talking about the ice cream or children, Son." John looked at his only child.

Daniel shook his head. “No, I didn’t, Dad. I didn’t miss anything.”

“Oh, Son, you can’t keep yourself here forever. At some point you have to let yourself feel again.”

Daniel looked at his father. Gen had been gone two years. He needed longer than that to move past his wife of twelve years.

“I can’t do it right now, Dad. Not yet.”

“Soon, huh?” he looked to the children’s rooms. “The kids. They aren’t getting any younger. Raven was three when she lost her mother, about the same age as Elizabeth’s son, David. He was a year old when he lost his dad.”

“Daddy?”

Daniel saw his daughter as she poked her head out of her door. “On my way, Raven.” He turned and looked to his dad. “I love you all very much. You are all I need.” He went to his daughter’s room and shut the door.

“That’s where you’re wrong, Son. You need love.” He turned and saw Tayler looking at him through his open door. “And you, Tayler, need to be sleeping. Let’s tuck you in, my boy.”

He moved to his grandson’s room.

Chapter Six

Elizabeth tucked her four younger children into bed and kissed them good night. David complained about his stomach hurting. She checked his temperature and noticed he was running a low-grade fever. He also said he felt a little sick and through the day this belly had hurt more when he moved.

She gave him some medicine. "If you don't feel better in the morning, I will take you to see a doctor, alright, sweetie?"

"Okay, Mommy."

Elizabeth saw him wince, but he closed his eyes. Walking out the door, she glanced to make sure the outer door was locked. She shut the door to the room partially and lowered the lights.

She went to lie down and rest. She lay there for a while, looking out of the window at the dark world. Sitting up, she pulled on a jacket. "Paul, David isn't feeling well. Can you check on him in a little bit? I gave him some medicine and that should be working. I need to walk for a bit. I've got my phone on me in case anything happens."

"Ok, Mom." Paul was on his laptop checking the family finances and playing games. "I love you."

"I love you, too."

She pulled the door closed behind her and walked down the hall. She opened the front door of the B&B, and padded her way out onto the sidewalk. She began to walk down it, pulling up her hood.

She passed The Dip and then the chapel. She ended up at the bench where she had talked to John's son. She sat there for a while and watched the street light. It was quiet.

Daniel was lying in bed and the house was quiet. Too quiet. The bed was lonely and cold He sat up and pulled on a jacket, pulling up his hood, tying his hood tightly. Walking softly, he went to his father's room and poked his head in.

"Dad?" He heard his father moan. "I'm going to go for a walk. I have my mobile. Be back later."

"Alright, Son."

Daniel shut the door and walked out of his house, locking it behind him. The street was silent tonight as he walked down the sidewalk. He made his way to the bench he was on the night before. As he looked up, he saw someone on the bench. It must be Elizabeth. He considered turning around but decided not to. Instead, he ambled over to the bench and sat down on the other side of it.

Elizabeth had pulled her feet up and placed them on the bench. She pulled the jacket over her body and brought her head down to her knees.

"You're going to stretch out my jacket, Elizabeth." He had looked to her and saw his favorite jacket pulled over her legs. He wondered if she were cold but instead decided to tease her.

Elizabeth looked to the man at her side. "I was going to give this back to you," she said, offhandedly, "I guess I forgot. Sorry." She was quiet for a moment and then said, "Wandering the streets tonight, Clark Kent. What's on your mind?

Lois Lane?" She chose to ignore his earlier statement. She put her head back on her knees.

"Actually, I was always a Batman kind of man. He always liked the blondes in the movies. But Superman is close enough." He laughed. "I like Superman."

"You would. Prefers solitude. Likes to be alone. That is how I envision Superman, Batman, too." She sighed, pulling her legs down to the ground. "You missed a lot today, Mr. Stark."

He laughed. He never considered himself Ironman.

"You missed lunch with your children and ice cream with them, too." She looked at him. "Why don't you want me to know who you are?"

He shrugged. "People usually don't see me for me when they find out who I am. When I am at my home, I can just be me and no one else."

Elizabeth shrugged. "We should all be who we really are when we are home. It is home."

He turned to her, angry now. "I can't do that when you are there! I have been away for a month. A month without my kids, without my father. Now you have them and I don't."

"What makes you think I have them?!" She turned to him now, angry too. She only had her family and no one else.

"My dad is enamored with you and my children adore you. Don't you see that? And now that I'm home I can't be with them when you and your family are around."

"Why, Tony? Why can't you be around us?" She was livid now.

"Because if you all knew who I was you wouldn't like me for me. You would like me for who I am."

"What does that mean?" She dropped her hands and opened her mouth at him. "I told you I don't care who you are."

"But you would if I told you who I was."

"Try me." She stood now and walked in front of him. She saw him drop his head.

"I can't." His voice was quiet, soft.

She moved down to her knees and saw him draw his face to his chest. He shook his head

"What if I told you I wouldn't flip out? I wouldn't go crazy. Would that help?"

His head didn't move this time. She moved her hands toward the tie on his hoodie and saw him flinch. Moving her hands more slowly now, she rested them on the tie of his jacket. She felt his eyes move to her hands.

"Can I…" She purposefully trailed off.

He sighed. She might as well know. Might as well get this over with. He nodded his head.

She pulled on one string and saw it fall to the front of his jacket. Pulling the other out, she saw it fall, too. She heard him hold his breath.

"You know this won't make a difference to me." She saw him duck to avoid looking at her. He nodded his head. She laughed. "You will always be Peter Parker or Bruce Wayne or Tony Stark or Clark Kent to me." She lifted her hands to his hoodie and rested them on the crown of his head.

"But what if I'm not the superhero? What if I am just an ordinary guy just doing what I can to make a living for my family?"

"Then that would make you a superhero in my book." She drew back his hood.

He looked up at her on her knees in front of him and saw her eyes closed. She couldn't see him. He was surprised. "Why are your eyes closed?"

"Because I am imagining what you look like, Mr. Stark, before I see you."

She brought her hands to his face. "Your hair is messy and short like Tony Stark's or Loki's. Maybe you're the bad guy." She knew her voice purred on the term "bad guy." She continued, "It is too unkempt for Peter Parker or Batman or Superman, sorry."

She moved her hand down the side of his face. Your jaw is long and lean. May be Tony or Loki." She moved her hands up his face to his eyebrows. "Uneven. Not Loki. His eyebrows are straight."

Her hand came back around to his face. "You, sir, are Tony Stark." She brought up his hood and tied it again. She pushed his head back down and opened her eyes. "Well, Mr. Stark, good evening."

He laughed. He had expected her to look at him with her eyes. Except she hadn't done that; she had "seen" him with her hands and then respected his privacy, his identity. "Why didn't you look at me?"

She laughed as she sat back up again, drawing her knees to her, stretching out his jacket again. "Because, Mr. Stark, I want to protect who you think you are. I want you to want to show me who you are instead of taking that right away from you. I want you to want to do it."

He looked at her now in amazement. She had respected who he was as a person. "Why?"

"Maybe because I want you to see me the same way I see you before I see you." She knew she had talked in circles. "Besides, if you are Tony Stark, AKA Ironman, I can't be Pepper. I would have to be someone else." She thought. "Maybe I could be The Mandarin, your arch nemesis." She laughed at that. "I could attempt to foil you at every turn." She stood now and placed her hands on her hips, spreading her feet apart. "That's it! I shall be The Mandarin and you shall be Tony Stark! We shall fight and I will overcome you!" She stood on the bench now, holding out her hand as if as sword was in it. "Stand now, Mr. Stark, and battle me!"

"Quiet down." He tried grabbing her, but she evaded him, scooting backward just a little

"You have to be quicker than that!" She gestured toward the front of him. "I stand in front of you now with you in your Ironman suit. You think you are invincible, sir, but I shall take you down!" She pretended to thrust her sword at him.

"Get down." He looked up at her now. "What are you doing?" He stood on the ground and he watched her.

"I am fighting you with my sword." She thrust and then parried.

"Ironman didn't fight with a sword, Elizabeth." He laughed and shook his head at this woman.

"I am," she put her hands on her hips, "The Mandarin! And I know that your suit is impenetrable to my sword! But I shall try, good sir, to beat you anyway." She went to thrust again and lost her footing. "Ah!" She felt herself falling.

"Elizabeth!" He caught her in his arms as she toppled sideways. "Are you alright?" He looked her over.

Elizabeth looked into his eyes. They were beautiful. "Are your eyes brown?" She shook herself and averted her gaze. "I'm sorry." She wiggled to get out of his hands. She felt her feet hit the ground. "I lost my feet, Mr. Stark, and fell."

She moved away from him now, on the ground, and held out her hand as if she had a sword again. "Just because you have shown me mercy, Ironman, does not mean I shall be your friend!" She pretended to thrust again and sidestepped his imaginative swipe with his sword. He wasn't playing along, but she pretended he was.

"Are you crazy?" Daniel looked at her and laughed.

"Crazy with power! Your power, and it shall be mine! Hahaha!"

She had no clue who Ironman was other than the few snippets of a conversation she had caught with her husband.

He laughed at her this time. A big laugh that found his hand out to hers. His sword was in his hand now and one hand was on his hip. She had never seen Ironman in her life. He knew he could have easily made that bet and won.

"I shall defeat you, Mandarin! You will not survive this encounter." They would swashbuckle as Ironman and nemesis.

"I shall defeat you!" He hopped up on the bench and moved closer to her.

"Nay! I shall be the one to defeat you and take all that you have. Stark Industries shall be mine! Bwahaha!" She leaned against the back of the bench and laughed, looking up into the night sky. She stopped laughing. Daniel was standing behind her now, but she hadn't heard him move. He was breathing down her neck. Every hair on her body rose as she felt his hand around her waist, pulling her close to him.

His other hand was at her neck, holding his invisible sword against it. "Nay, it is I that haveyou, Mandarin. Victory is mine!"

She had to think quickly! "You shall not have my throat, Ironman, no matter how much you thirst for my blood!" She moved back and pressed herself against his body. She heard him gasp and relax for just a moment. She ran out of his grip and moved to the other side of the bench. "You see, Mr. Stark, I shall always fight you and I shall always win! You cannot defeat me!"

Daniel stopped and beheld the woman in front of him. Her hair had come out of the long ponytail it was in and cascaded down her back. As she had fought him, it glinted in the moonlight. He couldn't take his mind off of it. As she had laughed he thought to play along with her and crept up behind her, pulling her to him. When she had pressed herself against him, he had been surprised at his reaction to her. Once he got over the shock, he narrowed his eyes at her.

"You think you can defeat me, Mandarin, but it is I that will defeat you." He held out his sword and advanced to her quickly.

Both pretended to thrust and parry until he had her against the back of the bench. His body leaned over hers and he pressed his sword against her long neck. He could feel the softness of her hair against the back of his hand.

"Do you admit surrender?"

She shook her head, her golden hair moving as she did. "Never!"

He moved closer to her again. "Say you surrender!"

She saw his high cheekbones and his brown eyes. His small mouth and straight nose. His uneven eyebrows with his arching left one. She looked down. She shouldn't have noted those things. Her face burned. "Nay!"

He brought his hands to her shoulders and she saw his eyes drop. "Say you surrender to me!"

Her own eyes dropped and her already quick heartbeat began to race faster. What was going on? "Nay." She felt breathless. Didn't he hear her heartbeat pounding?

There was a silence between them and she saw his head moving toward hers. She held her breath, knowing this was wrong. She closed her eyes.

The sound of her phone ringing found him flinging himself from her. She jumped to the side and fumbled it out of her pocket. She looked to the ground.

"Hello," she said, her voice shaky. Did she really almost kiss a man she had never laid eyes on?

"Mom? It's David. He's still running a fever. His stomach looks… bigger and he has started being sick." Paul sounded worried.

"I'm on my way." She pushed "End" on the phone and her eyes darted to Daniel. "It's my son, David."

Chapter Seven

She turned and ran down the street toward the B&B. As she ran she tried to think. She had a few things for him but not a lot of medicines. She hadn't even found a physician for the kids yet.

Elizabeth hurried into the B&B, went to her room, and knocked on the door. "Paul, please let me in." The door swung open and she shut it behind her, locking it. "What's going on, Paul?" She looked over to her oldest son.

"I heard David say he was thirsty so I went to get him a drink. I bent down to kiss him and I noticed he was warm. I threw all of the covers off of him and took his temperature. It was one hundred one degrees. He says his stomach hurts worse."

Paul was worried, but he knew his mom was the healer in the house. She nodded her head, looking around. What should she do? Elizabeth grabbed the phone book and searched for the nearest hospital. It was at least an hour away. She remembered passing it on the way here.

She threw the book from her.

Picking up the phone, she dialed the only person she could think of. When he answered, she could have wept. "Reverend, David is sick. I think he needs to go to the Mercy Hospital. Can you help me?"

The Reverend was watching his son grab the keys to his car. He had heard Daniel come running in and bound up to his room. He had told him David was sick and that he was on his way there. John had gotten up and just as he was going to answer his son, the phone rang.

"You bring the other kids to me, Elizabeth. I will watch them while my son takes you to the hospital. Get them ready, my dear. They will be fine here." He hung up the phone. "Hurry, Daniel."

Daniel ran out the front door of his home and drove to the B&B. A man and woman were standing inside and had cups in their hands. He walked up to them.

"Elizabeth Seraphim—which room are she and her family in?" He looked down into her face.

"Room nine and ten. Why?"

They began to follow him and he pounded on the door. "Elizabeth! Open up the door." He pounded on the door again and it opened. He looked to the teenager and then moved past him. He heard the boy gasp, recognition in his eyes. "Where is he? Where is David?" He made his way over to Elizabeth and picked up her son. He didn't look at her. "Are your children ready, Elizabeth? Dad will watch them."

Elizabeth watched her son. "Yes, yes." She gathered her children and ushered them out the door.

"My car. It's the blue one at the end." He held the little boy in his arms. He unlocked it and moved everyone into it. He handed the little boy to his mother. "I'm going to take them in to my dad and then we are going to take David to hospital."

He parked his car and moved the kids out. His dad was already standing at the front door.

"You all know my dad. I will be with your mum." He saw his dad move the kids into the house.

"If you need anything, call me."

He got back into the car and threw it into drive. He saw Elizabeth, now in the back seat, holding her son. Her eyes were closed and she was mouthing words. When she opened her eyes he saw her look into his. Immediately she dropped her eyes.

"The nearest hospital is an hour away. I think his temperature has gone up more." She felt her son shiver. She pulled him closer to her. "You've got to hurry." She laughed crazily. "I don't even know your name. You are driving my son and me in the middle of the night to the hospital and I don't even know who you are."

"Does it matter, Elizabeth?" He felt if he had to he would tell her. If he had to.

"No. Not really. I just want my son to be well." She looked down to him and began to sing to him. It was a hymn they had sung in chapel the Sunday before. It was one of David's favorites. She sang to him all the way to the hospital.

As they pulled up to the entrance, she heard Daniel shut the car off then he took David from her hands. He rushed the little boy into the hospital.

Elizabeth was shaking as she made her way with the man carrying her son. He had found a physician and they had whisked him away.

"Wait!" She went to go after him and she felt Daniel pull her to him.

"Does he have any allergies, Elizabeth? Tell me, does he?" He looked down at her in the bright light of the hospital.

Elizabeth looked up at him now. She wasn't noting his features. She was looking for her son in his face. She blinked and she felt him shake her violently.

"Elizabeth, your son David, does he have any allergies?!"

She blinked again. They just took her son and the man in front of her was asking if he had any allergies.

"Penicillin." She blinked, still looking at him, not really seeing him. "David is allergic to penicillin."

He let go of Elizabeth and caught up with the nurses. He told them of the boy's allergy. A few of them blushed as they recognized who he was.

"But you're…" one of the female nurses said.

He was afraid this would happen. "Yes, I am." He took a breath and tried to calm down.

"This boy is allergic to penicillin. Don't give him any." He turned then and made his way back to

Elizabeth. She hadn't moved. He put his arms around her and pulled her to him. "They know, Elizabeth. They won't give David any penicillin. He will be okay." He stroked her long blonde hair.

"I just want my son, Tony. I just want my son." She laid her head on his chest.

"Your son is going to be fine. They will take good care of him. You'll see." He kept stroking her hair.

He wouldn't tell her, but this was the hospital that he found Gen's body in. He had to come here to verify that it was her.

Now a little boy of a woman he barely knew was here and as much as he knew that little boy's life was precious, the memories of his wife are what occupied his mind now. He tried to push them down and amazingly, moving his hand through this woman's hair helped to calm him.

Elizabeth felt the man holding her as his hand moved through her hair. She had no idea who he was other than that his arms were wrapped tightly around her and he was whispering words of comfort to her. It really didn't matter that she didn't know his name; he was there for her son and her.

"Thank you, Mr. Stark. For everything you have done." She didn't move her head off of his chest but brought her arms around him.

He took a deep breath and dropped his face to her hair." Call me Daniel."

Elizabeth stopped and listened to his heartbeat, smelled the scent coming off of him. He smelled like warm chocolate, her favorite. She found herself drawing in his scent.

"Is Daniel your real name?"

He sighed. "Yes, but that is not what others outside of my family call me."

"I am not in your family, Mr. Stark, so I don't know what to call you. Should I call you what others call you? What is that? Maybe I should call you that."

Elizabeth didn't know what to call him other than Tony or Mr. Stark. Somehow the man in front of her had become Ironman to her.

He thought for a moment. "No, just call me Daniel, alright, Elizabeth?" He wanted her to call him by his name and not his stage name.

"Alright," she laughed, "but I still want to think of you as Ironman." She pulled him to her tighter.

"Mrs. Seraphim?" A male voice called her name and she turned from Daniel, going over to the man who called her name.

"This way, please." He led her into a room off to the side and closed the door.

Daniel looked at the closed door and felt his body drop. As he stared at the door, he wished he knew what was going on behind it. He strained his ears to listen but heard nothing.

A few minutes later, the door opened and Elizabeth walked out. The physician was talking quietly with her and she was nodding her head. He smiled and went on his way.

Elizabeth walked up to Daniel but didn't look at him. The light was too bright and she didn't want to see him. She motioned out the front doors and looked into the night. Daniel followed Elizabeth out of the front doors and stood alongside her, not touching her.

"They have checked David over. They are waiting for the tests to come back, but they think it is appendicitis. They want him to rest until they can run a few more tests on him. They won't let me see him yet."

She wanted to see her son and had asked the physician. He had told her they were almost done prepping him and when they were through she could see him.

"Appendicitis?!"

"They are working on him now." She turned to him. "Listen, thanks for the ride. I really appreciate all that you and your father have done for us. I know having eight children in the house is a lot and

I think he struggles more than he lets on, Daniel. I'll have them make their way back to the B&B so they can stay there until David and I can come home. Mabel will keep an eye on them." She looked back into the night.

"Dad can watch them, Elizabeth. He likes kids. You know that. Yours seem nice to him."

"It would be an inconvenience. I don't want him to go to any more trouble than he already has." She looked back to the drawstring of his hoodie.

"It's not an inconvenience. Dad will watch them and I will stay as long as you need me."

"You can't. You know you can't, Daniel. Your life can't stop because a stranger's son is sick."

He didn't know why, but her thinking of him as a stranger bothered him. "Stranger? Do you think of yourself as a stranger to me?! I am Ironman, Mandarin. I am no stranger to you." He laughed and saw her mouth lift.

"I know. I'm just saying," she let out a breath. "I hate hospitals. My mom, my dad, my brother, and my husband all died in a hospital." She walked away from him a little, glaring up at the building.

"I know," his voice was low and sad. "The last time I was at this hospital was to claim my wife's body." He thought to walk up to her and put his arms around her but didn't.

Elizabeth looked at him now. "Your wife's…" She looked down. "But I thought you said your wife was away."

"She is away, Elizabeth, and she isn't coming back." He was the one to glare at the building now. "I got a phone call while I was shooting, the kids were all at school. I had to leave set to come here and tell them that the body I saw on the table was my wife's." He wanted to hit something, he was so angry.

She moved up to him and put her arms around him now. "I'm sorry, Daniel. I know what that's like, having to say goodbye to a spouse." She laid her head on his chest and closed her eyes, saying a prayer, hoping it drove away some of his pain.

He restrained himself from touching her. She didn't feel like Gen and that's who he wanted holding him right now. But she was soft and warm and she smelled so good.

"Elizabeth, I have things I have to do today, but I will have my mobile on me at all times." He put his hands on her face and slanted it up to his. "If you need anything, and I mean anything, you call me."

Elizabeth nodded her head. "Alright, Daniel."

He took her mobile phone out of her pocket and saved his number into it. "This is my personal mobile phone number. Only a handful of people have it. Don't give it to anyone. This is just for you."

He looked down at her as he slipped it back into her pocket. He knew he was taking a risk giving her his personal number, but he trusted her to do the right thing.

She nodded her head and smiled. "If you don't want anyone else to have it, none shall, Mr. Stark. Your secret shall be kept safe. But you realize you just gave your nemesis your number. Was that a wise thing to do, Ironman?"

He thought about it for a moment. "I think, Mandarin, that you are more than my nemesis." She felt her breath catch as the doors opened.

"Mrs. Seraphim?" She saw Daniel drop his head. "Mrs. Seraphim? We have your son settled. You can see him now."

Elizabeth hit the doors running.

"Where is he? Where is my son?" She looked to the person who relayed the information.

"He is in Room 48. We have his fever down a little, but he is still warm. We really are doing all we can."

Elizabeth knew the person had used their voice to sound calm, reassuring. "Thank you."

She opened the door and walked into the room.

"Mommy!" David was lying on a bed. There were a few things hooked up to him and some tubes running to a point in his arm. She reached out to hold him in her arms.

"Hey, baby. Mommy loves you."

"I love you too, Mommy." His eyes looked past hers. "Is that Danny…?"

Elizabeth saw her son's eyes widen. "Yes," she interrupted, "this is Daniel." She turned, now realizing he had followed her. Inwardly she was glad he was here.

"But, Mommy, he…"

Daniel winked at the little boy and said, "I know. How are you feeling, David?"

"I'm fine, sir."

"Daniel. Just call me Daniel." He knew the boy knew him by Danny, but he wanted the boy to know his real name.

"Okay, Daniel. I am feeling a little better. My belly still hurts and I'm sleepy." He settled his head back on his pillow. He felt his mother's hand in his. "Will you sing to me, Mommy? Sing me Jesus Loves Me, that's my favorite." He closed his eyes.

"Of course, David." She moved up to the head of his bed and began to sing softly to her son. Before she knew it, he was fast asleep.

She ran her hand across his forehead. He did feel cooler than he did before, but he was still warm. She kissed him on the cheek and sat back in the chair, holding his hand.

Daniel had seen the exchange between Elizabeth and David. It was obvious she loved her child and he loved her. He saw her still holding the tiny hand as she gazed at her son.

He looked down to her other hand and he noticed that it was curled in on itself. He had the strangest urge to hold it but didn't. He just watched as Elizabeth looked at her son.

Daniel looked around for another chair and pulled it up next to hers. Together they both watched the little boy as he slept. He did reach down then and took her hand. It laced itself through his and he heard her sigh.

After a while, Elizabeth began to tire. It had been a long night and the adrenaline had begun to wear off. She felt the hand leave hers and heard the scrape of a chair. She felt a hand wrap around her shoulder and pull her to the body it belonged to. Her head fell on his chest and still she held on to her son's hand. She picked up her head and looked at him.

He said, “It’s been a busy day. Why don’t you rest? I’ll watch over Davey.”

She looked down at his chest. “Don’t you have to leave?”

He shook his head. “Not for a little while. Why don’t you rest while Davey does? If he wakes, I will let you know.”

She knew she should argue with him, but instead she leaned against him again. “Alright, but just for a moment.”

Chapter Eight

"Elizabeth?" She heard the sound of a voice calling her out of her sleep state.

"Elizabeth?"

She opened her eyes and looked to her child's bed. It was empty. She stood up now, wide awake. "Where is my son?"

"They took him to run some more tests. Dad is sending one of the people from the church to sit with you. I have to leave, but my phone will always be on." He looked down into her eyes. "You remember what I told you about my number?"

She nodded her head and smiled. "Your secret is safe with me, Mr. Stark. I shall protect your identity at all costs, sir."

"That was not spoken like a true nemesis. You are going to have to work on that, Mandarin." He smiled with her.

She knew that smile. She liked that smile. She looked down at the floor before recognition flashed in her eyes. "Did they say when they would be back?"

"I was told the tests wouldn't take long." He heard the door open and he smiled at the man walking through it.

"Hello," Deacon Wayne said as he walked over to the two people in the chairs. They were sitting next to one another and the man had his arm around Mrs. Seraphim.

Elizabeth stood up and felt Daniel's hand drop from her shoulder. "Good morning, Deacon Wayne. Thank you for coming by." She smiled at him.

"I would like to sit with you and David for a while, Mrs. Seraphim. Reverend Templeman called me and asked if someone could. I find myself at a day off and I would like to be here with you and your son."

"Thank you, Deacon Wayne. It was very thoughtful of you." She turned to Daniel and eyed the tie on his hoodie. "Do you have to leave now?"

Daniel looked at his watch and over to Deacon Wayne, smiling. He didn't feel the smile that moved across his mouth. He should have. This was the perfect opportunity for Elizabeth and Deacon Wayne to get to know one another.

"Yes." He sighed, finding himself not wanting to go, but he had three things he had to do today. "But remember what I said." He looked to her pocket, where her phone still was.

Elizabeth nodded her head. She laid her hand on his wrist and looked into his eyes. "I will. Thank you, Daniel. For everything."

Daniel smiled at Elizabeth and then turned and walked out of the room, shutting the door.

"Good morning to you, Mr. Celebrity."

"Deacon Wayne," she chastised him. "Thank you for offering to sit with me today, but if whatever has you upset is going to bother you, then you can leave."

She didn't know why, but what he said to Daniel's back bothered her. Yes, Daniel should have acknowledged the other man, but that gave Wayne, a Deacon of the church, no right to be mean to him.

“I’m just saying, just because he is a celebrity and the Reverend’s son doesn’t give him a right to be rude.” He laughed nervously.

“I understand, Wayne, but I am pretty sure he had a lot on his mind.” She walked toward him, keeping her distance. “I really do thank you for coming by. I appreciate the company.”

He took her hand and as he did the door opened. Since Daniel had walked out of the room, something kept telling him to go back and speak to Deacon Wayne. He ignored it until he got to the front doors. Turning then, he made his way back to David’s room.

Pushing open the door, he saw Deacon Wayne holding Elizabeth’s hand. He looked to the joined hands and then to Elizabeth. He felt his eyebrows furrow as he looked to Wayne.

“I just wanted to say good morning, Wayne, and thank you for offering to sit the day with Elizabeth while I couldn’t.” He looked at their hands again and then to Elizabeth. “I will see you as soon as I can.”

He looked at their hands again, then and pulled the door closed, hard, behind him. He heard the door bang as it hit against the frame. Several heads looked his way and recognition flashed across their faces. More than one looked around frantically, probably for pencil and paper.

He sighed. He was going to be later than he thought, now, as the first person walked up to him with both items in their hand. He smiled and became Danny Tensley, the actor. He could probably spin this to make it look like he was visiting the sick children in hospital.

As he chatted and signed the first of many autographs, he thought he would need to protect Elizabeth and David from questions. He moved to the nurses' station, chatting and signing autographs. He asked the staff where he could find a few more children to visit with while he was there.

Some of the women blushed and said they would take him to the children's rooms personally. He would need to call his agent, he thought, as he smiled and laughed with the people around him. He hoped Deacon Wayne would keep Elizabeth in the room for a little while longer.

He would need that just to clear the hospital.

Daniel made his way home and was not surprised to find his children already at school. Elizabeth's children were at the kitchen table with textbooks in front of them, quietly working. His dad was standing in the doorway.

"Hello, Dad." He walked up to his father, looking at Elizabeth's children. "Homework?" He nodded to the kids.

He had already called his agent and had reworked his day. His stops were closer together, so that gave him less time to prepare for each one. The car for the day would be here in half an hour.

John stood and watched Elizabeth's children. "Good morning, Son. Yes. Paul insisted to walk to the B&B this morning to get the children's books to continue their lessons. I told him I would drive him once I dropped off Tayler, Olivia, and Raven at school. Once we were back, they all sat down, prayed, and started their lessons."

"How did they know what to do?" He watched the children working and writing quietly.

Occasionally one of the children would ask and answer a question.

"Elizabeth. Paul said when she pulled them out of public school in America she ordered curriculum for them and they started then. She made out a whole year's worth of lesson plans for each of the children, even David."

Daniel watched the children as they studied. "Alright, Dad." He turned and nodded his head. "I'm going to shower and be off for the day. I'll stop by when I can, to see all of the kids, but I would like to go to the hospital as soon as I can."

He looked at the children. Paul, Lily, Ben, and April looked up and saw Danny Tensley standing in the doorway. Lily gasped and felt Paul touch her hand, then she looked down at her books. Ben and April saw the exchange and looked to their books, too, sneaking glances at the celebrity standing in the doorway.

Paul looked up and smiled at Danny Tensley. What was he doing here? "Good morning, sir."

Daniel saw all of the kids' heads pop up now. Lily and April blushed and Ben smiled.

"Good morning. How are your lessons going?"

Paul leaned back in his chair. "Fine. How is David?"

"He is with your mother. They are running tests. They are going to keep him there for a few days so you will all stay here. Dad will make sure you have everything you need from the B&B. I have a few things I have to do today and then I will be home for a little while, then back to the hospital to see your mother and brother."

"Thank you, but I can take care of my siblings while Mom is with David." Paul didn't really know the man in front of him, but he did know the Reverend. The Reverend hadn't mentioned staying there until David came home.

Daniel looked to his father and said, "I think it's best for you children to stay here while your mom is caring for your brother." Daniel turned to walk out of the room. Twenty-five minutes to the car. He would have to hurry.

"With all due respect, sir, I can take care of my siblings until my mother and brother come back." Paul's hackles were raised. He had seen his mother take care of them. Now it was his turn.

John stepped forward, looking at the boy. Paul was sixteen and responsible, but if something happened to one of them, he would not know what to do without his mother being there.

"I would appreciate it, Son, if you would stay here with me and my grandchildren until your mom can return with your brother. I know it will take a load off of her mind to know you kids are being taken care of by the pastor of the church." He smiled, his crooked teeth showing now. "It will help her to help your brother."

Paul settled now. If being there would help his mom, he would do it. "Alright, sir," he looked to the Reverend, then to his siblings. "Let's get back to our studies, guys."

He watched until Lily, Ben, and April's heads dropped back to their books. He knew they were sneaking glances at the man standing at the doorway.

"Thank you, Paul." John nodded at the oldest boy. He looked to Daniel now, gesturing him to the foot of the stairs. "I know you have to leave, but how is David?" He glanced toward the children at the kitchen table.

Daniel crossed his arms. "He is not much better. The hospital thinks he has appendicitis. They have him comfortable until the tests they did come back."

"How is Elizabeth?"

"Lizzy is holding it together for him."

The old man's eyebrows perked up and he smiled. "Lizzy, is it?"

"Elizabeth. Mrs. Seraphim. Oh!" He threw up his hands. "I don't have time for this." He turned and started to make his way up the stairs. "I told her to call me if anything changed."

"Call you?"

Daniel stopped and turned toward his father. "Yes. I gave her my mobile number." He really didn't want to have to admit that to his father. He didn't know why. He turned to walk up the stairs again.

"Did Deacon Wayne make it to the hospital before you left?" The Reverend had his reasons for calling Deacon Wayne. He held back a smile as he saw his son stop and turn toward him again. A thundercloud had formed over his head.

"Yes. They were holding hands before I left. Does that make you happy, Dad?" He turned and stormed up the stairs, slamming the door to his room.

Reverend Templeman laughed quietly as he watched his son's retreating back and heard the door slam. He laughed a little louder now, wondering how his son was going to work his appointments, his children, and Elizabeth Seraphim into his day. The last, John was sure, would occupy his son's mind for most of the day.

Chapter Nine

Daniel showered, dressed, and got ready to go for the day. He made his way down the stairs, five minutes early for the car. He pulled out his phone and texted Elizabeth.

Any news on David? I am getting ready to head out my front door and start my day.

Three stops and then back home for a bit. Then to hospital.

He sent the message and waited for a reply. He tapped his foot and looked out the window just in case the car was early. It wasn't. He was about ready to send another text when Elizabeth replied.

No. Still waiting. Deacon is still here and we are breakfasting in the cafeteria. He really is a nice guy. I see now why he is the Deacon of the church.

Daniel grasped the phone and restrained himself from throwing it. Deacon was having breakfast with Lizzy! He closed his eyes and calmed down. Loosening his grip on the phone, he sent another text.

Thinking good thoughts for David the rest of the day. You have my number call or text anytime. If I am recording I may not get back to you right away.

He was about to hit "Send" when a thought came to mind. He added another part to the text.

Glad Deacon Wayne is there with you. He is a nice guy from what my father says. He likes large families too. Wants one of his own one day. Know where he can find one? I am here when you need me.

Ironman

He waited to see if Elizabeth would reply to his text and when she didn't he restrained himself from texting her again. He had already told her if she needed him, he would be there for her. What else could he say? Have a good day with Deacon Wayne. Hope you get a marriage proposal before the day is over. No, probably best not to ask those questions or make those statements to her.

He slipped his phone back in his pocket and saw the car pull up. Roger stepped out of the car. "Dad, I'm off." He opened the door. "Have a good day, kids!" He shut the door behind him.

Another good thing about Roger was that Daniel didn't have to pretend to be a celebrity with him. He could just be Daniel Templeman. "Good morning, Roger. I trust you are well." He looked the other man in the eye as he slid into the seat of the car. He saw Roger shut the door.

Roger Blain slid into the driver's side of the car, started the engine, and pulled out of the drive. He liked Danny Tensley, although Roger knew that was not his real name.

Danny was sharp and industrious. A self-starter. It was his greeting that threw Roger off this morning. Usually he got a "good morning," but today Danny had asked him how he was doing. Something in his life must have changed.

"I am well, sir. Yourself?" His thick Scottish brogue was much like Danny's, except Danny had lived in England long enough that he could slip in and out of accent fluidly.

"Good." He looked out the window and felt for the phone in his pocket. "You know the plan for the day, Roger?"

"Yes, sir." He rattled off the stops and times flawlessly. "Then back home."

"Good." Daniel felt for his phone again and decided to take it out of his pocket. He began flipping it over in his hands, wanting it to ring or chime, but it stayed silent.

His first stop was an interview. The questions had already been scripted and he knew his answers. It seemed he was always asked the same questions. He always had the same answers; he just rephrased the words, making the host or hostess laugh with his smile and charm. He played the part of Danny Tensley well.

He saw the studio building and then looked down at his phone. He opened a new text to Elizabeth.

Any news? I am getting ready to head in for my first interview of the day.
Ironman

He waited and there was no response. He sent another as the car pulled into the spot.

If there is any news don't hesitate to text or Call me. I am here. How is Deacon Wayne?
Ironman

No response again. He frowned. Roger got out to open his door. He smiled as the door opened and he became Danny Tensley, the actor. People were chanting his name. He slipped his phone deep into his pocket, its weight reassuring him it was there. It was time to play his part.

After the interview, he stopped on the way out to sign a few autographs and take some pictures. Roger opened the car door for him and he slid in. The tinted windows hid the world from him as he pulled his phone out of his pocket. Ten a.m. Two more stops to make in less than three hours.

Looking at his phone, he noticed there were no calls or messages. It had been four hours since he left the hospital and Deacon Wayne had come to stay with Elizabeth for the day.

Why hadn't she texted him? Maybe Deacon Wayne was charming her as she waited for David to come back to the room. Maybe they had found something out and Wayne was comforting her. He opened his messages and sent another text.

First interview over. It went well. How is David? Any news yet from tests? Are you alright?

He waited through two red lights, flipping his phone over faster and faster in his hand. He knew he couldn't call the hospital and ask about David Seraphim, and Lizzy wasn't texting him back. He sent another.

Sorry to interrupt your time with the church Deacon but I would like to know what's happening with David. Text me back when you get this, Mandarin.

Ironman

He waited again, flipping his phone faster as they approached his next destination. Another interview: this time about a popular television show he had been on. He was still famous for that run. He had a good time with it, but that time was over and he was moving on to other projects.

He knew these questions and answers were scripted, too. Same thing here. Smile, charm, and give the people what they wanted. Leave. Let them see Danny Tensley the actor for just a little while and then leave them wanting more.

His phone vibrated. He turned on the screen and looked at the message icon. He moved his finger over it, opening the message. It was from Lizzy.

No news on David yet. Tests were run and back in room. He is hungry but the doctors want to wait on solid food for now. On limited overseas calling plan, Mr. Stark. Cannot reply to every text.

Your Nemesis, The Mandarin

He felt the car pull up to the curb and this time a bigger crowd awaited him. He smiled, pulling on the façade of Danny Tensley, and slipped the phone in his pocket.

He smiled happily now. He was going to make a phone call when this interview was over. Lizzy would be so surprised.

Roger opened his car door now and Danny Tensley stepped out of the car, smiling and happy. He couldn't wait for this interview to be over, but he wouldn't let it show. He beamed and posed, signed more autographs, and flashed his devastating smile as he made his way into the studio.

Later, slipping back into the car, he pulled out his phone. No messages. No texts.

Going through his list of Contacts, he found what he was looking for and called the number. After being on the phone for a few minutes, he hung up, smiling at himself. Sometimes it was good to be a celebrity.

He sent a text to Lizzy.

It will be alright, Lizzy. David will be fine, you'll see. How are you? You did not mention that in your last message. Is everything going well between you and Deacon Wayne?

Ironman

He held the phone in his hand now, not really paying attention to where Roger was taking him. He was ready for his day to be over. He wanted to see his children and then be at the hospital with Lizzy, but his life was in the way.

He loved his job and what he did. He'd dreamed about what he wanted since he was a kid, but right now he wanted to be somewhere else and he couldn't.

His phone was silent and he opened his messages again. He knew he had about a thirty minute drive to the next destination. He also knew that the request he had made on the phone earlier should be fulfilled very soon. He smiled. His phone vibrated and he almost dropped it as he fumbled to turn it over and read the message.

The doctor has David on an IV drip. He says his belly hurts. We never like to see our children sick, do we? Deacon Wayne is fine. He says to tell you "hi."

Your Nemesis, The Mandarin

Daniel looked out the window and thought about the text. He smiled and opened a new message to Lizzy.

Wish Davey was feeling better. Tell Deacon Wayne I said "hi", too and that we celebrities always have time for our fans. (Yes, I heard that this morning as I was leaving.)Last stop of the day. Will text when this is over. Text or call if you need me before then.
Ironman

Chapter Ten

Roger had been watching his client all day. He was nervous and seemed fidgety. This was not his charge's usual self. "Care to talk about it, sir?" He looked into his rearview mirror and then back to the road.

"What?" Daniel looked from his phone to his driver.

"You have been cradling that phone like a lover all morning, sir. Is something happening?" Roger genuinely was concerned for Daniel, not just as a client, but as a friend.

Daniel looked down at his phone. Cradling his phone like a lover? He shook his head. No, he wasn't. "I don't understand what you are asking, Roger."

He looked back at Daniel again and back to the road. "I think, sir, that you have met someone, sir."

"I have a new friend, if that's what you mean." He looked out the window, still flipping the phone around in his hands.

"A lady friend?" Roger laughed. He would bet Danny Tensley was smitten.

"She is a woman, yes." His phone vibrated and he felt the car pull to the side of the road. He did drop it this time and heard Roger laugh. He looked up to the other man and saw him straighten his face, a knowing smile still on it. Daniel opened the message.

Doctor says surgery early in morning—an obstruction. Please ask your father to call the congregation for David and say a prayer. I'm worried, Ironman.

Your Nemesis, The Mandarin

Daniel had to stem the rising panic. He had to do this interview. "Hold on, Roger," he said to the man. Luckily Roger hadn't gotten out of the car yet. He dialed his father's number. "Hello."

"Dad, Lizzy just texted me. David has to have surgery. Something about an obstruction. She has asked if you would ask the congregation to pray for him." He tried not to sound desperate, but he became fidgety.

"Let her know I will, Son. Also let her know we are praying for her, too."

"I will, Dad, thank you." He ended the call.

Roger looked into the rearview mirror at his client. "Lizzy, huh? Pretty name." He saw Danny glance up at him as he held his phone. He looked mad. "Not meaning anything by it. But this David. Her son?"

"Yes." He nodded his head, already starting a text to Lizzy.

"Let her know I will be praying for her, too, and her son, Mr. Tensley." He was already forming the prayer in his head.

Daniel looked up from his phone to roger. "You're a spiritual man, Roger?"

"Yes, sir. I will light a candle for her and her son."

Daniel made eye contact with the other man. "Thank you, Roger." He checked his message.

Will be there as soon as I can. Have last interview to do then on my way. Talked with Dad, he is having congregation praying for him and you. My

driver Roger says he will light a candle for you and your son.
Ironman

He hit "Send" and looked out over the crowd. He put on the mantle of Danny Tensley as he put the phone in his pocket. Looking to Roger, he nodded his head. Showtime!

Daniel slipped back into the car. The interview took longer than expected and his phone had vibrated several times while he was in the studio. He pulled it out of his pocket now.

There were three messages, two from a number he did not recognize. The first was from Lizzy.

Daniel. David's fever has spiked again and the doctors are saying they might do emergency surgery this afternoon if they can't bring the fever down. Say a prayer for my son.
Your Nemesis, The Mandarin

He opened the second message, from the unknown number.

Daniel. Thank you for the phone. I don't know how or why but the guy who delivered it said it had unlimited calling and texting for this country already on the line. David's fever climbing. They are taking drastic steps now. I'm scared, Ironman.
Your Nemesis, The Mandarin

He was almost afraid to open the next message. This was also from Lizzy.

David has stabilized. His fever is still too high. Still talking surgery before early morning. Can't stop shaking. Know you are busy but wanted you to know. Thank you again for the phone.

Your Nemesis, The Mandarin

He looked up and saw the questioning expression on Roger's face. "I need to be home, now," Daniel said, dialing the number to Lizzy's new phone. He was thankful Roger was his driver.

"What's wrong, sir?" Roger pulled from the curb, already planning the shortest route to Danny's residence.

Daniel pulled the phone to his ear as it rang. "David is worse. I have to get home and change before I go to the hospital." The phone rang until it went to the voicemail that was not set up yet. He ended the call and hit redial.

"I'm sorry to hear that, sir. I have lit a candle for them at the church. God has heard our prayers."

Roger was driving carefully, yet now he was pushing the speed limit.

Daniel nodded his head. "I hope he hears them, Roger."

Voicemail again! He searched his phone for the number to the hospital and found it. He had not deleted it from his phone since they had called him about Gen. He dialed the number.

"Mercy Hospital Information Desk, how may I help you?" Under any other circumstances the woman on the other end of the phone would have sounded nice and helpful.

Right now she stood between him and Lizzy.

"Lizzy," he stopped, glancing up at Roger. "Please page Elizabeth Seraphim."

"Who may I ask is calling?"

He had to think. He couldn't use any of his names. "Ironman."

The lady on the other end of the line sighed. Her voice when she spoke next sounded irritated. "Seraphim? Ironman? Is this a prank call?"

"No! Page Lizzy Seraphim and tell her Ironman is calling her and to answer her phone!" He waited. After a bit of silence he heard the woman switch connections and then the line went dead. He heard Roger laughing in the front seat. "What is so funny, Roger?"

"Sir, do you know what Elizabeth means?"

Daniel scowled at the other man, who then said, "It means 'pledged to God' or 'my God is an oath.' Seraphim means 'angel.' David means 'beloved.' And if she knows your father and has asked for his congregation to pray…" He shook his head. "You, sir, are in love with a spiritual woman. Do you even know what you are doing?"

Daniel became angry. "I am not in love, Roger. And yes, I know she is a spiritual woman. I'll thank you kindly to keep your thoughts to yourself." He looked out the window, flipping the phone around in his hands. When it rang, he answered it, purposefully making his voice gentle.

"Lizzy, tell me what's happening."

"They have moved his surgery to this evening. They say something is going on and they have to remove the blockage soon." Lizzy sounded worried and stressed. He looked at Roger driving the car and then out the window. He knew Roger was listening and he was almost home.

"I have to stop by the house and then I am on my way. Is Deacon Wayne still there?"

"Yes. We have already gone to the chapel here in the hospital and Deacon Wayne led the prayer for my son. Now we are reading scripture together and to David." She sounded surer now.

"I know David will be okay, Daniel, but I just need…"

"It was nice that Deacon Wayne was there to help the two of you, Lizzy." He knew he wouldn't have led Elizabeth in prayer for her son. He knew a little scripture but not enough to help her and her child. It sounded like Deacon Wayne had everything in hand, probably literally.

"Do you still want me—to come to the hospital, Lizzy?"

"Yes! Yes, please."

He waited, debating on what to do. Should he stay away and let Deacon Wayne take it from here, or go to the hospital like she wanted and he seemed to need to do?

"I'm on my way soon, then, Lizzy."

"Thank you, Daniel."

He looked up and saw Roger's eyes look down. He reread the last three text messages from Lizzy.

"You know, I was married once." Roger's voice came from the front seat. "She was a beauty. Long fiery red hair that tangled just by looking at it. "Fiona would brush it and then shake out her hair and it would tangle again." He laughed. "It would drive her crazy! I loved it."

He winked at the other man. "She died. Taken from me. I could never see her again."

Daniel waited. He knew Roger had a point to this story.

"If I had the chance to find love with someone who believed, not only in me but in God, I would grab on to that woman with both hands, sir. I would not let her go for all the Deacon Waynes in the world. I would fight for her, no matter what I had to do." He sighed. "I will always love my Fi, but this new woman would be my love, too."

Daniel continued looking at Roger until the other man moved his eyes back to the road.

"But he prays with her and reads scripture, Roger. I can't do that. I can't be that man."

Roger looked into the rearview mirror until Daniel looked up at him. Two Scots now stared one another down, one big and brawny, the other tall and wiry.

"Can't, or won't, sir?"

Daniel felt himself become angry. The car pulled up to his house and he opened his own door. He heard Roger's open, too. "You've crossed a line, Roger. Don't presume to tell me how to pursue my love life."

"I was just saying, sir." He crossed his arms, coming full height. If that man didn't know what wonderful thing was in front of him, he didn't deserve it.

"I won't be asking for you to drive me anymore, Roger." If his driver wanted to play the Scotsman, so could he. "From now on, do not take me anywhere, you got it?"

Roger nodded his head. """Aye. And I will not be asking for you, either. Stubborn man!" He moved to the front of the car and opened the door. "And another thing, since I won't be driving for you or interfering with your personal life, when you are done dangling this woman along, know that I will continue to pray for your soul, too, sir. That you find someone to help you on your way to the Lord." He opened the door, got in and slammed it, pulled out of the drive and moved off.

Chapter Eleven

Daniel turned toward the house and moved to the door. Opening it, he saw his dad at the kitchen table with Elizabeth's children. Their heads were bowed and his father was leading the prayer with them. They were all holding hands.

He could never be that man, he thought. The man to lead children in prayer, comfort them spiritually, answer questions.

He glanced at the clock. Two-fifty. The hospital was an hour's drive. He needed to hurry.

He changed and made his way down the stairs to the front door. As he looked down he saw Elizabeth's children standing in front of him. Paul walked up to him.

"Are you going to see my mom?"

Daniel had already had a trying day. He nodded his head, looking at the teenager. He saw Paul and the other children extend their hands to touch him.

"What are you all doing?"

The other boy looked at him. "We are going to pray for you, sir. That God use you to help our mother and our brother. To bring them home to us."

Daniel watched as all the children closed their eyes. He looked around for his father. He looked back to the boy who had just spoken. "What if I don't believe in your God?"

The littlest girl looked at him. She appeared to be about nine or ten years old. "You may not believe in God, but God believes in you."

Daniel looked at all of the children and saw them nod their heads. The other girl spoke this time. "And He will use you whether you believe in Him or not. He doesn't care that you don't because He believes in Mom and David."

"Be quick then, children, because your mother has asked me to come up to the hospital."

He saw all the children bow their heads and the oldest one began speaking. As Paul prayed, Daniel felt his head bow and his eyes close.

He wanted to believe that all the things that Paul was saying were true. That he could be used to help Lizzy and David, that David would be made whole again, and that, although he didn't know how, God would be brought glory through the situation. The children all ended with, "Amen."

He felt the need to hug them and he did. "Thank you, children. I'll let you know if anything changes."

He pulled the door open and shut behind himself. He felt a tear fall and he wiped it away. Those children had a great faith.

His drive to the hospital was faster than expected and as he exited the car, he pulled up his hoodie and slipped on his shades, hunching his shoulders, trying to appear shorter. He went straight to David's room.

As the door shut behind him, he heard Lizzy crying. He saw David's bed empty and made up. He looked over to see Lizzy in Deacon Wayne's arms. Deacon Wayne was holding her like a china doll and whispering to her.

He made his way over to the two people. He looked only to Lizzy. "Where is David?"

Panic set into his chest as he surveyed the woman in front of him. He saw her cry louder and pull herself out of Deacon Wayne's arms. He stalked up to her now and put his arms up to her. "I said, where is David?" He looked over at the bed and to her. She looked up to him with sad, broken eyes.

"No," he whispered. He pulled her to himself. "No! No, not David. No!" Not another person for her to lose, a child this time. Didn't this God have anything better to do than to take everyone this woman loved? "Not David."

He moved her away from him a little and pulled off his sunglasses and pushed the hoodie off of his hair. There was no one to hide from in here. He heard Wayne lock the door.

"Lizzy," he waited for her to look at him. He made his voice gentle for her now. "Lizzy, where's David?"

"They took him, Daniel." Elizabeth looked at the man in front of her. She knew why he looked familiar now. But she didn't care that she knew who he was. She looked at the bed and then to Daniel. She started to cry again and felt herself shake.

"Who, Lizzy, who took David? Tell me." He didn't want to picture the little boy's lifeless body lying on the bed but he did in his mind's eye.

"They came in and took him to surgery, Daniel. Just a few moments ago." She sniffled. "They said it couldn't wait any longer."

He looked down at her. David wasn't dead! Daniel pulled her to him and hugged her tightly. Pulling back just a little, he said, "Tell me what you need. Anything that I can get you is yours."

"I don't need anything, Daniel. Deacon Wayne and I were just going to the chapel to pray." She looked to Deacon Wayne, standing now by the door.

He took her hand and walked over to the door. "Where is the chapel?"

"It's down the hall, Daniel, and to the right. There is a sign above the door marked 'Chapel.' Elizabeth and I have been in and out of there all day today."

Daniel eyed the man and then Lizzie. "You come with us, Deacon. Teach me how to pray with Lizzy and then we are going to pray for David. All of us. Isn't there a scripture verse about two or more people praying together or something like that?"

Elizabeth nodded her head. "Yes."

"You," he swung his head around to Deacon Wayne, "are going to be our 'or more' once you have taught me how to pray with Lizzy." He unlocked the door and began to open it.

"Wait!" She shut the door before he could open it all the way. She moved her hands to his hoodie and pulled up his hood, tying it. She found his sunglasses in the pocket and slipped them on him. She reached up and hunched his shoulders. "Now, Mr. Stark, you are ready to face the public." She smiled at him and saw his lips tug upward.

"What are you two doing?" Deacon Wayne looked back and forth between the two people in front of him.

"I am suiting up Ironman so he can face the world, Deacon." She had looked over to him and smiled. Now she looked back over to Daniel—

Danny Tensley, as the world called him. "Can't have Mr. Stark going into this place unprotected, can we?" She raised her eyebrows and bit her lower lip.

"No, we cannot, Mandarin." His eyes followed her teeth as they slid over her lip. He pulled her closer to him as he opened the door. He made his way to the chapel and heard Wayne walk in beside them.

"Wait, wasn't The Mandarin Ironman's nemesis?" Wayne looked between the two of them.

"Yes, he was." Elizabeth nodded her head, smiling at Daniel as she went down to her knees. She tugged him down with her and he fell to his.

Wayne made his way to his knees beside Daniel. "What happened?" He looked between the two of them. He knew he was missing something.

Daniel let go of Lizzy's hand long enough to take off his shades and hoodie. He laid them aside. "Ironman thought he was challenging The Mandarin, but in reality he was meeting Penny." He saw Lizzy tilt her head. He could bet she had no idea who that was.

"Who is Penny?" She looked to Daniel as he shook his head, still smiling at her. She saw him look to Wayne and heard them chuckle.

"That, I can't tell you, Lizzy." He looked forward at a tall cross with a man whose hands and feet were nailed to it. The man up there looked sad. "But you can tell me about this guy." He turned to her. "I've heard about him my whole life but I really don't know who He is."

She looked to the representation of Jesus on the cross.

"That, Mr. Stark, is a man not unlike yourself." She looked back at him. She knew who he was but she didn't care. "He was God hidden in a mortal frame." She touched his jacket and eyed his glasses. "When He shed that body He became who He truly was: God." Daniel looked back at her.

"When we first met, Mr. Stark, you wouldn't tell me who you were. Jesus went around telling everyone who He was, but they didn't believe Him." She sighed. "I wanted you to tell me who you are—that's why I wouldn't look at you with my eyes, I looked at you with my hands and my heart. Jesus wants you to look at Him with your heart, too, Tony, and see Him for who He truly is."

She looked back at the statue. "This is just a representation of the physical form of God. Like the hoodie and the glasses you wear, but He shed His physical form like you shed your persona to become Daniel Templeman, not Danny Tensley, the actor. He played the part of a man so we could empathize with Him and He with us. Just like you wear that hoodie and those glasses to look like everyone else, Jesus had a mortal body so He could blend in with us."

"But he didn't have to, Lizzy. Dad always said He didn't have to come to Earth and die for our sins."

"That's right. Just like you don't have to be an actor; you do it because you love it. Jesus didn't have to come to Earth and die for us, but He did it because He loves us."

He looked into her eyes and wanted to believe her. "But what if we pray and He doesn't hear us?"

She laid her hand on the side of his face. "He always hears us, but sometimes we get a 'no.' and we should use that 'no' to glorify Him."

"Do you want your son to die?" He shook with anger now.

"No! No, of course not, but if he does, I will mourn him because I made him in my body as God has made me and would mourn my passing. But if I love Him like I say I do, I have to follow Him no matter what happens in my life."

"I don't know if I can do that." He looked deeply into her eyes now.

"You loved your wife, Daniel." She saw him nod his head. "Did she ever make a mistake?" He nodded his head again. "Did you stop loving her just because she messed up?" He shook his head. "God loves you more than that, Daniel. More than you loved your wife, more than I loved my husband. And no matter their faults and mistakes, we still loved them, didn't we?"

"Yes."

"That is how we should love God. We should trust that no matter what happens in our life, He loves us and will take care of us. We don't have to like it, but He does ask us to love Him."

"I want to pray, Lizzy, and ask Him to help David." He took her hand again and bowed his head. "But I don't know how, Wayne. Would you help me?"

Wayne looked at Mrs. Seraphim and smiled. "I sure will, Daniel." He reached for Mrs.

Seraphim's hand and for the second time that day, he held it.

Chapter Twelve

John had just gotten all the kids down when the phone rang. “Hello.”

Daniel still had hold of Lizzy’s hand and wouldn’t let go. “Dad?”

“Yes, Son?”

“David’s surgery went fine. He should be home the day after tomorrow. Are you alright with the kids until then?” Daniel was so happy and he could see Lizzy’s face glowing.

“Sure. Sure. Do what you have to do, Son.” John paused. “I am so happy.”

“Let all the kids know.” He squeezed Lizzy’s hand, resisting the urge to kiss it as she pushed herself up on her toes.

“I will, Son. Good night.” John hung up the phone and held his hand over his chest.

Elizabeth pulled Daniel to her and hugged him. The surgery had been slotted for two hours and it only took an hour and a half. The surgeon said he had to remove the appendix and it was a fairly in-and-out procedure. It was minimally invasive, so David would be out in a couple of days. They had called John as soon as they heard the news. Deacon Wayne went home shortly after that.

Daniel could feel Lizzy’s enthusiasm as he held her. The physician said David should sleep the rest of the night so they could head home and shower and rest. They would start with him around eight in the morning. He knew that like himself, Lizzy had not fully rested in the last twenty-four hours.

“Lizzy?” He looked down at her now. “Let’s go home and come back tomorrow. The physician said we couldn't do anything until tomorrow early, anyway." He saw her looking at him now. "We'll stop by the B&B and you can pick up some clothes. You can stay at my house for the night and we will drive up early in the morning."

Elizabeth looked around herself. "What if they need us tonight for something?"

"We will give them both your mobile numbers, that way if they need you they will call you."

He took her hand and began to open the door to David's room.

"Hang on there, Mr. Stark, you have to become Ironman." She reached for the ties to his hoodie and he moved her hands away from him, holding them.

"No. No more hiding, Lizzy." He looked down at her. If she could accept him in Clark Kent form, so would he. "One thing, though, Lois Lane." He looked at the door and then back to her. "Being with a celebrity is exhausting. You always have to be on the lookout for cameras, and people make up things about you all the time. If you walk out these doors with Clark Kent, Ms. Lane, you have to be prepared for that."

She leaned over to him and smiled happily. "I have the one thing those people don't have, Clark. My faith in God. He is going to see me through whatever happens in my life and I love Him for that."

"Most days you won't find God outside of the doors—you find a pit with vipers." He laughed and then winced. "They sting and it hurts."

She made sure her hand was in his. "Then we have to remain strong, Mr. Kent. Never let go of God and our faith."

"You forgot, Ms. Lane, I don't have God." He looked at her and sighed.

"Not yet, Mr. Kent, but He has you and for now that's enough." She leaned toward him again. "Now take me back to the B&B so I may grab some clothes and shower."

He smiled goofily at her. "As you wish."

Elizabeth laughed. "Oh! Good one. 'As you wish.' Princess Bride! Great movie! You know what that meant when he said that to her, don't you?"

"Of course I do, Ms. Lane." He pulled her to him.

She retreated a step and frowned. "I can't." She felt the mood shift and saw him withdraw from her. "I'm sorry." She looked to him. "I…"

"Let's just go home, Elizabeth." He slipped on his sunglasses and pulled up the hood to his hoodie, tying the string, hunching his shoulders. He walked out the door.

They stopped at the nurses' station and gave their numbers to them. Elizabeth told them to call if there was any change.

All the way to the car there was silence. Neither of them spoke as he opened her car door and shut it behind her. She watched as he slipped off the shades and threw them into the recessed area of the dashboard. Off went his hoodie, too; that went to the back seat.

She watched him as he turned out of the hospital parking lot and started down the road. He had withdrawn from her again. She didn't like the feeling.

"Hey," she reached for him and saw him flinch from her touch. "What's wrong?"

He said nothing as he drove down the road. He was driving but not really watching it. He was angry. Roger said he was leading her on and it was she who was leading him on. All this time.

"Did I say something, do something wrong?" She watched him watching the road.

"I thought we were going somewhere, Elizabeth."

"I am back to being Elizabeth, am I?" She looked at the road. Great, put her back in the box with everyone else. Awesome!

"When I said 'as you wish,' I knew what I was saying. You just didn't want to hear it. Fine!" He was angry. He knew he had just said he loved her, but she didn't love him.

"That's not true. Don't think for me! It's not that I don't want to hear you say that. I just can't hear you say that."

He looked at her and then the road. "What?!"

Her voice was small and timid. "I can't say 'as you wish' to you, Daniel."

"Why?! Why can't you say it? Do you not feel it? Do you not care? What?!" He pulled the car over, pocketed the keys, and got out. He moved over to her side of the car and opened the door. Pulling her carefully out of the car, he stood her against it. "Tell me!"

Elizabeth shivered. She could feel his anger like some sort of tangible thing. "I can't tell you I love you because you don't have Christ in your life, Daniel."

Daniel became angry. "But you said I did. You and your children said He was in my life even if I didn't want Him there." He stopped for a moment and thought. "This goes back to the… unequally yoked, doesn't it?"

She looked at him, amazed. "You know about that?"

"Preacher's kid, Lizzy! Preacher's kid. Can't grow up in front of the pulpit without hearing a few things and some of it sticking. Like the three-fold cord." He crossed his arms and looked at her.

She nodded her head. "Yes, Daniel, it has to do with being unequally yoked. You don't believe and I do. We can't be together." She turned her head. It hurt to look at him right now.

"I can't do it, Lizzie. I can't believe in this being in the sky who chooses to grant wishes if and when he feels like it. I can't. Not even for you." He crossed his arms as he looked at her.

He saw her looking back at him.

"I didn't ask you to believe in God or Jesus, Daniel. I didn't ask you to invite Him into your heart just like you or I made a place in our hearts for our spouses." She moved to lay a hand on the side of his face and he moved from her. "I would never force you to make that decision. It would have to be a decision you would have to make yourself."

"And if I don't want to make it?" He walked up to her and looked down at her. "I can't be with you—is that what you're saying?"

She swallowed the lump in her throat and nodded her head. "Yes, Daniel, that's exactly what I'm saying." She saw him back away from her. "But we can be friends. Good friends, if you want."

She watched him walk away from her, screaming into the night. She was glad they were on a deserted stretch of road. Suddenly he turned and stalked back to her. She had moved around to the back of the car and now she was against it.

He moved up against her and looked down at her. "What if I don't want to be your friend? What if I want to be your lover?" He bent his head down and she moved her face from his. His face fell in her hair.

She felt a tear run down her cheek. "Then I'm sorry, Daniel. I can't do that. I can't be that to you."

She felt her head pulled back to his. He looked down to her mouth for the longest time and then into her eyes. "Get in the car, Lizzy." He let go of her and saw her move from him.

"No, Daniel. I won't do it. I can't be next to you." She wrapped her arms around herself. "You pull me out of the car and tell me you love me. And then you expect me to get back into the car like nothing happened?"

"Do you want me to tell you that I don't love you? That everything I just said wasn't true? Because I can't." He moved up to her slowly with his hand out. Placing it on her cheek now, he stroked her cheek with his thumb. "Your children are at my home waiting on their mother. Davey is at the hospital and he loves you very much. Let's go home and see them and then tomorrow morning go back and see Davey."

She looked into his eyes. Nodding her head, she allowed him to take her hand. He opened her door and helped her inside the car. Shutting her door, he slid in behind the wheel. Turning on the engine, he checked behind him and pulled out onto the road.

The rest of the car ride was silent as they were both lost in their own thoughts. Elizabeth watched the road as it moved past her, kicking herself for rejecting him. Except for his lack of faith in God, he was a great guy. She would try to make it work with him if he believed, but he didn't.

Daniel was watching the road. This woman grated on his nerves with her very presence. She made him believe in someone again, and then took that away from him. It had been a long time since Gen's death and this woman was a shining example of what a woman should be. So why did it bother him so much?

Chapter Thirteen

He pulled up to the B&B and turned off the car. Elizabeth turned to look at him. "I can stay here tonight, Daniel, if you want."

He was looking at the road and not her. He pulled in a big breath of air and continued looking at the road, exhaling. "No. If they call you, you are going to need a ride to the hospital." Yes, that was why she had to go home with him.

"I can call Deacon Wayne and ask him if he can help." She looked at him now and saw his countenance change. He looked at her and he was angry again.

"Of course you can, Elizabeth, you can call Deacon Wayne for anything, can't you? A ride to my house, to the hospital, to the church, to the altar. And he will give it to you."

He turned to her and moved himself closer to her. "And do you know why? Because you are a good woman. You have a beautiful heart and are great with kids. Which brings me to my next point: you have kids—five of them—and Deacon Wayne wants a big family. That's why he drives around that huge vehicle, waiting for a woman of faith like you, with all your children, to marry him."

He turned and looked out the window. "I'll wait in the car for you."

Elizabeth turned and shut the door behind her and walked into the B&B. She saw Mabel as she stood at the counter. Elizabeth smiled a false smile. "Oh, child, how is your son? I have been praying for you and him." Mabel touched Elizabeth and stood back.

"He is fine, Mabel. I just need to grab a few things and then head back." In the morning, she silently added as she turned to her room.

"Of course, of course. Is there anything we can do?"

"No, Mabel, thank you." She entered her room now and threw a few things in a bag. She put it by the door and sat down on the bed.

Daniel had called her a good woman and said she had a beautiful heart. He had said he loved her. He was a great guy, but she knew she couldn't commit to him. Not without his faith. Why did her belief in God always have to be what held her back from what she wanted? She knew that God would let her marry Daniel and they would probably have a good life, but he would not be what she needed.

She pulled the phones out of her pocket and inspected them. No calls, no texts. She put them back and grabbed the charger for her phone. She stood then and picked up her bag.

Walking through the hall, she told Mabel good night and walked out the front door of the B&B.

As she walked up to the car, Daniel got out and took the bag out of her hands. He put it in the back seat and opened her door.

"Thank you." She sat down in her seat and heard him close the door to the car.

He pulled out of the B&B and drove the short distance back to his house. Pulling into his drive, he dropped the garage door.

When he got out of the car, he made his way over and opened Elizabeth's door. He watched her get out as he opened the door and grabbed her things. He escorted her into the house, shutting the door behind her. He walked her to his room and put her bag down.

Elizabeth walked with Daniel as he moved through his house. She looked around herself now. Daniel's room was cozy. It had a king-sized bed with a soft comforter on top. Along one wall stood a woman's vanity with a jewelry chest off to the side. An open walk-in closet was on the opposite wall next to the bath. One could shower and then change, walking into the bedroom after.

Elizabeth looked to Daniel now, watching her. "What am I doing in here?"

"Dad said the kids have taken the two guest rooms. You can sleep in here tonight." He turned to his dresser and began to rummage through it.

She watched him going through the chest of drawers and he pulled out a set of clothes. It was a T-shirt and pajama bottoms. He turned to her. "Would you like to shower first? I know you haven't had one since yesterday when all of this started." He watched her, waiting for her to make a decision.

Elizabeth picked up her bag and walked over to the door of the bath. Turning in the doorway, she looked at him. She knew who he was. He was Danny Tensley, the actor, but her brain refused to see him that way. Instead she saw Daniel Templeman, the man. She saw that he was lonely despite the façade he put on for others.

"I haven't thanked you yet for everything you have done for me and my children today. It was very thoughtful and very much appreciated. I don't know what we would have done without you and your father." She smiled at him. She had realized she had not shown how appreciative she was to this man.

He smiled at her. "I know you are, Lizzy. You and your family are very special."

Elizabeth smiled at Daniel. She wished she could bring herself to form a closer relationship with him but she couldn't do it. She turned and shut the door behind her.

Daniel looked at the shut bathroom door and grimaced. Hearing the water run in the shower, he sat down on the bed. He was used to women in his profession being a little more open to relationships.

He liked to date actresses, women who were more used to his profession and the hours he had to keep, the life he had to live. Most of them wanted nothing to do with God, much less ever brought God into the workplace, and they definitely never talked about Him.

That was one of the things he loved about Genessa. She had been an actress and understood the life he had to lead. She led that life, too, even after she had Tayler, Olivia, and Raven. She liked being a wife and mom, but she loved acting, too.

He looked to the bath door as he heard the water turn off. He wondered if Lizzy could handle his life, his career. Work was work and home was home. Would she understand that he knew that distinction? Or would she be jealous of whomever his leading lady was at the time?

Elizabeth was dressing and considering the man outside the door. She knew he was an actor and that his life was one of hard work and dedication. It often would take him from those he loved, and sometimes for long stretches.

It must be hard on him, she thought as she looked into the mirror. She remembered the times her husband and she had to be apart. It was hard on both of them, but they stayed together and loved one another despite the distance. They always welcomed one another home and loved on their children when they were all back together.

She picked up her brush and moved it through her long blonde hair. It was thick and wavy, reaching her lower back. It was hot in the summer, but she didn't mind. The winter months made it all worthwhile as she let it hang down her back and she loved it as it flowed through her fingers.

Mostly dry now, she brushed her teeth. It felt so good to have clean teeth again. She kept gum in her bag to freshen her breath and clean her teeth, but the feel of the brush cleaning them was heavenly. She finished and laid her brush on the side of the sink for tomorrow morning, should she still be there.

She opened the bathroom door and saw him sitting on the bed. He smiled as he gazed at her and she smiled back at him.

"Thank you for letting me go first. It felt wonderful." She glanced back into the bathroom. "I straightened everything up when I was finished."

She moved over and set her bag down on the makeup table's seat. Watching him in the mirror, she saw him slip into the bath and shut the door.

Pulling her Bible out of her bag, she sat down on the bed and opened it. She had been reading in the book of Proverbs and tonight found her in chapter thirty-one. This was the part that talked about the virtues of a good woman.

She loved reading her Bible before bed. It helped to relax her and set her mind at ease. She and her husband used to do this together. They would each read a little of their Bibles before bed. They would pray together and then he would curl up next to her, telling her that he loved her. She would tell him that she loved him and they would kiss. Their love for one another knew no bounds.

Their life had been hard, but they had God and that was enough for both of them. They had taught the children that no matter what happened in their lives, He was in control and He would take care of them. They may not always get what they wanted, but they would always have what they needed because God would take care of it.

She turned the page and finished the passage. She laid the open Bible on Daniel's bed and closed her eyes. This was one of her most favorite times during the day: the chance to talk and listen to God. She always wanted to hear from Him and she liked talking to Him.

Daniel opened the door to the bath. The lingering scent of Lizzy fresh from the shower was new. Turning, he saw her toothbrush on the side of the sink. It was red—a bright red.

He smiled, liking the color. Gen always liked more subdued colors, but the red in the midst of the blues and greys was like a bright spot of hope. It looked right on his sink and he refrained from touching it. He didn't feel worthy of touching something as personal as her toothbrush.

He looked at her as he stepped out of the bath. She was sitting on his bed, a white gown on and eyes closed. He saw a book on the bed. It was a Bible, on his bed! He saw tears slip down her cheeks and she nodded her head. More tears and a brief smile. He saw her rock herself and smile bigger now. She laughed and opened her eyes, looking straight at him.

Chapter Fourteen

Her time with God tonight had been so precious. He had assured her that all would be okay and that He would take care of not only David but the other children and her as well. She knew those things, but to have Him tell her was an incredible honor. He had said something to her to make her smile and then she could feel Him hold her in His arms. She loved the feeling of love that surrounded her when He did that.

Peace. That was the look on Lizzy's face, he thought, as her eyes pinned him where he was. He felt he could not move from her gaze. He felt his knees try to give and he steadied them.

What was it about this woman that made him think now about his life? He had a good one and he loved his father and children. His career was good and he liked where it was going.

But the look of Elizabeth Seraphim sitting on his bed made his knees start to shake a little.

She truly did look like an angel. Her long blonde hair falling behind her white gown covered her entire body. Her robe, tied at the waist, hung open just a little and he could see the lace at the top.

Elizabeth looked down at her gown and brought it closed. She looked back at Daniel. "I didn't expect to be in my nightclothes around anyone but my children."

She looked down again. The gown was long and flowing, gathering at the waist and falling to her feet. She stood now, needing to move around. "So where will you be sleeping tonight?"

She looked back at the bed and saw the Bible still on it. Going back over to it, she bookmarked it and shut it. She turned to slip it back into her bag.

"What were you reading just now?" He looked to her Bible. Whatever it was seemed to help her. He looked to her face.

Elizabeth swallowed as she looked at Daniel. She held the Bible up to her chest now.

"Proverbs," she cleared her throat, "Proverbs 31."

He nodded his head. "The Sayings of King Lemuel and The Wife of Noble Character." He watched her as her eyes became big. "Preacher's kid. Dad would preach that message at least twice a year, more when Mom was alive." He sat down on the bed and looked at her. "He used to look at Mom when he read the Epilogue about The Wife of Noble Character." He smiled. "*A wife of noble character who can find? She is worth far more than rubies. Her husband has full confidence in her and lacks nothing of value. She brings him good, not harm, all the days of her life. She selects wool and flax and works with eager hands. She is like the merchant ships, bringing her food from afar. She gets up while it is still night; she provides food for her family and portions for her female servants. She considers a field and buys it; out of her earnings she plants a vineyard. She sets about her work vigorously; her arms are strong for her tasks. She sees that her trading is profitable, and her lamp does not go out at night. In her hand she holds the distaff and grasps the spindle with her fingers. She opens her arms to the poor and extends her hands to the needy. When it snows, she has no fear for her household, for all of them are clothed in scarlet. She makes coverings for her bed; she is clothed in fine linen and purple. Her husband is respected at the city gate, where he takes his seat among the elders of the land. She makes linen garments and sells them, and supplies the merchants with sashes. She is clothed with strength and dignity; she can laugh at the days to come. She speaks with wisdom, and faithful instruction is on her tongue. She watches over the affairs of her household and does not eat the bread of idleness. Her children arise and call her blessed; her husband also, and he praises her: 'Many women do noble things, but you surpass them all.' Charm is deceptive, and beauty is fleeting; but a woman who fears the Lord is to be praised. Honor her for all that her hands have done, and let her works bring her praise at the city gate."* Elizabeth looked up from her Bible which she had opened when he recited the verses from memory. She was amazed. She had just read those verses from her Bible. She didn't even remember all of that. "How did you know that?" She looked up from her Bible.

"When you hear it at least twice a year since you were born to sixteen years of age, it tends to stick. When I met Genessa, my wife, she fit those verses." He shook his head. "She didn't not believe in God, but she didn't take the kids to church and neither did I. Dad did. And when she and I were home on Sundays, we spent those days together. It was quiet and nice."

"You loved her very much, didn't you, Daniel?" She slid her Bible back in her bag and then turned to look at him.

"Yes, I did." He saw her sit on the vanity seat. "She and I met twelve years ago." He smiled and blushed. "We met on set on a television show I was filming. She was only in one episode and the entire time she was there I couldn't bring myself to talk to her. I would stumble over my own feet and mess up my lines. Every time." He laughed louder. "Once filming was done, she asked me out. That's all it took. A few months later, we were married." He paused, remembering, and Elizabeth watched him as he talked about his wife. "She could always make me laugh and I could make her laugh, too. She had black hair and was an excellent mother."

"Did you ever visit her on set?"

"No. We agreed being as we were both actors that we wouldn't do that. Sets are closed for privacy, so we agreed what happened on set stayed on set."

"Why?" Elizabeth was fascinated.

"Because sometimes as actors we have to do things in the script that we wouldn't do in real life but our characters would. Neither of us wanted to see the other do anything like that, even though it was just our character acting as they would have."

Elizabeth had a burning question to ask. "Did you ever have to compromise what you believed in to do your job?"

He looked at her now. He tried not to become angry. Yes, there were many times he had to do things that he didn't want to do for his job. But he did them anyway. He wanted to be honest with her. "Yes."

Elizabeth regarded the man in front of her. Daniel Templeman had done things as Danny Tensley that he didn't want to. He looked sad. "How did you deal with that?" She moved over to the bed and laid a hand on his.

He shrugged his shoulders and sniffled. He smiled, but it wasn't real. "You do what you have to do and then you leave the set. You leave behind that character and become who you know you are." He noticed her hand on his. "When I leave this house on my way to whatever I have to do, I become Danny Tensley, the actor. I affect who he is as a person, but when I am home I am Daniel Templeman, the husband, father, and son. When I take on a role on set, I become that person. Do you understand?" He knew there were many outside his profession who didn't separate a character he played from who he was as a person.

She nodded her head. "Yes. For my kids, I am mom or mother. For my husband, I was his wife. For our friends and family, I am Elizabeth," she looked into his eyes, "or Lizzy."

She looked down at his hand and blushed. She moved her hand from his and stood again. She leaned her back against the wall and pushed her hands to it. "You add another dimension and become someone else to play a part and when it's over you become Daniel Templeman again. I get it."

He looked at her, nodding his head. He missed the feel of her hand from when she had touched his. He saw her look at the clock. Eleven-thirty.

"I guess we should be getting some sleep, Daniel. You said you would drive me in the morning. Are you sure your schedule is clear for that?"

He nodded his head again. "Yes. I have some things to do the day after, though."

That would be the day David would be released if all looked well. He saw her smile.

"Good. Thank you." She watched him watching her again. "Sleeping arrangements. Am I on the couch? Are there blankets there?"

He shook his head. "You are going to sleep on the bed."

She watched him as he stood. "Where are you going to sleep? I don't want to…"

He walked up to her and smiled. "On the floor." She watched as he pulled a blanket and pillow to the floor. His carpet was plush and soft.

"I should take the floor, Daniel." She grabbed a pillow and blanket now. She felt his hand on hers and she looked up into his eyes.

"No. You take the bed. I'll take the floor, Lizzy. I want to be near you if the hospital calls. Do you have the phones charging and on?" She shook her head no and moved to do that.

"Let me." He took the phones off the side table and plugged them in. Next he made sure the ringer was on high. He laid them on the table and turned to her. "All set. I have an alarm set for six a.m. I want to see the kids off to school and then we will leave. That alright?"

"Of course. It will give me a chance to read scripture to the children before I go."

Read scripture, really? "The children read the Bible in the morning?" Sitting down on the floor, he looked at her.

"Yes. Actually, it is part of their curriculum. They have a part of their schooling they do during the day that is a study at one place or another in the Bible." She lay down on the bed, turning her head to the side so she could look at him.

"God is very important in your and your children's lives, isn't He, Lizzy?" He didn't understand why the big man in the sky was so important to them.

"Yes." She closed her eyes. "There were so many years my husband and I did not have God in our lives. Those were bad years, Daniel. When we both found Christ, He turned our marriage around. Instead of other things being our focus, He became our focus. We found when we put our eyes on Him, He brought us closer to one another." She opened her eyes and saw him looking at her. "What?"

"Gen and I were close. We had our rough patches, but we stuck together. I think we made it." He smiled.

"I think you did, too, and that was great, but my husband and I found we needed more. We needed God."

Her voice had been so honest, so pure. He laid his head on the pillow and then propped it up with his hand, his elbow on the blanket under him.

"So when you didn't have God in your lives it was harder and when you did, it was easy. That must be nice."

"If it was easy, Daniel, he would still be here with me and David wouldn't be in the hospital."

She sighed, laying her head on the pillow now. "We had just bought a house when he was killed." She shivered. "We didn't even have a chance to make it our home. That would have been easy. But when he died, we sold it all, we all decided on a country and David picked this town. We got our visas, packed a bag, and moved here. We have a few things in storage, but the majority of our things we sold. We have a new life now."

How can you just accept the fact that God took your husband from you, Lizzy? Aren't you angry at Him for doing that?" He knew he was upset at God for taking Gen from him, from their children.

"No, I am not mad at Him. I don't like it, but I'm not mad. There is no reason for it. It won't bring him back to us. But I have faith God has something else for me." She yawned. "I have to believe that, Daniel—that He is taking care of me and my children."

"Is that what gets you through the day? Leaning on Him? Using Him as your crutch?" He looked at her now. She was smart, capable. She really didn't need God.

"Is he what gets me through my day?" She considered that. "I would have to say 'yes.' I believe He guides my steps. He opens doors for me to walk through and closes them when I don't need to go in them. Not physically, although there were times I couldn't do something and later found out that it wasn't a good idea, so...." She shrugged. "I lean on Him all the time. When I lost my mother, my father, and my brother, I needed my husband, but I also needed God. My husband was very good to me. He prayed with me, for me. He helped me in my relationship with God as I tried to help him."

She had tried, too. "Is God my crutch?" she shook her head, "not so much as He is my helper. I mean I believe He takes care of me and my children and doesn't allow anything to happen in my life that He doesn't first see."

"You truly live a faith-filled life, Lizzy. We can't all do that, though. Trust God for everything like you do." He knew he didn't. Everything he had, he made happen.

"I wouldn't do it any other way, Daniel. If I don't take my time to talk to Him, listen to Him, I slowly become a person who isn't such a nice person. I have been this person so long that I know that other person I could become is still waiting for me. She will always wait on me to turn my back on God. And I won't do that for anyone, anything."

"It must be nice to have your conviction, your principles. I don't think I could believe the way you do." He saw her close her eyes.

Elizabeth opened her eyes and reached out her hand. She saw Daniel bring his hand to hers and clasp it. "You could, Daniel. You could have that same faith in Him. You had that faith in your wife. You could do the same thing with God."

She smiled at him and closed her eyes again. She liked the feel of his hand in hers. She opened her eyes, yawning again. "I want to pray, Daniel. I want to pray for David and your dad. And then I want to pray for your children and for you." She closed her eyes again.

He saw her eyes close and missed the feeling of her eyes on him.

"Lizzy," he whispered and saw her eyes open. "If I pray with you, would God hear me?"

She nodded her head. "Yes, Daniel. He would hear you. I believe that."

"Would you… speak out loud so I can hear what you say? I remember what Deacon Wayne said this afternoon but I don't think it would be the same prayer we said then." He wanted to know how she prayed.

"Yes, Daniel. The key to talking with God is listening to Him as you speak and then afterwards. As much as I want to talk to Him, He wants to talk to me," she squeezed his hand, "and you." She smiled. "But the main thing is that He is your friend. And just like I wanted to speak to my husband every day," she blushed, "often during the day, He wants you to speak to Him all day long, too. It doesn't have to be fancy, just tell Him how you feel. Let me start…"

She closed her eyes and thought of her Heavenly Father. "Father, I love You and thank You for everything in my life. And tonight I thank You for my good friend, Daniel, and his family…"

She opened her eyes and looked at him. His eyes were closed, too. She closed hers again. "Father, thank you…"She finished her prayer shortly afterward and opened her eyes. She saw

Daniel open his, too.

"Lizzy," he squeezed her hand, "that was truly beautiful. Thank you."

He contemplated this woman in front of him. Of all the things she said, one thing stood out in his mind. She had thanked God for everything He gave her and everything He had taken away. He didn't think he could do that. He heard her sigh and her breathing become regular. She was beginning to fall asleep. "Good night, Mandarin."

"Good night, Ironman." She could feel herself getting very sleepy.

Daniel looked at their joined hands and felt hers relax. He moved closer to the bed and gripped hers more tightly. He couldn't bring himself to let her hand go. He watched her as he fell asleep. She truly was a Proverbs thirty-one woman.

Chapter Fifteen

Elizabeth heard a strange sound and opened her eyes. It took a moment to acclimate to where she was. She looked around the room and heard the sound again. She looked to the floor.

Curled up into a ball on the floor was Daniel Templeman. He was crying and she could hear him.

She moved from the bed to the floor, her long white gown trailing with her. She touched Daniel's shoulder and saw him sit up. His arms came around her and he pulled her to him, his lips meeting hers. She struggled a bit and then relaxed. Her body moved closer to his and she could have sighed.

Daniel was dreaming of his wife. He had made his way to the hospital to claim her body. Roger had driven him and he remembered being in shock. Was he really on the way to see his dead wife?

He stood in the hospital and saw her lying on the cold table. She wasn't moving and her chest was still. He didn't want to believe it was her. He felt his father's arms come around him as grief overcame him. He turned to look at his dad and instead saw a woman in white.

She was beautiful, his wife. Her hair was longer and in the dark she looked a little different, but he didn't care. Gen was here and alive in his arms, so he didn't question it. He pulled her to him and sighed as his lips found hers. She was sweet and tasted like berries. That was not Gen's taste, he thought as he kissed her. Gen tasted like sunshine and summer. He didn't question the fact that his wife was here and he could hold her.

He drew back from her a little, his eyes still closed. He heard the woman in his arms gasp and his eyes flew open. He wasn't holding Genessa Templeman, he was holding Elizabeth Seraphim.

"Lizzy?"

Elizabeth looked to Daniel, trying to remember who she was. She had heard, read about how good a kisser Danny Tensley was, but now she realized they were greatly understating his ability. He wasn't just great, he was brilliant! She steadied herself when he let go of her.

"Daniel."

He sat up now and moved away from her. "I'm sorry." He wiped the tears from his eyes, on his face. "I was dreaming about Gen and then you were there." He gestured around himself. "It's dark in here and I thought you were her."

She had taken off her robe when she had lain down in the bed. He could see why. The gown she had on had a lot of lace to it. The solid material covered the essential areas, but it was still sheer. He turned from her, finding her robe, he held it out behind him.

Elizabeth looked at the thing in Daniel's hands. She looked down at her gown. "Oh, Daniel," she could feel her cheeks burning, "I'm so…" She slipped on the robe, tying the tie, covering herself.

He heard the material moving and then peeked over his shoulder. When he was satisfied she was covered, he turned around again. She was still beautiful except now her lips looked puffy. He looked somewhere else.

"It's okay, Daniel." She moved away from him. Her heart was racing and her pulse was pounding. She knew she had to move away from him. He was fire and if she stood too close to him she was going to get burned. She saw him pin her with his look.

"No, Lizzy, it is not okay. I shouldn't have kissed you. That wasn't right."

Yes, he wanted to, but not that way. He wanted their first kiss to be better. He didn't want her to have him thinking of her as his dead wife. He wanted her to know he was kissing her. He regretted kissing her now. He really had thought she was his Gen.

Elizabeth stood at the other side of the room now, away from the bed. She wasn't stupid. She wasn't going near that thing right now.

"Sometimes I miss her, Lizzy, and I dream about seeing her…" He paused. "She was always so full of life and energy. That seeing her on the table, not moving…"

He tried to stop the tears that fell from his eyes but they fell anyway. "And I can't…" He turned his head. He didn't want to show anyone how he felt about the loss of his one true love.

Elizabeth watched Daniel. He was hurting and he missed his wife. She moved to the other side of the room, laying a hand on his shoulder.

"Where you have made peace with your husband's death, I can't make peace with losing Gen. I can't accept that God in all His wisdom would take her from me and our children. I can't do it, Lizzy."

She heard all the pain and struggle in his voice. She laid her head against his back and brought her arms around his chest.

Daniel felt Lizzy's head lie against his back and then felt her hands on him. Her hands clutched at his shoulders and he brought his hand to cover hers, needing something real to hold on to.

"Sometimes I have these nightmares…" He shivered. "Then I stay awake the rest of the night. It's not so bad during the day, but it's the nights that are the hardest, Lizzy." He dropped his voice. "That's when I miss her the most."

Elizabeth brought herself closer to him and squeezed his shoulders with her hands. There was a silence in the room. The sound of them breathing filled the quiet.

"I miss my husband in the night, too, Daniel," she said softly. "When the kids are awake and I can focus on something, I do alright, but it's the night that I think of him the most." She squeezed his shoulders again. "That's when it hurts." She felt a tear slip down her cheek.

Daniel heard the pain in Lizzy's voice and turned to bring her to him. He felt her slide her hands around his chest and lay her head on it. He brought his arms around her and held her, too.

His head dropped to the top of hers.

"What do you do, Lizzy, when the nightmares start and you feel like you can't do it without him? When your heart hurts so badly that you can't breathe?"

She sighed and sniffled loudly. "That's easy," she said, lifting her head and smiling a watery smile at him. "I pray. I pray and ask God to help me. And He does." She smiled wider. The stabbing ache lessened. "And then I can go on, Daniel. My heart doesn't hurt as bad and I can breathe again."

He broke the embrace, grabbed her hands, and pulled her back to him. "Pray with me, Lizzy. Help me to breathe again. Help my heart not to hurt so terribly." He closed his eyes as he had seen her do.

"Always, Daniel. I will always pray with you." She closed her eyes as she felt his head drop to hers, his forehead resting against hers. "Father, we love you…"

As Lizzy prayed, Daniel could feel a peace settle over him. The pain he felt did lessen and he felt a restfulness move into him. When the last word was uttered from her lips, he knew it was the last because his father finished with that word: "Amen." He felt content. Lizzy was right.

His heart did hurt less and he could breathe more easily. He opened his eyes and looked at her. He breathed in. "Thank you, Lizzy." He exhaled.

Elizabeth looked into Daniel's brown eyes and smiled. "You're welcome, Daniel." She went to move away from him and she felt him hold her more tightly. She looked at him.

"Why did you do it, Lizzy? Why did you ask God to rule your life?" He looked into her blue eyes. Blue eyes and blonde hair. Gen had brown eyes like he did.

Elizabeth sighed. "Because it was time, Daniel. I had been running from Him for so long that it was time for me to come home and He knew it. So he made a way."

"How did you come home? I mean, I can come here. See my father, my children, but it doesn't feel like home anymore, not without Gen." He knew he was giving so much of himself away to this woman.

She walked him over to the bed and sat down. "Remember what I said about my husband and me giving our lives to Christ and Him changing our marriage?" She saw him nod his head.

"Well, it was my husband who found God first, Daniel. He had this great faith. He didn't know God when we got married but when he found Him, it changed him. Slowly. He lost a lot of things giving himself over to the Lord, but he gained so much more."

She sighed, remembering. "I saw a change in him and I liked that change. So when he asked if I wanted to know God, I said yes. Once I found out who He was, that was it. I was all in. I gave my heart to God and never looked back since."

"How did that take you home?" He still had hold of her hand.

"Because I knew then that a house is just a place. That home was wherever God wanted me to be. Home was where my husband was, where my children were. Once I knew Him, he helped me to see what was truly important and for that I am very grateful."

"Do you think God wants you here right now? That He wants David sick and lying in a hospital bed?" He didn't see how God could think that was alright.

"I think sometimes we have to be where we are for Him to have us where we need to be. I think in

His wisdom, He has a purpose for David to be where he is. It's not up to me to ask why my son is there but to ask how my son being where he is can help God."

"So he put your son in the hospital to help Himself?" Daniel was confused.

Elizabeth shook her head. "Let me put it this way: have you ever been given a difficult role and found out at the end of it you were made a stronger actor because of it?"

He nodded his head. "Yes."

"You knew what you were getting into with the role, didn't you?" She looked into his eyes. She really was just guessing how his life worked as an actor.

"Yes."

"But you did the role, read the lines, acted out the parts no matter how tough it was, and got through it. You didn't like it, but you did it anyway. Then when it was all said and done, you had honed your skills a little more because you did that tough part. So the next time you were offered a role that was just as challenging, you knew what to do."

"Yes."

"That is kind of how God works. When I gave my life over to Him, He didn't tell me it would be easy. He just said He would always be beside me to help me through whatever I had to face." She smiled. "And He has. Every time."

"So if I make that decision—to make God the ruler of my life—it won't get easier, it'll get harder." She nodded her head. "But He will help me through whatever I have to do." She nodded her head again. "I would have to think about that, Lizzy."

He knew he should stand, but he didn't want to. That would mean he would have to let go of her hand and he liked the feel of her hand in his.

"That's fine, Daniel. He will wait for you as long as you need. But it's a limited-time offer. Because when you die, there won't be a second chance."

"You mean if I don't ask Him into my heart...."

"The Bible says if you don't make Him Lord of your life now, when you die you won't be able to." She didn't know any other way to put it.

He stood now, letting go of her hand and moving to the floor. He didn't know if he could do that. He wanted to think about it. "Thank you, Lizzy, for everything." He wanted to hold her hand again but he wouldn't push it. He had a lot to think about.

"You're welcome, Daniel." She saw him lie down on the floor facing her and she lay down on the bed facing him. "Do you feel better, Daniel?" She saw him nod his head as he closed his eyes. She saw him breathing regularly now. "Good night, Daniel."

He smiled. "Good night, Lizzy," he muttered sleepily.

Chapter Sixteen

He could hear it: the morning alarm. He rolled over to turn it off and realized he was on the floor. He looked up to the bed and noticed that it was empty and made. He stood and turned off the alarm, noticing the phones were gone and so was Lizzy's bag.

Had something happened to David and she was gone? He ran to the stairs and, taking two at a time, he made his way down them. "Dad! Dad!" He rounded the corner to the kitchen and saw Tayler, Olivia, and Raven at the table. His father was setting their food in front of them and said, "Good morning!"

Daniel smiled. He had missed his children. He realized then that he hadn't seen them very much in the last few days.

They all descended on him now and he hugged them, holding them tightly. He held them in his arms. John said, "Alright, kids, to the table. Prayers and then eat. I'm going to talk to your dad." John watched as the children prayed and then he ushered Daniel to the living room.

"Where is Lizzy, Dad? Her stuff wasn't in my room this morning and the bed is made."

He waited impatiently for his father to answer.

"She slept in your room last night? I wondered where she slept." He continued nodding his head, half smiling.

"Nothing happened, Dad. I was on the floor and she was on the bed."

"Oh, no, Son, nothing happened. I know Elizabeth."

"Where is she, Dad? Did she leave?"

John looked toward the open front door and nodded his head toward it. "Why don't you see for yourself?"

Daniel moved toward the door and looked outside to the porch. Sitting on the porch were Lizzy and her children. They all had Bibles open in their laps and were reading from them. As he watched, they would read a little and then Elizabeth would speak to them.

He watched her as she helped the kids understand the passages they had read. He remembered his own mother doing the same thing with him. He remembered he believed then and that everything was much simpler. His faith was stronger and childlike. He wondered if that were the same for Lizzy's children.

They bowed their heads now and he could see Lizzy's mouth moving. He wondered what they were praying for. He felt like he wanted to be a part of that group of people who were praying but held himself back. When they lifted their heads, he smiled as he saw the peace on Lizzy's face.

They all stood and made their way to the front door. He saw Lizzy look at him and smile. He returned it. The children all came through with a "Good morning, Mr. Templeman" and wound around to the kitchen. He turned to look at Elizabeth.

"Good morning, Daniel." She had known he was watching them as they did their devotion and prayed on his front porch.

"You were gone, Lizzy." He saw her turn her head toward him. "When I woke up you weren't in bed and it was made. Your bag was gone, too. I thought…"

He stopped himself from walking up to her and taking her in his arms. He thought something had happened to Davey and needed Lizzy's reassurance.

"Remember I said I could read to the kids this morning?" She saw his nod his head. "That's what we were doing. I got the kids up at five-thirty and we began reading together. We just finished when you came to the door."

"Oh." That's right, she had said that. "Have you had breakfast yet?"

"No. I was hoping to eat with the kids before we left."

He took her hand. "Let's do that and then dress." He looked at her robe. No one had dressed yet for the day. She seemed to glow in the early-morning light. Her hair shone and the white gown looked bright as the sun's rays caught it.

"I am hungry. Once your children are on their way, can we see David?" She felt him leading her to the kitchen.

He picked up a plate and handed it to her. "Of course."

She took the plate from him and laid on two pieces of toast. Filling a cup with tea, she went over to the table. She hadn't noticed, but the table seated twelve. Her children were seated, as were Daniel's, and John was seated, too. That left four chairs. They were all next to one another.

Elizabeth sat down next to her oldest son and she saw Daniel sit down next to Raven. His children had seated themselves on one side and hers on another. John sat at the head of the table.

They all ate and laughed. Questions were asked about David and she answered them. One-by-one, Daniel's children left the table to dress and get ready for school. Elizabeth watched her children clean the kitchen and move their books to the table.

"Alright, guys, Daniel and I will be off in a bit. I am going to dress. Any questions about anything the last couple of days?"

She looked her children over and noted that David was not among them. She could feel tears begin to well up in her eyes.

"No, Mom. We are fine." Paul looked to his mom. She was feeling more than she let on. "Why don't you get ready?" He turned her from his siblings. "I'm taking care of things here, just make sure Davey is alright." He guided her toward the stairs.

She bent down and took her bag. She had laid it there when she had awoken this morning, just in case the hospital called. The phones were inside it and the ringers were on high.

"Are you sure, Paul? I know it's a lot."

Paul hugged his mother. "Of course. I love you, Mom."

Elizabeth looked up to her son. "I love you too, Paul. Thank you for everything." She took her bag and walked up the stairs. Looking around, she saw a bath and started to walk toward it. She felt her hand grabbed again and looked toward Daniel.

"Your toothbrush is in my bath." Actually he didn't know if it was. He hadn't been in there this morning, but he hoped she had forgotten it.

"No, it's not. I grabbed it this morning before I left your room." She started to turn again and felt him pulling her toward his room. "I can dress in this bath."

"And I can stand outside while the paparazzi take pictures of me when I don't want them to, but it doesn't make it right." He guided her toward his bath and moved her inside. Her hat and gown were still on the sink, but he wouldn't mention that to her.

"Why don't you get ready while I find my things? I don't need it right now anyway." He turned and walked through the adjoining closet and shut the door leading to the bedroom.

Elizabeth heard the door to the walk-in shut and looked to the shut bath door. She changed quickly, straightening as she went. When she emerged a few moments later, he was sitting on the bed.

"You look nice." He looked her over. She must like red. She now had on a red shirt and blue jeans. Red sandals completed the outfit. She had pulled her hair back into a ponytail that slid down her back.

"Thank you." She felt herself blush. "I'll be downstairs when you are ready." She moved to walk out his door.

"Lizzy," he saw her turn to look at him, "I know you have a strong faith, but how are you really doing with all of this?"

Elizabeth looked at him and then at the floor. The door was shut and she was sure the kids and John were downstairs. "It's hard, Daniel. I used to lean on my husband when things looked bad. He was the one with the bigger faith. Now…" She looked at him, smiling, but didn't feel it. "I am learning to lean on God instead. And it's okay. But I miss the feel of my husband's arms around me. It was comforting and I drew strength from that."

"You could… you could hold me, if it helps, Lizzy. I know I am not him but if it helps you, I would do that." He would do that for her.

"Thanks, Ironman."

He smiled and moved away from her. "I am going to dress. Meet you downstairs in a bit."

He moved away from her now and into the bath, shutting the door behind himself. He dressed quickly and moved through his routine. He saw her hat and gown still on his sink. He thought to move it but decided not to. There was a lot to do this morning and he was just going to bring her back later. She could pick it up then. When he was finished, he walked out his bedroom door and down the stairs.

He could see the pain in her eyes and knew she was trying to hide it from him. His children walked to the door and he saw Lizzy pick up her bag.

"You don't have to take that with you, if you don't want." He could feel his dad's eyes on the two of them. "We will be back later and you can get it then."

Elizabeth shook her head. "I may need something in it today. I packed an extra outfit." She looked toward the kitchen where the kids were already doing their assigned work. "I may stay tonight and then find a ride back to the B&B tomorrow."

"I can drive you up early in the morning before everything starts for me."

"Thank you." She walked up to him and laid a hand on his wrist. "I don't want to impose any more on you, Daniel." She looked to John and smiled. "Either of you."

She went to move her hand and felt Daniel's cover it. He stepped up to her and smiled down at her. "It's not an imposition, Lizzy. I want to."

"Let's just see how today goes and then decide. Thank you for the offer, Daniel."

John watched as his son and Elizabeth talked as if he weren't standing in the same room. He could swear Elizabeth really liked his son and that Daniel reciprocated those feelings. He had seen how they talked low with one another and how they moved toward one another.

He was happier than a kid at Christmas! Daniel and Elizabeth seemed so right for one another. She was smart and caring and his son was supportive and intuitive. They would be a good match. He smiled bigger and looked at the clock.

"Well, you two had better pop off." He moved them toward the door and saw their hands drop. Oh, well. He bet before the day was over they would be touching again. "And let us know what's going on with Davey. Can't be kept in the dark. And don't worry. I'll take the kids to school today."

"I will, John," Elizabeth said, already feeling Daniel taking her hand and guiding her toward the other side of the car. "Thank you for letting my children stay with you."

"Anytime, my dear, anytime." He saw Daniel open her door and shut it behind her. He looked up at his son now.

"Thank you, Dad, for everything. I have my phone and Lizzy does, too." With that, he shut his car door and opened the garage door.

John watched as his son and Elizabeth pulled out of the garage and the door closed. He laughed out loud. He had seen his son taking care of her. Yes, he bet there was something in store for his son and the mother of the children who were sitting at the kitchen table. He knew that, if he had his way, there would be wedding bells in their future.

Chapter Seventeen

Daniel settled back into the car and his hand twitched, wanting to hold hers again. Instead he put it near her. She had her hands in her lap and was looking out the window. He could bet she wasn't really in the car with him now.

"What are you thinking about, Lizzy?" He watched her for a moment and then the road.

She shook her head and felt a tear slide down her cheek. The memory going through her head was painful and she didn't want to talk about it. He did reach for her hand then, and felt her fingers lace through his. She squeezed them but looked out at the road. She looked sad, like she was remembering something painful.

"Are you thinking of your husband?" He had softened his voice and glanced to her and back at the road.

"No." her voice faltered and cracked. "I was just thinking of David."

"What about him, Lizzy?"

"David is not my husband's child, Daniel."

He looked at Elizabeth and then back to the road. "What?!"

"The kids don't know how David was conceived." She looked at him. "My husband knew and we moved past it."

"How was David conceived?"

She shook her head again. "I'm not a good woman, Daniel. Not as good as you think." She sighed, continuing to look out the car window. "It doesn't matter now. What matters now is that something did happen. I love David and even though this thing happened, I still love him."

Daniel was quiet for a moment. She didn't want to tell him. He wasn't sure what to do about that. An affair. Was that how Daniel was conceived?

He could see she had calmed down a little. "God is a forgiving, God, Lizzy, you know that. Whatever happened, He has forgiven you."

He saw her turn to him and scowl. "I don't want to talk about it anymore." She turned from him. Only her husband and she knew the truth.

"Have you heard from the hospital this morning?" He knew they were close to the hospital now and would be there soon.

"No." She felt strung-out and tight. "I unplugged the phones this morning and put them in my pocket. There was nothing on them this morning. Why did you give me another phone, Daniel?"

He pulled into the parking spot and moved over to open her side of the car. He shut her door and walked her up to the entrance. Moving through the doors separately, they both made their way to David's room.

"I did a few commercial spots for a mobile company a few years ago. One of the things I had in my contract was I could get a new phone with unlimited service for the rest of my life, up to five phones. They agreed to that and a few other things."

"So you get a new phone whenever you want it and you don't have to pay for the service on any of them. Sweet." She saw him open the door to David's room. "Thank you, Daniel."

She looked to David's bed and saw it was empty. Opening the door, she made her way to the nurses' station. "Where is my son? Where is David Seraphim?"

The nurse at the station was looking at a chart in front of her and looked up now. She opened her mouth and then looked past her to the man beside her.

Elizabeth turned to Daniel. In all the excitement of the morning, he had forgotten to grab his hoodie and sunglasses. She had seen the nurse recognize Daniel and knew the woman was going to get excited. Instead, Elizabeth took the initiative.

"Danny!" She gawked at him, turning from the nurses. She saw no one coming down the hallway. "Danny Tensely in the same hospital as my son!" She moved up to him and clutched onto him. "Can I get a picture of you with him?!"

She moved him into the hallway and into a waiting room. Luckily it was empty. She had played the fangirl, pulling and tugging at him. Touching him and mooning over him. She let go of him now and moved away from him.

He had seen what she had done and almost burst out laughing. Now he was standing in an empty waiting room. There was a small window on the door. He would bet news of his being in the hospital would move through quickly.

Elizabeth opened her bag and pulled out his jacket. "Here." She threw it to him, looking at the door. "Sorry about that. I thought she was going to come unglued." She didn't hear him moving. She turned around to him. "Why aren't you putting on the jacket? Someone could come through the door any moment."

"You still have my jacket?" She shrugged, blushing. "I'm not going to wear it, Lizzy." Grinning, he remembered he had made up his mind while he was dressing this morning that he was done pretending with her. He'd decided that when they went out that day it was as Daniel Templeman and not Danny Tensley.

"What do you mean you're not going to wear it? People are going to be crawling all over this hospital, Daniel, to see you. Probably very soon."

"I don't care, Lizzy." He looked at her, waiting for her to get it.

"But they will see you…"

He walked up to her now and put his hands on her upper arms. He looked down at her. "I don't care if they see me with you anymore. I don't care if tomorrow there are pictures of you and me on the front page of every magazine in the country."

"You can't mean that, Daniel. That would mean something. Something that isn't happening right now. With us. I know they would say, think things that are not true or real. Do you want that?"

"I would want that with you." He pulled her to him. He didn't care if she wanted him to have God in his life or be saved, he wanted everyone to know he had found a treasure and he intended to keep it.

She smiled a sad smile at him and laid her hand on the side of his face. "I know you do, Daniel. But you know I can't. Not right now." She took her hand off of his face and picked the jacket up out of his hands. "I don't want your name, your career to be hurt because of me."

She felt him stand still as she slipped the jacket on his shoulders. She looked into his eyes as she zipped it up, pulling the hood up. She tied it and smiled at him. She moved away from him and to the other side of the room, looking out the window.

The door to the room burst open and a group of people looked around the room. Daniel had dropped his head and slouched as he wandered over to a magazine rack, picking one up.

The nurse from the station ran over to her. "Mrs. Seraphim, where did Danny Tensley go? He was just with you." She looked around and saw a man reading a magazine.

Elizabeth saw Daniel sitting now on a deep chair, pretending to read a magazine. She affected excitement.

He was amazing!" She saw all the heads turn to her now, away from Daniel. "He took a TON of pictures with me and my son. Then he said he was heading to a little chapel outside of town. I think he said the pastor's name was Reverend Templeman. I think the town is about an hour away. If you hurry," she smiled as she saw the crowd begin to move out of the room, "you could probably catch him." She sighed as everyone moved out of the room. She ran to the door. "I am the luckiest woman alive!"

When she saw the last person round the corner, she burst out laughing. She couldn't help herself. People were just plain crazy sometimes. She turned and came face-to-face with an angry man.

Daniel was mad. He had once again told her that he would want something with her and she pushed him away. This time literally. He reached out and pulled her to him. What was it about this woman that made him want to scream at her and kiss her at the same time?

"Do you know what you just did?!"

"Yes. I became your phone booth, Clark Kent." She moved to move out of his arms. "You're welcome."

"You just sent them to my father's church."

"Yes, I did. And if you let of me, I can call him and let him know he is going to have company very soon. I bet about half of this floor, probably even this hospital, just emptied of staff just to see where Danny Tensley is going."

He looked at her. She was smart. She just sent a large group of people to her father's church. He bet his father would have something to say to them when they got there. Probably something about how God loves them.

He pulled her to him again and looked down at her. She had just saved him. He let her go but stayed beside her now.

Elizabeth pulled out her phone and dialed John's number. "Reverend Templeman?" There was a pause. "Yes," she smiled, "I know I can call you John. Listen, a large group of people are on their way to your church to see Danny Tensley." She looked up to Daniel and winked. "They may be ready to hear a man of God when they get there." Pause. "Uh-huh. Can I talk to my son, Paul?" Silence. "Thanks." Silence again. "Hi, Son." She smiled wider. "I need you to be a reclusive celebrity trying to worship God in church today, just for a little while. Daniel and I just got to the hospital and he was swarmed." Yes, it was a bit of an exaggeration. "Thanks, Son." She hit "End" and turned to Daniel. "I bet your dad is preparing a sermon now, just for Danny Tensley." She sighed. "And I bet it will be a packed house."

He pulled her to him and kissed her. He knew it was a conscious choice this time. It was either this or scream at her, and this seemed a lot better and more fun.

He felt her push at him and then slowly she relaxed in his arms. She tasted like berries again. He slowly moved himself away from her, looking into her eyes. "We need to see your son, Lizzy." He took her hand, hunching his shoulders and dropping his face to the floor.

Elizabeth tried not to trip as she followed Daniel out the waiting room door and into the hall. She didn't want to like him kissing her, but she did. A lot.

Daniel tried to concentrate on where he was leading Lizzy but it was hard. She felt so right in his arms and she smelled so good. Fresh-picked berries, straight from the vine.

He moved away from her when she approached the nurses' station. Where there were at least half a dozen nurses there before, now there were two. He would have bet a lot of them suddenly had to leave. He hid a smile.

"I am Elizabeth Seraphim. Could you tell me where my son, David, is?"

She saw Daniel, out of the corner of her eye, lean against the wall. She knew why he did it. He was trying to distance himself from her. She saw the nurse look up at her and then over to him.

"Yes, Mrs. Seraphim." The nurse smiled. "You were the woman fortunate enough to have a run-in with the famous Mr. Tensley." His voice was dripping with sarcasm. "Sent half the nurses in the hospital off to wherever they were pointed to, just to see him. Celebrities are just people. They put their pants on one leg at a time just like the rest of us." He looked down at a chart. "David was taken for some tests about an hour ago. He should be back soon."

Ronald LaStat ogled the woman in front of him. She was short but pretty. Her eyes were blue, but it was her long blonde hair that was the draw for him. "I hope he is okay."

Elizabeth noticed his change in attitude and felt herself take a step back. Not that she found the tall, red-haired man in front of her unattractive—she didn't, but he just wasn't what she wanted. She felt herself take another step back.

"Do you have any idea when he should be back in his room?" She smiled weakly at him, hoping she looked like she wanted to go to her son's room.

He looked at the other nurse now at the station. "Should be any time, Mrs. Seraphim. You haven't by any chance had breakfast already? I have a morning break coming up soon and I would love your company."

Elizabeth nodded her head and felt a hand slide into hers. She knew the feel of Daniel's hand. She sighed in relief.

"Yes, actually, I have, thank you. I haven't seen my son all night and I am worried about him." She turned and made her way to David's room, shutting the door behind her.

The sound of the door opening behind her caught her attention. Daniel walked in and dropped his hood, smiling at her. "He was cute. He could have bought you a second breakfast. You should have taken him up on it." He laughed as he saw her gape at him.

She laughed, too. "Not my type, Daniel. Too, I don't know, tall." She was grasping at straws. She liked tall men.

Daniel looked down at himself. His six-foot-three-inch frame was far from short. "Guess I'm out then, aye?"

"I don't know. She looked him over, shrugging. "You might do."

"I would like to."

"I think, Daniel, under the right circumstances, you would do very well."

She felt trapped in his gaze but she wouldn't tell him that. She smiled at him.

He knew what those circumstances were but he didn't want to talk about that right now. Right now he wanted to talk about their kiss, but he probably wouldn't do that, either. He made his way over to the large window in David's room and looked out at it.

"I'm sorry, Daniel. I know it doesn't seem fair to you and I don't expect you to do anything. I don't want you to feel obligated in any way for anything."

"It's okay, Lizzy. I don't expect anything from you except your friendship. For now."

The sound of the door opening and something rolling came to her ears. Lying on the bed was her son David. She felt Daniel move up next to her, so close she could feel him.

She stood still until they stopped moving around the room. She looked at the nurse nearest her. "Why is he sleeping?"

She smiled at Elizabeth and then looked to the man. She couldn't make out his facial features as his head was bowed and he was looking at the floor.

"Mild sedative. Should wear off in a little bit. He will be a little groggy when he wakes up. I bet you two were worried about him. Lucky little boy to have his mom and dad here when he wakes up. I bet he has been missing you both." She smiled to Elizabeth and then to the man. "The doctor should be in later to talk to you both." With that she turned and left the room, closing the door behind her.

Elizabeth walked up to the bed and smoothed back the hair on her son's head. Making sure there was a little room on the bed, she lay down beside him and took him in her arms.

Daniel had watched Lizzy as she touched her son. She loved him and he knew it by every touch she made to him. "Who is his father, Lizzy?"

He considered David now and saw a resemblance to her but not like her other children.

He didn't see it before. He wondered who the boy's father was and why he had no ties to the little boy.

Elizabeth shook her head and closed her eyes, a tear slipping down her cheek. "I don't know, Daniel," Elizabeth replied, her voice barely above a whisper.

"What do you mean you don't know?" His mind was racing now. How could a woman not know who the father of her child was? Oh, he knew of ways a woman could not know who her child's father was, but none of those profiles seemed to fit her. "How does a woman like you not know who the father of her child is?"

"Probably because the man who helped create David snuck up behind me, pressing his hand over my mouth." She blew out a breath. "I was visiting a small hospital. A friend of mine had a child, and I was on my way out when it happened. He pulled me into a room and shut the door. He blind–folded me and taped my wrists together. I heard the lock click and then…" She shivered. "I tried fighting back. I did! But when he was done, I heard the door open and he left. I was broken and bleeding, Daniel. I never knew who he was."

Daniel had become angrier as she talked. "You mean to tell me that David was the result of a…"

"Yes." Elizabeth had to stop him. She didn't want to delve into this too much in front of David, even if he were just sleeping. "My husband knew that David was not his but he loved him and we raised him as ours anyway."

She closed her eyes again. "There were a lot of complications as the result of what happened, but our faith played a large part in what got us through it. Of course I had a lot of testing done and they all came back clear, but I just wonder if whoever it was sees David and wonders if he is his son."

Daniel had played a lot of roles in his time, but if it ever came to something like that, he had always rejected it no matter how good the role looked. "I'm sorry that happened, Lizzy." He knew she was sturdy but that she was also fragile like a china doll.

"It's okay. I don't remember any more than what I told you. Just a hand, a gag, blindfold, lock clicking, a lot of pain and the door opening." She paused, shuddering at the memory. "I didn't… We weren't… intimate… after. I couldn't… not after what had happened. My husband was sympathetic… patient, and waited for me to be ready." She shrugged. "It wasn't long after that I found out I was pregnant. He knew the child wasn't his. He didn't care and he chose to love David."

She laughed. "He even named him after himself, David, meaning beloved. He became our beloved. Instead of seeing him as this thing that happened as the result of something so horrific, he became this gift to us. So we treasure him each and every day."

"Could they not tell who the man was?"

"No. She shifted her eyes to the floor. "They ran his DNA through the database but they haven't caught him yet."

He couldn't imagine something like that happening to his Lizzy. She was a sweet woman with an even temper. She was good to her children and to those around her. Who would want to do something so terrible to such a beautiful woman?

Elizabeth felt her son move a little and looked down to him, smiling. "Hey, Davey."

She saw him look up sleepily at her. "Mommy."

"Hey, Baby. I love you."

His little face formed a wincing smile. She carefully moved him to her. She saw him close his eyes and fall back to sleep.

Daniel moved closer to the bed and he took the little boy's hand.

Chapter Eighteen

It was a little while later that the door opened and Daniel let go of David's hand. Lizzy and David had been resting, but now he saw her moving as the door opened. He turned to the man in the white coat as he came in.

The physician saw Danny Tensley standing next to his patient. He watched him drop the little boy's hand and move away from the bed to the window. He looked now to the woman sitting up and moving away from her son.

"Elizabeth?" He couldn't believe it. "Elizabeth Seraphim?" When he had read the chart earlier he knew the name Seraphim sounded familiar. It was an unusual name and he knew one other Seraphim the entire time he had been a physician. He smiled at Elizabeth.

She moved off the bed now and over to him as she spoke. "Doctor Reynolds? What are you doing here? I thought you were in the States."

"I was, but I came over for some work." He looked to Danny and smiled. "Good morning, Mr. Tensley."

Daniel nodded his head. The man in front of him knew Lizzy and acknowledged him as a person. The latter he appreciated, the former he questioned.

"Where is your husband, David?"

"He died a few years ago, Doctor Reynolds." She looked to Daniel and saw him move over to her but not touch her.

Doctor Reynolds frowned. "Well, he will be missed. David was a great man." He eyed Danny and then looked to his patient. "He seems to be doing well. His surgery went better than anticipated and his tests look good. He should be up and moving today and if all looks well, he should go home with you tomorrow. He should be good as new, Elizabeth. If I may." He gestured toward the window.

Elizabeth moved over to the window with Doctor Reynolds. Daniel could see them talking in quiet tones and he saw Lizzy tear up. The man put a hand on Lizzy's shoulder and he saw her sniffle. He nodded at her now and smiled. Together they moved back to David.

"I should be back in to check on David before the day is over. Have a good day Elizabeth, Mr. Tensley." With that, Doctor Reynolds left the room.

Elizabeth knew Doctor Reynolds would not let the hospital staff know Daniel was in the room. She breathed a sigh of relief.

"He knew you, Lizzy." Daniel couldn't help but stare at her.

"Yes. After I was attacked, he was there. He followed my case until I went home. He was very good to me and David. He was asking me how I was doing with all of this. With what had happened, David, losing my husband. He truly is a good physician."

Daniel watched her move over to the bed. "I saw you with him. You were sad."

"Of course I am sad, Daniel. None of this should be happening, in my book. I mean, I know appendicitis happens every day and so does losing people we love. So many people move through their day, every day, without someone to care for them, but that is them and not me."

She was looking at David now. She knew she would do whatever it took for him. "Sometimes it's hard to remain strong for everyone, Daniel."

Daniel walked up to Lizzy. He pulled her into his arms and laid his chin on her head. He hadn't realized she was so much shorter than he. "I am Ironman, Mandarin. You can lean on me and I will hold you up."

Elizabeth laid her head on his chest. "Thank you, Daniel, but I think as my nemesis you should be trying to keep me down." She smiled despite the circumstances. "I can't bring myself to lean on you too much, Daniel."

She sighed. "Please understand that it's not that I don't want to, but if I do then I would expect..." She went to move out of his arms and she felt him holding her tighter.

He put his hands on her shoulders and looked down to her. "You let me worry about my heart, Lizzy. You just do what you have to do. I am here for you." We can work on being enemies later." He laughed quietly. He knew they weren't enemies but new friends.

She looked up at him and laughed, too. "Alright." She moved out of his arms and over to the bed. She looked down at her son. He was still sleeping. "Why didn't you pull up your hoodie when Doctor Reynolds walked in?"

He walked to her and stood beside her. "I told you, Lizzy, I didn't care who knew about me and you."

He looked to David now. He knew she didn't care that David was her son with some unknown man. She loved this little boy anyway. His hand moved into hers.

"But what about the newspapers and tabloids, the paparazzi. Don't you care about that?"

"Doesn't matter. As long as you are here."

Elizabeth squeezed his hand and let go of it. Moving to the bed, she saw David move again. "Hey, Baby. You want to sit up?" She saw him nod his head. "Alright, let Mommy help you."

She moved her hands under his shoulders and helped him to sit.

"Mommy?" His eyes were open now and looking at Daniel. "It's Danny Tensley, Mommy." Elizabeth noticed her son's voice sounded stronger. "He's from that TV show we like to watch." She saw he was moving more and smiling. He was excited to have one of his favorite TV actors in the room with him.

"Yes, he is." She looked at him and saw him smile at her.

"Why is he here, Mommy?" Her son had looked to her and smiled. She saw Daniel sit down on the other side of her son's bed.

"Careful, Baby." She touched his little hand where the IV still was.

"I am, Mommy. But, it's Danny Tensley. You wanted to meet him for so long. You and Daddy loved watching all of his shows."

Elizabeth blushed. Yes, she and David had watched all of the things Danny Tensley had been in. She loved Daniel's acting style and thought he was very handsome. But she had never told Daniel Templeman that. Her son David had just taken that upon himself to do just that. She felt herself get redder.

Daniel restrained himself from laughing out loud at Lizzy as he looked at her. She had not said a word about seeing things he had been in. She was blushing now, her cheeks the same color as her shirt. She was embarrassed. He could see her looking at her son's hand.

"Your mum has seen television and movies I have been in, Davey?" He watched the little boy nod his head.

"Oh, yes. You are Mommy's favorite actor. She knows all about you."

David was very enthusiastic now in telling Daniel all about his mother. Daniel looked to Lizzy. He saw her bring her lower lip under her teeth and he knew she was avoiding looking at him. "Really?"

Elizabeth could feel Daniel staring at her. She looked at David and purposefully avoided looking at Daniel. She knew about this man sitting to the side of her but she wouldn't tell him that. Instead, she changed the subject. "How are you feeling, Sweetie?" She leaned over and touched his face, softly.

"My belly hurts, Mommy." He moved over to Daniel now, all eyes on him. "But I am alright. Jesus was with me and He kept me safe." He smiled a big smile.

"I know He did. There were so many people praying for you."

"I know, Mommy, He told me." He looked to Daniel again. "I liked that movie you were in, Mr. Tensley, where you were that detective. Mommy and I used to sit down and watch it all the time." David moved to Daniel's lap and felt the man sit him in it.

Daniel smiled down at the boy. He had a feeling Lizzy knew more about him than she let on. "Yes. I was Detective Russell Baker. I loved playing that part, Davey. Did you have a favorite thing that happened?" He moved the little boy so they could be eye-level with one another.

Elizabeth listened as David and Daniel talked about their favorite parts of the TV show. She smiled when Daniel told what she was sure was a wildly flamboyant story about the TV show. David listened with anticipation. She could see her son's eyes shining with joy.

Danny Tensley was David's favorite actor, too. And to be sitting on his lap listening to him tell a story was making him very happy, too. Elizabeth laughed when her son did and saw Daniel's eyes catch hers more than once. Eventually, David looked at his mother. "I'm sleepy, Mommy." He leaned over and reached for her.

She took her son from Daniel's arms and laid him carefully on the bed. She saw his little eyes close and held his hand. "I love you, Baby."

He smiled a sleepy smile at his mother. Opening his eyes for just a second, he looked at Daniel and smiled. "I love you too, Mommy."

Elizabeth saw her son fall back asleep and couldn't help but smile at him. She loved her little guy with all her heart. She touched his face again and leaned down to kiss his forehead.

Daniel watched Elizabeth with her son. Her love for him came through with her actions and words. He knew what it was like having someone do that for him. He felt something in his heart when he looked at Lizzy. He knew he wouldn't name it because then he would have to claim the feeling.

"So you have seen all my television shows and movies?" He saw her blush again and smile. He knew he was teasing her. "All this time I thought you liked me for me and you were just in love with the actor. Fangirl." He saw her look to him, getting redder. He laughed quietly.

Elizabeth heard Daniel talking to her. Yes, she had seen all of his stuff that she could. She didn't think of him as the actor, though, she thought of him as the man. She knew he was kidding with her. She could hear him laughing.

He reached over and took her hand. She was looking at Davey again. "You never told me you knew me. And you know all about me too. My, my, Lizzy, you must know a lot about me."

She knew she couldn't get any redder.

"You know my birthday?" He watched her, waiting for her to answer.

Elizabeth nodded her head.

"When I was married?"

She nodded her head again.

"Davey has told me you have seen TV and movies with me in them." He watched her. He knew he was teasing her unmercifully now.

"Yes." She looked up at him. "Yes, I know you as the actor. But I don't see you that way, Daniel. I just see you as Daniel Templeman, the man." Why did she feel the need to justify herself?

He laughed quietly. "The man. I am progressing on your scale, aren't I?" He sighed dramatically.

"No." She stopped. "Yes." She glared at him. "Stop." She looked at David, blushing. "Yes, I knew your work. But when we met, I only knew you as who you are right now, not as someone who played a part. To be honest, my brain won't connect the two. You the actor and you the person. It just won't do it."

"Could you do it, Lizzy? Could you see yourself with me?" He knew he wasn't talking about forever. They hadn't known each other long enough for that. But he would see where their relationship would go if she wanted to.

"I don't know." Elizabeth looked at David. She actually had thought about it and she knew what was holding her back.

"Yes, you do." He pulled her hand a little toward him and he saw her look at him.

She swallowed and looked into his brown eyes. Yes, she did know but she wasn't going to tell him. "I made a decision when David died, Daniel. I decided that I wouldn't date." She saw his look of confusion. "I made the decision that if I found the guy I wanted I would wait for him to ask if he could marry me. No playing around, no guessing. I had to know for sure that he loved me enough to commit to me."

Daniel looked at Lizzy, confused. "How would he know if you were the one without dating you first, Lizzy? Wouldn't he have to get to know you and your family, your life?"

"Yes," she blushed now for a different reason, "but my thought was that God would tell him, Daniel. That He would tell him that I was the one and that He would tell me that." She turned from Daniel. "I know it sounds crazy to you, but it makes sense to me." She tried to tug her hand out of his, she looked at him again.

"It isn't crazy, Lizzy. You should know what you want after being with David for so long. And you should wait for that man. He would have to love you and everything that had to do with you. He will indeed be a very fortunate man." He squeezed her hand and looked to David.

The little boy was sleeping peacefully now. Daniel moved a piece of hair out of the boy's eyes. He wanted Davey to be able to see his mother when he opened his eyes.

She knew she had allowed Daniel to take liberties with her. Ones that she had told herself wouldn't happen. But she had let him do so anyway. She liked Daniel Templeman. He had a warm smile and a loving heart. He was kind and gracious to those he met.

Daniel and Lizzy sat at David's bedside and watched him sleeping. Daniel knew that this little boy was so special to Lizzy. Now he knew why. It must have been terrible, what she had gone through, but she never told her children. She was strong.

David stirred a little while later and looked to his mom. He looked to the other person and smiled at him. "You're still here, Mr. Tensley."

"My friends call me Daniel, Davey." He smiled down at the boy.

"Alright." He looked to his mother. "Mommy, I'm hungry.

"I know, Baby. I'll ask the nurse if you can have anything." She looked for the call button.

"I can go ask if you want, Lizzy." He stood and let go of Davey's hand.

Elizabeth leaned over to Daniel and pushed him gently back on the bed. "Oh, no, Ironman, you will draw too much attention to yourself. I'll go ask. Is that okay, Davey, that Daniel stays with you while I talk to the nurse?" She smiled at her son, moving to the door." She already had her hand on the door.

"Yes, Mommy."

"I'll be back in a minute." She looked to Davey and Daniel already talking and wondered if they heard her.

Chapter Nineteen

She made her way over to the nurses' station and saw the same nurse there that she had talked to earlier. "Hi. My son would like to know if he can have something to eat."

Ronald LaStat turned to look at her and smiled. "Hello, Mrs. Seraphim." He looked down at her son's chart. "Your son is approved for clear fluids. I believe there will be a soft tray for his lunch. Doctor Reynolds would like to have him up and moving after he sees him this afternoon."

"Thank you, sir." She turned and felt his hand on her arm. She pushed herself away from him. She felt her heartbeat quicken and her pulse race. Adrenaline poured through her system and the hair on her arms stood straight up.

"Are you alright, Mrs. Seraphim? I'm sorry. I only meant to give you this." He handed her the booklet on guest services. "I did say your name, Mrs. Seraphim, when you turned around. I honestly thought you heard me."

Elizabeth could hear her heart pounding in her chest. She nodded her head but couldn't bring herself to talk. She hurried back to her son's room and shut the door behind her. She knew she was shaking but tried to bring herself under control.

She looked to the bed and saw Daniel look up at her, smiling and laughing. She saw his demeanor change and his countenance darken.

Daniel was laughing at some joke that Davey was telling him when he heard the door open. He turned his head and saw Lizzy. Her eyes were wide and one hand was on her chest.

Something had happened.

He stood and went to her, taking her in his arms. "Lizzy?" He tried to catch her eyes with his, but she looked away from him. "Lizzy, what's wrong?"

He let go of her and put one hand under her chin, bringing her face up to look at him.

Elizabeth knew she was in her son's room and that she needed to pull herself together. She could feel Daniel looking at her and one hand holding her face. "Daniel." She looked at him and then her son, pulling him to her. She felt his arms come around her. "I'm just so happy," she knew her voice was shaky, "Davey is getting better."

Daniel held her and gasped. This was the first time this woman lied to him in the few days he had known her. Something must have bothered her. He leaned his head to her ear.

"Lizzy," he whispered, "you're shaking. Is something wrong with Davey?" He felt her shake her head no. He said, "Something happened. You're shaking and scared. I can feel it."

Elizabeth smiled at her son and turned her head. "I can't talk about it right now, Daniel. Not in front of Davey. Just hold me for a moment until I stop shaking, please. Davey needs to think I am happy for him."

He pulled her more tightly to himself and began stroking her back. With a false bravado, he said, "Doctor Reynolds gave your mum such good news about you this morning, Son. She is just happy for you." He could feel her shaking begin to subside.

Elizabeth began to move out of his arms and felt his hand catch in hers. She smiled at him, feeling more in control of herself. They made their way over to her son's bed. She felt Daniel sit down behind her as she sat on Davey's bed.

"Doctor Reynolds says you can have lunch in a little bit." She smiled as she took his hand. Hers had stopped shaking and she could feel Daniel right behind her.

"Yay! Mommy, Daniel says when I leave tomorrow I can stay at his house until I am better."

Daniel had been talking to Davey about maybe staying at his house for a little bit when he got out of the hospital. He hadn't had a chance to discuss it with Lizzy yet.

"I told him I would talk to you first," he said, feeling her sit up a little straighter. "I can talk to Dad about it."

"You don't have to do that, Daniel. We have our rooms at the B&B."

"I know, but," he took a deep breath and laughed, looking at Davey, "It's not every day a celebrity asks you to stay at his home." He winked at the boy, a half smile forming on his face.

"Besides, Raven likes to play with Davey. She could take his mind off of this." He looked to her. "Say yes, Lizzy."

Elizabeth had halfway turned and she watched Daniel as he talked. When he had finished, she had a feeling he was asking her for more than just a few more days. She found herself looking to Davey. "Is that what you want to do?"

"Yes, Mommy. I like Daniel and Tayler and Olivia and Raven. I like Reverend Templeman, too." David looked to Daniel. "He looks like you, Daniel."

Daniel leaned forward and set his chin on Lizzy's shoulder, smiling. "Can I tell you a secret, Davey?" He had lowered his tone conspiratorially. He saw the little boy nod his head.

"Reverend Templeman is my dad."

"Really?"

"Yes." He saw the little boy's eyes grow larger and smiled as his hands found their way to Lizzy's side. He didn't touch her with them. "Wow, Mr. Tensley, you have a great dad."

Daniel heard the awe in the little boy's voice.

"Yes, I do, David."

"Why don't you come to chapel, Daniel?"

It was such an innocent question that Elizabeth was caught off guard. She looked to Daniel and could see him forming an answer.

"I need to, don't I, Davey?"

"Yes, sir. Mom says Sunday is the best day of the week."

Daniel looked to Elizabeth. That would be something she would tell her children, he thought smiling at her. "Your mum is right, Daniel. Sunday is the best day of the week." He looked back to the boy.

"Will you come to church with us this Sunday, Daniel?"

Davey looked so hopeful that he couldn't tell him no. "I will most definitely, Son."

David smiled as there was a knock on the door. Elizabeth made her way over to it as the door swung open. She saw Daniel move closer to Davey and pull himself in on himself.

It was Davey's lunch. She took the tray from the person and smiled at him. "If it's alright, I would like to give it to my son." He handed her the tray and backed out of the room. "Thank you." As she made her way over to the bed, she saw Daniel sit up straighter and smile.

"Lunchtime!"

Davey cheered and Elizabeth smiled. They prayed, even Daniel, and all through lunch, she helped her child eat. He had always had a good appetite and he ate everything quickly. Elizabeth took the tray from David and placed it on the table by the bed. As she did, she heard her son and Daniel laughing and talking quietly.

She heard the door behind her close as she stood next to it, watching her son and Daniel. She saw Daniel smile and laugh with him. He launched into another story about Detective Russell Baker. He stood and danced around the room, laughing as he described the character.

Elizabeth laughed, too, wondering if that was how he was with his own children. She bet he was a good dad when he was home. She laughed again when she saw David laughing with Daniel.

She saw Daniel sit on the bed and move the same piece of hair out of her son's eyes. Her husband David had had long hair, too, and her son wanted hair just like his dad's. Daniel's hair wasn't short, either, but not as long as David's dad's was.

"Mommy?" She saw Davey turn to her and so did Daniel. They looked good together. "When can I go home?"

Elizabeth stepped over to the bed. "Doctor Reynolds says tomorrow, David. Is there room for Mommy on the bed?"

"Oh, yes, Mommy."

Elizabeth lay down next to her son and pulled him into her arms. "I love you, Baby."

"I know, Mommy. I love you, too."

She felt her eyes close as she held her son in her arms. She loved the feel of her child in her arms. As she drifted off, she heard, "Mommy is sleepy, Daniel."

The sound of Daniel's voice came to her, too, as the last vestiges of consciousness faded away. "Yes, she is, Davey. Mommy is pretty when she is sleeping, Davey."

Chapter Twenty

Elizabeth opened her eyes and looked around the room. It was empty and she ran to the door. She looked around the corner to the nurses' station and saw someone new there. That was a relief. She made her way to it, looking around. .

"Where is David Seraphim? I was resting and when I woke up he was gone."

The nurse sitting at the desk looked at her. "Your husband took him for a little bit of a walk around the hospital."

"My husband?"

"Yes. Tall fellow, hoodie pulled up, studied the floor the entire time I was talking with him, would only nod his head." The nurse observed Mrs. Seraphim as she took off. "He seemed a nice enough fellow. Shy. They are around her somewhere."

Elizabeth took off at a run. Daniel was not her husband. She trusted him to look after David, but she wanted to be the one to help her son.

As she rounded a corner, she saw Davey and Daniel. Daniel was on his knees, keeping pace with her son. She started forward and then stopped. They were so happy together, laughing and joking. She could see them smiling at one another. Daniel would drop his head to David's side or the floor if someone came near.

She stood back a little so they couldn't see her. She watched them as they came closer and then moved past her. She had ducked into a corner to avoid them but heard Daniel encouraging Davey as they came by, moving back to his room. She trailed behind them and followed them back to his room.

She shut the door behind her as she saw Daniel settling David back in his bed. They were still laughing and now they looked at her.

"I went for a walk, Mommy, with Daniel."

"I saw you. You did very well." She saw his eyes close.

"I had to be very careful with my belly, but Daniel helped me. He is a good helper, Mommy. He took good care of me."

"I know he did, Sweetie." She looked to him. "Daniel takes care of everyone he loves, David." She saw Daniel smile at her as she rethought her words.

"Daniel loves me, Mommy?" He opened his eyes briefly and looked at Daniel. Elizabeth opened her mouth, but Daniel beat her to it.

"Of course I do, Davey." He looked at the boy. He was so much like his mother. Daniel saw David smile.

"I love you too, Daniel." With that, the little boy fell asleep. Looking to Elizabeth, he saw her looking at him.

Elizabeth moved over to the window and looked out of it. When she had awoken, she was afraid for her son. When she had seen Daniel helping him, she was touched. And when she heard Daniel tell her son he loved him, it was almost too much. She felt a tear slip down her cheek.

Daniel moved over to Elizabeth and put his hands on her shoulders. He had seen the tear and wanted to comfort her. He brought himself to her. "Lizzy?"

"Thank you, Daniel, for helping David. That was thoughtful, but you don't have to do it." She turned to him. "The nurse at the station thought you were his dad. Twice today someone has called you his father. You're not." She felt him drop his hands.

"Do you know why I don't want to date, Daniel? Because I don't want a parade of men in and out of his life. I want one man who loves me and him—all of my children. I want one man in my life committed to staying with us. I don't want my children to become attached to someone just to have him leave them." She shook her head and stepped back from him. "I won't do it, Daniel. I won't have my children hurt if I can avoid it."

Daniel eyed Lizzy. He knew what she was saying. She had thought this through and he understood where she was coming from. He took her shoulders again and moved up next to her.

She moved her head away.

"Is that what you think I'm going to do, Lizzy? Tell Davey I love him and then turn my back on all of you?" He let go of her shoulders and turned her face toward his. "Is that what kind of man you think I am?"

"I really don't know what kind of man you are, Daniel." She saw him looking down at her. "We met in the dark and I told you more about my life than anyone knows. I don't care that you are famous and I can see you are good with not only my children, but you love your own. But I really don't know anything about you."

"Davey says I am your favorite actor." He softened his voice, smiling at her a little. "You must have done your research on me."

She blushed, nodded her head. She had done more than enough research on this man.

"Do you know where I was born?" He saw her nod her head. "Do you know who my parents are and when my mother died?" She did. "You knew who my wife was and who my children were, didn't you?" She nodded her head again.

"Fangirl," he said, teasing her.

Elizabeth looked at him, blushing. "I never knew in a million years, Daniel, that I would feel this way about you."

Daniel lifted his head at her words. "How do you feel, Lizzy?"

"I didn't…" She widened her eyes and tried to move away from him.

"How do you feel about me, Lizzy?" He stepped forward, bringing his arms around her.

He was looking down into her blue eyes. "Tell me."

Elizabeth shook her head. His eyes were hypnotizing her.

"It doesn't matter, Daniel, I can't…" She tore her eyes from his and looked at the floor. She felt him bring her face to his. There was only a small space between them.

Daniel looked into her eyes. "I know you can't, Lizzy. And I know why. I understand." He smiled. "But I won't kiss you again."

He saw her frown and he looked at her mouth. He knew the feel of her lips, the taste of her kiss. "I want you to be the one to do it. I want you to be the one to pull me to you and kiss me. It has to be your choice." He looked into her eyes. He could feel her breath on his face. "I want you to choose to kiss me."

She shook her head. "I won't do it, Daniel. I won't choose to kiss you. I can't." She looked to his mouth as she had seen him do to hers. His lips looked so inviting. She felt herself moving forward toward them. She saw his lips curl into a half smile. She shook herself and moved back from him. He wouldn't let go of her shoulders.

"You will, Lizzy. You will kiss me. You won't be able to stand it anymore." He felt his heart hammer in his chest. "You will pull me to you and press your lips against mine."

He saw her shake her head. He moved his forehead to hers and closed his eyes. He didn't want to see the denial in her eyes. "You will, Lizzy. And I will wait for it. I will wait for you."

Elizabeth didn't want to believe Daniel. She didn't want to believe what he said to her was true. She didn't want to think she would ever do that to him. But even as she denied it in her head, her heart was telling her different. She knew her head was lying. The lie in her head moved to her mouth. "I won't do it, Daniel." She opened her eyes and moved out of his arms toward her son.

Sitting down on the bed, she turned to look at him. "I won't kiss you." She shook her head, looking to her son. "That will never happen."

"You know what else will never happen, Lizzy? Meeting your favorite actor, one you know all the facts about, and falling in love with him." He saw her turn her head toward him. "I know you don't love me right now, Lizzy, but you will."

Elizabeth closed her eyes and shook her head. Her heart laughed at her head. Liar!

Daniel went around to the bed and sat opposite of her. He looked at her as she looked at her son. "I'm not going anywhere, Lizzy."

He looked at Davey and as much as he wanted to, he didn't reach for her hand. There was silence in the room until shadows began to fall over it.

Another knock at the door and Elizabeth made her way over to it. Dinner was here. She took the tray and carried it over to the bed. She saw David stir and look for her. Immediately his eyes found Daniel's. "Daniel, you're still here!"

Daniel took David's hand. "Yes, I am, and I am not going anywhere for a long time." He looked to Lizzy, smiling. He saw her smiling, too, but at her son.

Elizabeth looked to her son as she heard Daniel speaking to him. She smiled when she saw him smile. "Dinner is ready, sweetie." She sat the tray down and saw Daniel sitting David up to eat.

"Thank you." She glanced in his direction and then back to David. She uncovered the tray. "Your favorite. Jell-O!" She smiled as she saw the look of disappointment on his face. "I know, but Doctor Reynolds wants you to take it easy for a little while."

She took his hands and felt Daniel lay his hand on her and then one on her son. "Let's thank God for this food," she smiled at him and then Daniel, "and then when Doctor Reynolds says it's okay, I'll get you a cheeseburger. How does that sound?"

David laughed and nodded his head. Elizabeth looked to Daniel and laughed. She took his hand now as he took David's. "Let's pray." The three of them bowed their heads.

Chapter Twenty-One

Dinner for Davey went well. David ate everything on his plate and proclaimed he was full.

Doctor Reynolds came in a little while later and said David should be able to go home tomorrow morning. She saw Doctor Reynolds' eyes drop and then he bid them goodnight, saying he would see them in the morning for discharge instructions.

Elizabeth turned to Daniel and then her son. "Did you hear that, Sweetie? You get to leave tomorrow."

David clapped his hands and then looked down. "Mommy, why are you holding Daniel's hand?"

Elizabeth looked down at her hand and moved it out of Daniel's. She felt Daniel squeeze it as she let go of him. She missed the feel of his hand in hers. She hadn't even noticed that she was holding his hand.

"Maybe Mommy likes the feel of my hand in hers, Davey." He turned to Lizzy and then David.

"Do you like Mommy holding your hand, Daniel?"

"Yes, Davey, I like the feel of Mommy's hand very much." Even now his hand twitched to hold hers again. When Doctor Reynolds had been speaking, she had slipped her hand in his.

"I like Mommy's hand, too, Daniel." He looked to the two of them. "If you like Mommy's hand, you should hold it."

Daniel looked to Lizzy, laughing. Her son had just given them the okay to hold hands.

"Out of the mouths of babes, Lizzy."

Elizabeth moved to her son. “You know what I think?” She saw him shake his head. “I think it is time for a story.” She settled in beside him, taking his hand and holding it. “Tonight I will tell you of how Mommy and Daddy met and how God found them and showed them a great love.”

David giggled. “I like this story, Mommy.”

She felt Daniel situate himself on the bed. He took David’s hand and looked at her. She looked to him and then her son. “That’s because it is a good story, David, filled with love. Just like Mommy loves Daddy.”

Before Elizabeth knew it, visiting hours were over. She had made her way to the nurses’ station again, seeing the same nurse there who was when she asked about lunch. “Can I stay the night with my son?”

“No, Mrs. Seraphim. Doctor Reynolds left instructions that he rest this evening but you can come back at eight a.m.”

“Are you sure?”

“Take your husband home, Mrs. Seraphim. He has been in there all day with your son.” She smiled. “I saw them walking earlier. You have a devoted man in your husband, and you can tell he loves David.”

Elizabeth went to open her mouth to tell the nurse Daniel wasn’t her husband but decided not to. There would have to be another explanation on who he was if she did. Besides, tomorrow they would be discharging Davey. So she just said, “Thank you.” She turned to walk back to the room.

Opening the door and closing it behind her quietly, she heard Daniel say, "Will you show me how, Davey?" She stood against the door and watched her son and Daniel.

"Sure, Daniel." She saw her son reach out and take Daniel's hands. The two held hands as they bowed their heads. "Dear God, I love You and thank You for everything…" Elizabeth listened as Daniel prayed with her son. They thanked God for their good day and for their time together. They asked Him to bless their families and to help them have a good night. They asked to be safe through the night so they could wake to do His will tomorrow. Her son had finished with an "Amen."

Daniel looked up and smiled at her son. He said, "You are a very special little boy, David. More special than you know."

David smiled at Daniel. "I know that. God tells me all the time. He says He loves you, too, Daniel, and that He is waiting on you. He says it's a limited-time offer."

Elizabeth heard him gasp. Or was that her? She saw his head turn toward her with knowing eyes. He turned back toward the little boy. "God said that to you, David? You haven't ever heard that anywhere else?" Those were the same words Elizabeth said to him!

"Oh, yes, Daniel. God said you needed to hear that again."

Daniel looked to Elizabeth again, wide–eyed, then to David. "Would you tell Him I am thinking about it, Davey?"

"He knows you are, Daniel. Mommy." He smiled brightly, holding out his hands. "Daniel has prayed with me. I will be fine, Mommy."

Elizabeth was still in shock over what her son said to Daniel. "I know he has, David. Thank you, Daniel." She smiled at Daniel and saw him smile back at her. "We have to leave for the night, David, but I will be back in the morning."

She made her way to the bed and pulled the little boy into her arms. "I love you, Baby."

"I love you too, Mommy."

She pulled back from him and smiled at him. "Would you like me to sing to you before I leave?"

David leaned back in his bed and closed his eyes. "Yes, Mommy."

Elizabeth forgot about Daniel being in the room and sang to her son. She knew he loved the song, "Jesus Loves Me." When she finished the last verse, she saw him breathing evenly. She bent over and kissed him on the cheek.

Looking to Daniel, she took his hand and pulled him over to the door. Moving close to him, she zipped his jacket and pulled up his hood. Tying the tie, she winked at him and pulled him out the door.

She still had hold of his hand as they moved through the hallway past the nurses' station.

"Good night, Mr. & Mrs. Seraphim," she heard the nurses say. She thought to stop but didn't. She kept moving them out the door and to Daniel's car.

Chapter Twenty-Two

At the car, in the streetlight, Daniel unzipped his jacket and dropped his hood. He brought the woman who had dragged him out of the building close to him and held her in his arms. He breathed in her scent. Fresh-picked berries.

"I want to kiss you, Lizzy." He felt her breath catch and then become heavy. "I want you to want to kiss me. Right now. But I know you won't. I'll wait for you. I'll wait for you to want to—need to—kiss me and then I'll kiss you like you need to be kissed."

He pushed her back away from him. Her pupils were dilated. "Know this, Elizabeth Seraphim," he said as he bent his head down, "When I do, you had better be ready to be kissed thoroughly and for a long time."

She nodded her head at his words. She knew when she kissed him he would want it and he would hold her to him for a long while.

"Just so we're clear on that, Lizzy." He saw her nod her head. He had never used this much restraint with another woman in his life. He was used to women saying things to him, throwing themselves at his feet. Knowing this one woman—a good woman-didn't want him the way the others did not only intrigued him but drew him to her. He took her hand. "Let's go home."

As they pulled out of the parking lot, he had a thought. "There is this little restaurant in town. Everyone there knows me and I would like to take you there. You may not have noticed, Lizzy, but we haven't eaten since breakfast."

"Thank you, Daniel, but if it is all the same to you, could we just grab something and go home? I would like to see my kids before they go to bed."

He knew that family was important to her. "Are you sure you don't want something more substantial?"

"Yes, I am sure, but thank you, Daniel. Maybe some other time, alright?"

"It's a date." He pulled into a drive-through and they ordered their food. They prayed and then both ate in silence as Daniel began the hour-long drive home.

Elizabeth did not realize she hadn't eaten all day. She felt herself relax as the car moved down the road. She laid her hands in her lap and closed her eyes.

Daniel saw Lizzy lean her head back. He hated to disturb her but something had happened during the day that bothered him. "Lizzy?"

He saw her turn her head but not open her eyes. Sleepily she said, "Yes, Daniel?"

"Today at the hospital you came back into the room shaking. You told David it was because you were so happy for him." He saw her watching him now. "What happened when you went to talk with someone?"

Elizabeth looked to Daniel now. "A misunderstanding."

"What do you mean?" He watched the road but his attention was on her.

"When I went to the nurses' station, the guy we talked to this morning was there, the one who invited me to breakfast." She saw his head nod. "I asked him about David and then thanked him when he answered me. I turned around to go back to the room and he grabbed my wrist." She felt the car come to a stop in the middle of the road.

They were on that same stretch of road again, deserted still. She saw him turn to her, his eyes dark and glittering in the dim light. His mouth was set. "What?!"

"It was a misunderstanding, Daniel." She was awake now and lifted her head. "He told me he called my name, but I guess I didn't hear him." She shrugged. "He grabbed my wrist and I panicked. He said he was just wanting me to know about the guest services at the hospital."

She reached into her bag and pulled out the pamphlet she was given. She handed it to Daniel and saw him take it.

"He touched you, Lizzy." He knew he was the one shaking now. He felt like hitting the man. He hadn't liked him when he first saw him. "He shouldn't have put his hands on you."

He knew it was a statement. Her body was her own space and she should have someone touch her without being afraid of them.

"It was a misunderstanding, Daniel." She moved up to him and touched his shoulder, looking up into his eyes.

"No." He put his hands on her shoulders, moving his head down by hers. "If you ever feel that way again, Lizzy, you tell me. Do you understand? I won't have anyone making you feel unsafe."

"Yes," she blinked. He was mad! "Yes, Daniel. I understand."

"Are you alright?" He looked her over now. He knew if she wasn't, he would never see it. She would hurt on the inside and no one would ever know.

"Yes, Daniel." She moved closer to him, reassuring him with her presence that she was fine. He put his hands around her again and felt her move into his embrace.

"I want to pray for you, Lizzy, and then we will go home and see the children."

"Alright, Daniel." They got out of the car and leaned up against it. She laid her head on his chest, not missing the fact that he wanted to pray for her. She waited. She had not heard him start a prayer before.

He closed his eyes, his arms coming around her shoulders. One of his hands splayed in her hair. He hoped his prayer came out right. "Dear Lord, this woman in my arms loves you and I am getting to know You through her. Protect her and hold her in Your arms. She is so precious. More precious than she knows." He drew a blank now. Thinking, he added, "If she is afraid, please take the fear from her and help her to know You are always there for her." He paused. "And that I am, too." He paused again. "Amen." He held her for a few more moments.

"That was a beautiful prayer, Daniel. Thank you."

She knew she should step out of his arms but didn't. She looked up at him instead. The moonlight fell on his face and he was smiling.

He had a handsome smile. She had seen that smile on Raven and Olivia's mouth. He truly was a handsome man.

And he had just comforted her through prayer. She could get used to him doing that for her. She looked to his mouth again and felt herself moving toward it.

Daniel knew where her eyes were looking and everything in him was telling him to pull her to him again. Instead he heard himself speaking. "Lizzy?"

She was still looking at his mouth. Her eyes came up to meet his. She blinked. "Yes, Daniel?"

She pulled back from him now. She knew what she had almost done. She stepped away from him.

"We should get home, Lizzy." He didn't want to let go of her but he had to. He saw her nod her head.

"Yes, Daniel, we should." She stepped into the car and heard her car door shut.

The rest of the car ride home was silent. Elizabeth could feel the adrenaline coursing through her system. Her thoughts were racing at a hundred miles an hour. Today had been so good and to follow through with what she wanted to do earlier would have been wonderful. Wrong, but wonderful.

She closed her eyes. They were still less than halfway home. She would rest for a little while.

Home, she thought as she felt sleep begin to close over her. It was his home, not hers.

They had sold their home after they had lost David. They were wanderers now, without a home. She frowned. She looked forward to her heavenly home. Yes, she would think on that, she thought as she surrendered to sleep.

Daniel heard Lizzy's breathing even out and glanced over to her. He knew she was asleep. He remembered back to a few moments ago.

He wanted to kiss her. Everything in him was telling him to, but he knew it would have been wrong. So wrong. It felt like the wrong time. He knew he was attracted to her and she was attracted to him. He knew her ideals and principles that she stood on and for. If she had sacrificed them for him, he was afraid of where that would put her.

He reached over and turned on the radio. Instead of his usual station, he found himself scrolling through for a Christian station. He knew if Lizzy woke up, she would like to hear songs that talked about God.

Listening for a while, he found the music was good. They sounded a lot like his father's sermons put to music along with the love that Lizzy and her family talked about with him. He leaned back in the car as it moved through the night. He found himself easily finding the tune to some of the songs and humming along.

When he pulled into the garage, he turned off the car. When the door dropped, he made his way over and opened Lizzy's door. He leaned down. "Lizzy?" He shook her, but she didn't wake. "Lizzy?" She moaned and turned her head toward him. He bent down now and picked her up out of the seat. "Lizzy, we're home."

"Don't have a home," Elizabeth muttered, knowing she was half asleep. She felt like she was floating. She heard a noise and then a knock. She heard a door open then close. She felt herself moving up, still floating.

"You have a home," he said quietly as he gently shut his bedroom door behind him. He had seen her children come up to him as he carried her through the house. His dad motioned that his children were sleeping.

"Don't." She snuggled into the warmth of the cloud. "My home is gone."

"You have a home with me, Lizzy." He felt the catch in his throat as he spoke the words to her. He knew it was true.

"I want to have a home, Daniel." She began snoring softly as he laid her on the bed. He saw his father bring in her bag and set it down. Daniel mouthed the words "thank you" to his father and saw his father shut the door behind himself.

"You have it, then, Lizzy." He sat down on the bed and lay down with her. He felt her draw him closer to her. "Good night, Lizzy." He laid his head on hers, heard her snoring softly, and promptly fell asleep.

Chapter Twenty-Three

Elizabeth began to wake and felt a body curled around hers. It was long and at first she thought it was her son, Paul. She felt the hand around her waist and the comfort of a body next to hers. She opened her eyes and saw that it wasn't Paul.

Sitting up, she moved carefully off the bed and put her feet on the floor. The clock on the side of the bed read 5:15 a.m. She stood quietly, not seeing Daniel move, and picked up her bag.

As she closed the door to the bath, she didn't remember coming back or being brought to the room. She remembered the feeling of floating and thinking that she was dreaming. She knew now that Daniel must have carried her to his room.

She showered and saw her hat and gown on the sink. She hadn't noticed them before. She reached over and put them into her bag. She dressed and saw Daniel still sleeping on the bed.

Quietly, she shut the door to his room and made her way to the guest rooms.

The first door she opened contained her sons, Paul and Ben. Telling them "Good morning," she moved next door to the next guest room where Lily and April were. Telling them "good morning," too, she proceeded to go downstairs, knowing they would follow her when they were ready.

She went to the kitchen and saw John sitting at the table. He was drinking a cup of tea and looking out the window. John looked tired and lonely. She saw him look lovingly at the seat to his right and move his hand over to it. He looked sad. She wondered what he was thinking as he looked to the empty seat.

Putting on a happy face, she entered the kitchen. She went up to John and hugged him from behind. As she went around to the front of him, she saw his face pick up and smile at her. "Good morning, Elizabeth. I trust you slept well last night." He smiled and gestured to the chair to his right. "Sit. Sit. I'll get you a cup before the kids come down."

Elizabeth watched John as he made her a cup of tea. The sugar and honey were already on the table. He sat the cup in front of her and then took his seat.

"Thank you. I don't really remember sleeping last night." She blushed, remembering how she had awoken. "I don't remember coming in last night, either. I think the day really wiped me out." She took a sip of the tea and set her cup down.

"How is David, he doing better?"

"Yes. Doctor Reynolds says he should be released today. I am so happy." She slid her hand over to his and she saw him lay her hand on top of his.

"The entire congregation has been praying for him, Elizabeth."

"Before I came into the kitchen, John, I saw you looking at this place. Did your wife sit here, John, or was it Daniel's?"

John eyed where she was sitting.

"This table was supposed to hold ten children, Elizabeth, plus me and the missus." He laughed. "We wanted a big family with lots of children to love. She had so much trouble carrying Daniel that we decided not to have any more children. So Daniel stayed an only child."

She brought her other hand to his. "That must have been hard, John."

"It was. It was." He smiled a crooked smile at her. "The missus just started taking in kids from the neighborhood, children whose parents were gone for long stretches. Daniel may not have had sisters or brothers, but he always had someone to play with."

"Sounds like you were very fortunate to be here for those children when others couldn't."

"We were." He nodded his head and moved his hands away from hers. "With the addition of your family, this old table feels like it should."

Elizabeth drank the rest of her tea. "How was church yesterday, Reverend? Packed house?"

He laughed out loud. "So many people came to see my "son" worship. Your son did a good job impersonating. Just the right height and acted just like him."

Elizabeth laughed. "We have seen all of his movies, John." She blushed. "And a lot of extra things from what he has done. I think Paul just borrowed from your son's life."

John nodded his head. "I think you are right, Elizabeth. Now I know you and Daniel have been getting close. How are things between the two of you?"

She looked down at her empty cup. She didn't want any more. "I have told him just about everything about my life." She blushed again. "I still woke up next to him this morning." She held out her hands. "Not that anything happened, because it didn't. But I think he is doing okay with the information."

"Have you mentioned anything to him about God?" John had tried for so many years to help his son in that area. But ultimately it would have to be Daniel who made that decision.

"Yes. I told him our relationship could not progress beyond friendship without him knowing the Lord. I told him I didn't want to pressure him and that if he didn't, that was okay, too."

"If my," he scratched the back of his head, "if my son had a relationship with God, would you," he scratched it again, "pursue that with him?"

"Yes!" She looked around, glad no one was downstairs yet. "I mean, yes, John, I like your son very much."

John looked into her eyes. "Do you love him, Elizabeth?"

Elizabeth shrugged. "I don't know. The feeling I have for him is so new. I don't want to rush into anything."

"That's wise thinking. You should be sure my son knows the Lord and that you love him before you decide for sure, Elizabeth."

"He has prayed with us, John. Me and David, and last night he prayed his own prayer for me."

John smiled widely at Elizabeth. He knew they would be a good match.

"Have my children been good for you, John?"

"Perfect children. They are good kids. I like your children and their being here has made it like the big family I've always wanted."

"Thank you for everything, John. It has been so nice having them here while I try to be there for David."

"I know you are appreciative, Elizabeth. And what you are doing for my son is immeasurable." He smiled at her as he heard children on the stairs. "Sounds like your children are awake. Do you mind if I wake my grandkids and bring them to your reading? You could do it in here."

"The more the merrier."

She smiled at her children as they made their way into the kitchen. "Good morning!" She hugged all of them as they came through the kitchen, Bibles in hand. She watched them sit.

"I just wanted to let you know that your brother should be coming home today." She heard the kids cheer and then heard footsteps on the steps. "And we are going to have the Templeman children with us this morning. Good morning, Tayler, Olivia, and Raven." She looked to her children again. "Please find a buddy because this morning we are going to scripture-search before devotion."

Paul sat beside Tayler, Lily beside Olivia, and April sat with Raven. John sat beside Ben.

She smiled at the group of children in front of her.

"Hey, that's not fair." Paul gaped at Ben. "He gets the Reverend."

John looked innocent. "I promise not to tell him where it is exactly. Just nudge him along." He winked at Elizabeth. "Sometimes nudging works better, aye, Elizabeth?"

Elizabeth blushed and then looked to her Bible. Clearing her throat, she said, "Psalm 139. Go!" She saw each of her children helping one of the Templeman children. She knew what John saw now as she looked at the children.

Daniel awoke almost as soon as he felt Elizabeth leave the bed. One moment he felt the warmth of her body and the next she was gone. He had missed having someone beside him in the night. Curling next to Lizzy felt nice. He knew it was a feeling he could come to love.

Moving into the bath, he looked over to the sink and saw her hat and gown missing. He wondered why she had chosen to take them this morning. He missed having the items on the sink and seeing her red toothbrush lying on it.

The shower still held the warmth of Lizzy's shower. He had listened to her as she moved through her morning in his bath and room. He liked the sounds of her humming as she showered and dressed. He wondered if she realized that she did that.

He had already brushed his teeth and fixed his hair and was dressing now. He decided on his red T-shirt. It was in the back of his closet and he had almost forgotten it was there. Slipping it on with a loose-fitting pair of khakis, he chose loose deck shoes to complete the outfit. He knew he had two interviews to do today. Both were casual and didn't require him to dress up. He wanted to be back at the hospital in time to pick up Lizzy and David.

Making his way down the stairs, he heard the sound of his children's laughter. There was other laughter, too, and he heard Lizzy as she talked with all the children. They discussed what their plans were for the day. He heard his father chuckle.

Looking around the corner, he saw his father look at Lizzy. He saw the smile on his father's face. If he didn't know any better, he would think his father was smitten with Lizzy. Looking at his children, he could see them responding to Lizzy, too.

He saw their children sitting all mixed together now. John was sitting at the head of the table with Lizzy to his right. His mom used to sit there when she was alive.

Everyone laughed and he saw Lizzy look his way. She smiled at him and he felt himself answering her. He moved to the kitchen now.

"Good morning, everyone," he said. He moved to his children and hugged them. "How is everyone this morning?"

"Good mornings" were scattered around as he poured himself a cup of tea. He sat down by Lizzy. "Good morning, Lizzy."

"Good morning, Daniel." She turned her head to him and saw him smiling at her. She felt herself blush and looked down to her tea.

"So," he looked around at everyone, "what have I missed?"

He took a piece of toast off of the platter on the table. It was cold, but he didn't mind. He took a bite.

"We read scripture, Daddy," Raven said, her black hair bouncing around. "Mrs. Elizabeth read with us."

He winked at his daughter. “Did she now?”

“Yes, Father,” his son Tayler said. “She says we can do it tomorrow, too.”

“That she can,” he turned to look at her and saw his father smiling at him. “What?” He could swear his dad blushed.

“Nothing… Nothing, Son. Busy day?” John took a drink of his tea, hoping it hid the heat in his cheeks.

“I have two interviews and then I would like to be at the hospital when David is discharged.” He turned to Lizzy, finishing his toast and tea. “Would that be alright, Lizzy?”

Elizabeth didn’t turn to Daniel. “Of course.” She knew looking at him right now would cause her to start blushing all over again. “Do I need to call someone or will you still be driving me this morning, Daniel?” She wiped her hands and looked to him now, more in control of herself.

She refrained from gasping. He was so handsome! She put her napkin on her plate and stared at it.

He looked to Lizzy and waited for her to look at him again. He wanted to see her eyes as he talked to her.

“I told you I would drive you, Lizzy. What I say, I do.”

There was total silence at the kitchen table as all eyes turned to Daniel and Elizabeth. She swallowed as she looked at him and nodded her head.

Daniel restrained himself from touching her face. She was so beautiful in the morning. In the afternoon, in the evening, as she slept.

John cleared his throat and gestured for the kids to finish eating. As he watched, the children began to leave the table. Elizabeth blushed again and Daniel smiled a knowing smile at her.

"What time is your first interview, Son?"

Daniel looked around the table now. The children were all gone. When did that happen? He stood and took Lizzy's plate and cup as he took his.

"Ten o'clock, Dad. The car should be here around nine. The interviews are close together. Thankfully." He made his way back over to Lizzy. "Are you about ready to leave? Do you need to do anything before we go?"

He looked at the clock. It said 7:00 a.m. If he drove carefully, he would have time to run in and see David before he came back. He now had the drive down to forty-five minutes.

Elizabeth shook her head. "No, I don't think so." She looked to John and hugged him.

"Thank you again, John." She turned to Daniel. "I think I am ready to go."

He gestured toward the garage and when they had moved inside, he opened her car door. After she sat, he shut her door. The garage door went up and he pulled out of the drive.

Daniel watched Lizzy out of the corner of his eye. She was fidgety and nervous. He gripped the steering wheel. He had noticed that she had gotten quieter the farther they moved from his house.

"Are you alright, Lizzy?" He saw her nod and look toward the window. He did take her hand now. He felt her squeeze it. "No, I think you're not. Lizzy?"

She looked around herself. Her heart hurt and breathing was becoming a chore. The car was too enclosed and she found herself breathing in great gulps of air.

"Lizzy?" Daniel became concerned for her now. "Mandarin?"

"Stop the car, Ironman." She felt the bile rise in her throat. She knew she was going to be sick. Daniel signaled and pulled the car over. He saw her get out and run to the side of the road. On her knees she became sick. He followed her around the car.

"Lizzy? What's wrong?" Kneeling behind her, he brought his hands to her shoulders and felt her relax against him. She sighed in relief.

"I miss my husband, Daniel. My son is in the hospital and I remembered we talked last night about me not having a home. You said you would be my home. I can't do it, Daniel. You can't be my home, not like you are right now. I have to have someone lead me and my children. I have to have someone to answer my children's questions about God. I need someone to remind me that He loves me. Yes, you prayed with me and my son. You led me in prayer and that was sweet. But I can't do it, Daniel. I can't be with you and nothing come of it."

She turned toward the ground and became sick again. She knew it was stress. All of it had manifested and overwhelmed her.

He put his hands on her shoulders and pulled her back to him when she stopped. He knew it was all too much for her. "I'm sorry, Lizzy, if you felt like I was pressuring you. I'm sorry you lost your husband, that I lost my wife. I'm sorry your son is sick. I'm sorry you were violated. I'm sorry for so many things, but I am not sorry for telling you that I would be your home."

He steadied her and moved away from her. "I want to say 'as you wish' all day long to you, but I can't. Wesley told Buttercup that too. As you wish. He was really telling her that he loved her, as I love you."

He moved up to her. "I can't because you won't let me. I hold myself back from touching you, kissing you, pulling you into my arms." He laughed hysterically. "I loved the feel of you in my arms last night, sleeping. I remember waking up and looking at you, knowing you are there, knowing I have someone to hold, and going back to sleep with a smile on my face. I am not going to apologize for that, Lizzy."

Elizabeth looked up at Daniel and nodded her head. She knew what he said was true.

"Let's get you cleaned up and head to the hospital. David is waiting to see us."

He took her hand and brought her over to the car. He handed her a bottle of water he had in the front seat. He saw her rinse her mouth out a few times and then pull some gum out of her bag. He helped her into the car.

As they neared the hospital, he decided he was done pretending. He had told her he wouldn't kiss her again and he wouldn't, but he wouldn't hide his feelings from her anymore, either.

He pulled into a space and moved over to open her door. He knew he had left all his jackets at home. Today was about Daniel Templeman being with Elizabeth Seraphim at the hospital. He was going to visit her son and make his way through the interviews. Then he was going to come back for her and David.

Elizabeth looked at Daniel. "Your suit." She looked around and saw a few heads in the lot turn to him. They recognized him.

"Not today, Lizzy." He pulled her toward the hospital. No one had stopped him and for that he was grateful. "Today is about Daniel being with Lizzy. Only. If I get stopped or we get photo'd are you alright with that?" He stopped and peered at her.

"Yes." She nodded her head. "Yes, Daniel." She squeezed the hand in hers.

"Good."

He led her toward the doors of the hospital. He didn't affect Danny Tensley. He wouldn't. Not today. They made their way to David's room and he opened the door. Elizabeth made her way to her son's bed and saw he was awake.

"Hey, Baby. Good morning."

David's face brightened. "Mommy! Daniel!" He opened his little arms and felt his mother and Daniel move into them.

"Good morning, Davey. How are you this morning?"

He held the little boy in his arms. He liked the feel of David and his mother.

"Good." He let go of his mom but not Daniel. He felt Daniel take him into his lap. "They came in and took the needle out of my hand this morning, Daniel. I didn't like that thing."

"I don't like needles either, Davey." He had seen the twinkle in the boy's eye as he pulled him into his lap. "Are you ready to go home today?"

"I sure am, Daniel. I get to go to your house and see Raven. She's my best friend and she is in my Sunday School class." He moved closer to Daniel and laid his head on his chest.

"Mommy smiles a lot when you're around."

Elizabeth looked to the floor and blushed, smiling wider. She tried not to but couldn't seem to help herself.

"I think you're right, David. Look at Mommy, she's blushing." He saw her cheeks get redder. He looked down to the boy now. "I can't stay all day, David." He saw the boy frown. "I have some things I have to do, but your mum is going to be here for you." He brought the boy carefully to him. "If you or Mommy need anything while I'm gone, Mommy has my mobile number. You can both call me any time." He saw the little boy's face light up as he pulled him back.

"Really, Daniel? Any time?"

"Well," he met Lizzy's eyes, "anytime I can answer. I have to do two interviews today, but then I will be right back. I can talk anytime I am not in an interview." He looked to the boy, hoping he would understand.

"Alright, Daniel. Mommy and I are going to have fun, aren't we, Mommy?"

Elizabeth leaned down and picked up her son in her arms. She missed holding him. "Oh, yes, David." She looked at Daniel. "Shouldn't you be off, Mr. Templeman?"

"Yes, I should, Lizzy." But he didn't want to. He wanted to spend the day with Lizzy and David. He carefully took David from Lizzy's arms and took her hand.

"What are you doing, Daniel?" She looked at the man who was now holding her son.

"Clearing up a misunderstanding." He led her to the door. "Open it, Lizzy." She did.

Taking Lizzy and her son to the nurses' station, he saw the same man there from yesterday morning. Daniel pulled Lizzy to his side and held David in his arms. He saw the man look up to him and then to Elizabeth and David.

"Hello." Daniel smiled at the man, continuing to hold Lizzy and her son. "My name is Danny Tensley. I would like to thank you and the staff of the hospital for taking care of my fiancé and her son the last few days."

He saw the man look to Lizzy and then to him. "I just wanted to let you know that I have to be gone for a while and I would appreciate any assistance the staff can be to my fiancé and her son."

He looked pointedly at the man and saw him drop his eyes. "I understand that you probably have a busy day ahead of you, so I would appreciate you not being the one to assist my future wife. Do we understand one another?" He saw the man nod his head.

Another man had moved up to the nurse's side. He smiled at them. "Hello. I am the Floor Director. We had no idea, Mr. Tensley, that your fiancé had a son in our hospital. Please, Mrs. Seraphim, if you need anything, do not hesitate to ask."

"Actually," Daniel looked down into Lizzy's eyes smiling. "I was wondering if there was another floor this gentleman could work on today. I would appreciate it if he didn't come near my fiancé."

The Director glowered at Ronald LaStat. "Is there a problem, Mr. Tensley?"

"I want this man nowhere near my fiancé or her son." He ruffled David's hair playfully and the little boy giggled. "I will be back as soon as I give a couple of interviews and I would like to find Lizzy and her son happy."

"Of course, Mr. Tensley, anything for a celebrity like yourself." He attended to Lizzy. "Would you like anything, Mrs. Seraphim?"

"Just a lunch, please, when my son eats." She looked to David and smiled up at Daniel.

"Of course, Mrs. Seraphim. We will also have someone check on you every hour to make sure you and little David have everything you need."

The Director pulled out a chart and looked at Ronald. "Look at that, Ron, we are overstaffed today. Why don't you go home and take the day off." He reached for Ronald's badge and coat, taking them from him. "We will see you tomorrow."

He pulled the man out of the chair and walked him around the other side of the nurses' station. "Have a good day, Ronald."He turned back to Mr. Templeman. "Anything else you, your fiancé, or her son require?"

Daniel looked down at Elizabeth and over to the clock. He had exactly forty-five minutes to make it home for the car.

"No, thank you." He passed David off to Lizzy and looked down into her eyes. He waited for a minute and then bent down to kiss her on the cheek. He kissed David, too. "I love you both. I will see you soon."

Elizabeth watched Daniel round the corner, smiling happily. She swung her eyes back around to the Director. "Thank you for everything, Mister...," she read his badge, "Reynolds." She looked at his face. "Do you know Doctor Reynolds?"

"Yes, Mrs. Seraphim, he's my dad."

She laughed. She was meeting all the good dads: John, Doctor Reynolds, Daniel. "Thank you again, Director Reynolds."

Turning, she made her way with her son back to his room. She began settling David into bed and pulled his favorite book out of her bag.

"Mommy! You brought it!" He took it out of his mother's hands, looking over the cover.

Elizabeth felt the phone Daniel gave her vibrate. She pulled it out of her pocket. She opened the text.

I hope your day goes well. I do have two interviews today and then I will be back to pick you both up when Davey is released. Being a celebrity has its

perks sometimes. ;-) If either of you need anything, call or text.
As You Wish, Ironman

Elizabeth read the text and slipped the phone back in her pocket.

She knew what Daniel had done at the nurses' station was to make her feel safe. But they were not engaged and Daniel saying he loved her was only a ruse, but it still made her heart beat just a little faster to hear it. When she had looked up to him, she had smiled at the goofy grin and light shining in his eyes. When he said he loved her and kissed her cheek, it made every hair on her body stand on end and she could feel her toes curling in her shoes.

Thinking about the closing in the text, she wondered if he was still playing his part with her. He couldn't love her. Yes, he had said he wanted to tell her and couldn't. She knew that frustrated Daniel, but he couldn't know her well enough to love her.

She smiled at David and pulled him carefully closer to her. Taking the book from his hands, she felt him move closer to her.

"Alright, Baby, I am so excited to read to you today. I love you." She smiled down at him and kissed his nose. She loved him with all that she had.

"I love you, Mommy."

It was a little while later that a breakfast tray was brought into the room. The woman who carried it to the tray table saw Elizabeth and blushed. She kept eyeing her as she made her way over to her. "Hi. My name is Melody. I work with the kitchen. I was wondering, is it true that you are Mr. Tensley's fiancé?"

Elizabeth contemplated Melody now. Her features were a mix of envy and awe. She knew the next word out of her mouth was a lie. "Yes."

"Wow! You are just the luckiest woman alive." She blushed. "Sorry. I have seen everything he has been in and he is a really good actor."

"Call me Elizabeth. Yes, he is. What's your favorite role, Melody?"

Elizabeth tried not to fangirl over Danny. She knew she could in a heartbeat, but she could never do that over Daniel. Her heart did a different thing with him.

Her voice was dreamy and soft. "Oh, Romeo and Juliet. I could never picture a better Romeo."

"He did do a wonderful job in it." She had to restrain herself from becoming like Melody. To date, that was Daniel's best role in her own mind.

"Well, I just wanted to say that every woman out there," she pointed at the door, "envies you."

Elizabeth looked at the door. "Every?"

"Oh, yes, Ronald came to the cafeteria before he left and told us that Danny Tensley's fiancé and her son were in our hospital. Everyone in the cafeteria heard him. Of course by the time we made it to the floor he was gone and Director Reynolds sent us all back to the cafeteria. Thank you for your time, Elizabeth. I am going to get your breakfast tray now."

She left the room and came back in with a huge tray and a red rose off to the side. A silver cover was over the whole thing.

Elizabeth looked to the platter. "Is that mine?" It took two hands for Melody to carry it.

She sat it down on a second tray table.

"Yes. Director Reynolds was insistent on making sure you had what you wanted for breakfast. Let me get the cold tray."

"Cold tray?" Elizabeth was still in shock from the platter.

"Yes, we in the kitchen didn't know what you wanted for breakfast, so we made you a little bit · everything." She walked out of the room and back in with another tray of food.

"But this is so much, Melody." She had an idea. "What are your plans when you get done delivering all the food?"

"I get a break to eat my own breakfast."

"Why don't you bring two plates—regular sized plates?" Elizabeth laughed, gesturing to all the food, "and we will share this?"

"Really? I can have breakfast with Danny Tensley's fiancé?" Melody sounded in awe.

Elizabeth walked up to her and smiled. "How about you just have breakfast with Elizabeth Seraphim?"

"Are you sure?"

"Most definitely."

As Daniel walked into his house, he looked at his watch. Five minutes to the car. Traffic had been clear all the way home.

He pulled out his mobile and looked at it. No texts or calls. He headed up the stairs to his room and he came back down. He peeped out the window. Standing at the car was someone he didn't recognize. Where was Roger?

"Dad?" He looked into the kitchen and saw Lizzy's children studying. "Hey."

They looked up and smiled at him. "Hey, Daniel. Your dad is resting. We are being quiet and working." Paul looked at the man who he knew liked his mom.

"Is everything alright with him, Paul?"

"Yes, sir, he said something about a late night and wanting to lie down. He said he would be upstairs if we needed him."

"Alright. I have two interviews and then I am off to pick up Davey and your mum." He checked his pockets, making sure everything he needed was in them.

"Thank you, Daniel. Have a good day." With that, Paul went back to his work.

Daniel headed out to the car. "Good morning," he said as his driver opened the door to the car. There was no response from the man.

He sat in the back seat as the driver took off down the road to their destination. "Do you have a name?"

"Quimby, sir," was the man's curt reply.

Daniel noticed that Quimby kept his eyes trained on the road. "How are you this morning, Quimby?"

"I am fine, sir. How are you?" Very monotone.

"Good." He looked out the window. He missed Roger. He winced as he remembered why Roger wasn't there. He and Roger had gotten into a row.

The first interview was a short way away. He pulled out his mobile and texted Lizzy.

Haven't heard from you since the hospital, Mandarin, hope Davey is well. He looked good this morning. Kids are studying at home. Dad is resting, which he never does in the middle of the day. Odd. On way to first interview. Here if you need me.

As You Wish, Your Ironman

He waited for Lizzy to text back. She hadn't yet this morning and he wanted to hear from her. He felt his phone vibrate and turned on the screen.

Davey is still sore. Being a celebrity's "fiancé" is a little overwhelming though. Breakfast was delivered on two platters with a rose on the side. Melody was the woman who brought our food. She breakfasted while I helped David with his meal. Reading the Bible with David now. Talk soon. Your Nemesis, The Mandarin

He felt the car pull up to the curb. Looking out the window, he saw the usual crowd of people and frowned. The windows were tinted, so he knew no one could see in.

He wanted to be at the hospital with Lizzy and David. He wanted to hear her read to her son and see her play with him. He wanted to hold her hand.

But the call of the spotlight and people was alluring, too. Not as alluring as the sight of Lizzy sleeping, though. He sighed, smiling. He liked to watch her sleeping.

The smile was on his face now as he saw the door opening and he walked out into the crowd. He loved being an actor and couldn't picture himself doing anything else the rest of his life.

He posed for pictures, signed autographs, and smiled. Danny Tensley was the charmer. He knew how to work a crowd.

When the interview was over, he slid into the car and pulled his phone out of his pocket.

Nothing new. So he texted Lizzy.

First interview over. It went well and I had fun. On way to second and last one of the day. Missing you and Davey though. Having a good day?
As You Wish, Your Ironman

He held the phone, waiting for a response. He wished now he had something to read as he moved to his next destination.

He pushed an application on his phone that would download other applications with a search. He stopped and considered what he should download.

There were books out there of all kinds. He knew that any book he wanted to read was at his fingertips. As he looked at it, the phone timed out and he had to turn it back on again.

Knowing now what he wanted to read, he looked for and found the application and downloaded it, making sure it had what he wanted. Within that application, he found what he was looking for and sent the link to Lizzy's phone.

He smiled as he read it. He would always think of this text as theirs.

He was just about to his last stop when his phone buzzed again. He opened her message.

Thank you for the link. I try to be the Proverbs31 woman that it talks about but I don't think I achieve that sometimes. Davey was taken down for some last tests as he is to be discharged soon. You know since it has gotten out, yes it has, that I am your "fiancé" and David is my son. There have been flower deliveries all morning. LOL I have had all kinds of visitors from people I don't even know. It's kind of funny.

Your Nemesis, The Mandarin

He laughed. He figured something like that would happen. Opening his chat window, he felt the car pull up to another curb. Another crowd was there. He knew there would be more pictures and more signing. He smiled. He would be nothing as an actor without his fans.

As Daniel Templeman, he wondered where he would be as a man without Lizzy and her family. They had come to mean so much to him in so short a time.

He knew this interview would take around two hours. He was the second guest to be introduced of three, and he knew he would have to wait through the first and third before he could leave.

He texted Lizzy.

At second interview. Will be a long one, at least two hours. Will text when over. Will be taped in front of a live audience. Will have phone on vibrate. Text if you need me.

As You Wish, Your Ironman

He slipped his phone in his pocket and smiled as Quimby opened the door. He turned on the charm and Danny Tensley emerged. He smiled and waved, strutted and played.

His phone went off as he was taking the stage. He knew he couldn't answer it for at least two hours. During the interview, his phone vibrated at least four more times as he laughed and joked with the host and crowd.

At the car, he looked for Roger but only saw Quimby. He would have been able to talk with Roger about all of this and Roger would have given him some good advice. All he had now was the stoic Quimby who went about doing his job.

He opened the text window and saw five texts from Lizzy. The first was sent exactly an hour and fifteen minutes ago.

Just got release papers from Doctor Reynolds. We are free! Danny says he wants to go to the B&B for a little before we make our way to your house. Deacon Wayne is on his way to pick us up. Hope you are having fun taping.

Your Nemesis, The Mandarin

He had wanted to be the one to take Lizzy and Davey home! Angry now, he opened the next text.

Davey says to tell you "hi." I just want to thank you once again for everything, Daniel. You and your family have been a blessing to us. David is resting now, dressed and ready to go. He says he can't wait to see you and your family again. He says it feels like it did when his dad was alive. You have made my son smile.

Your Nemesis, The Mandarin

He couldn't help but smile at that one. He moved on to the next.

Deacon Wayne is here. Leaving flowers but have pictures, names, addresses of all who sent and stopped by. Am going to town when I get a chance

to pick up "Thank You" cards and send them to everyone. Will text you when we get back to the B&B.
Your Nemesis, The Mandarin

He found himself getting less angry now. Wayne had been there and was on his way home with them. Not home, he thought. To the B&B and then home—his home. That is where the Seraphim family belonged. At his home. With him.

But as he thought that, he thought of Wayne. Wayne had probably carried Davey out to his monstrously huge van. Buckled him to a car seat he had found for Davey as soon as he heard from Lizzy. He was talking with Lizzy as she and her son made their way back to the B&B.

Daniel looked at the clock. He thought he still had time to make it to the B&B before they got there. He opened the next text.

Daniel, just got back. Am at your house now. Hurry home, Daniel. We need you.
Lizzy

This message had a completely different tone. He dialed her number and waited for her to answer. He heard the phone pick up. "Lizzy? Lizzy, what's wrong?"

"I'm so sorry, Daniel."

He heard her sniffling. "Lizzy, what happened?"

"Paul went upstairs to check on John, Daniel. I called the hospital, Daniel, they are sending someone. Where are you?"

"My dad, Lizzy. What's wrong with my dad?" He knew what had happened even before she said the words.

"I'm so sorry, Daniel."

He heard her break down and start crying loudly now. His heart hurt that he was not there to comfort her. His father was gone.

"He's dead, isn't he, Lizzy?"

There was a quiet. "No, Daniel, he is just sleeping and visiting with God. We'll see him soon."

That's not what he wanted to hear. He gripped the phone harder. "Who knows, Lizzy, in the house?"

He looked at his watch. Three-fifteen. His children would be home soon, if they weren't there already.

"No one but Paul and myself. When your children came home, I sent everyone outside to play in the back yard. Paul is with them while I am with your father." He heard her crying. "I love him, Daniel—your father—and I never got a chance to tell him that. Oh, Daniel."

"I'm on my way home, Lizzy. We will take care of my dad together." He hung up the phone. "Quimby, how far are we from my house?"

"About fifteen minutes, sir."

Qumiby's voice grated on his nerves. He dialed the number to the booking agent. "Hey, Peter, this is Danny Tensley. Is Roger Blain still on payroll?" He paused. "Good. Good. I want him to be my permanent driver, Peter." He paused again. "No, no, Quimby is a good man. I would just like Roger

Blain as my driver from now on. I will pay extra for him, if I have to."

He ended the call and looked out the window, impatiently waiting while Quimby slowed the car.

He could have told Roger what had happened and Roger would have prayed with him, comforted him with words of wisdom. He knew nothing of this man in front of him. He was distant and cold.

Roger would have made it to his house in just a few minutes and held open his car door, offered him tissues. He knew that crow did not taste that good, but he would eat it for Roger.

Chapter Twenty-Four

When the car pulled into the drive, he collected his bags of goodies from the studio and let himself out of the car. He made his way into his house and put them inside the front door.

Taking the stairs two at a time, he opened the door to his father's room. He saw Lizzy lying over his father's chest, crying. He looked to his father, so silent and unmoving.

"Dad?"

Elizabeth didn't hear the door open, but the sound of Daniel's voice brought her out of her grief. Reverend Templeman was the best man she knew and he was gone.

Daniel made his way over to his father and saw Lizzy standing. She went to him and walked into his arms. He held her as he looked to his father. "He looks like he's sleeping, Lizzy."

He saw she had covered him and laid his hands on the bed. He truly did look like he was resting. He held Lizzy a little more tightly.

"That's because he is, Daniel. He's resting now with God." She tightened her arms around Daniel, too. As much as she needed to draw comfort from him, he needed her, too.

He knew the words she said, but they wouldn't register in his mind. "He's dead, Lizzy, not resting."

Elizabeth heard his words and knew they were true. His physical body was dead but his spirit was in heaven. She looked up at him. Her heart hurt and she knew that he needed to be comforted.

"Kiss me, Daniel," she whispered to him, blushing.

Daniel looked down at the woman in his arms. She was so familiar to him now. Like his family, she had become one of his own. He wanted to kiss her, but he didn't. He wanted their first kiss—technically not their first kiss, but he would always think of it as that—when she asked him to kiss her, to be a celebration of their love.

But he knew she didn't love him. He had to know if she did before he would kiss her. He pulled her to his chest.

"Not like this, Lizzy." He held her to him as he felt her tears on his shirt. "I want you to ask me to kiss you when you know that you love me as much as I love you. I want you to ask me when your heart can't stand to be away from mine as mine has felt the brief time we have been apart."

He looked down at her and then over to his father's bed. "Not when my dad has just died and we are both sad because he has left us."

He put his hands on her shoulders and pulled her to him. "I need to know that you love me, Lizzy. I know you don't see me as Danny Tensley the actor but as Daniel Templeman the man. I have to know that I am everything to you and that you can't live without me."

He took his hands off her shoulders. "That's when I'll kiss you. When you tell me you can't go on without me and that you have to kiss me or die. That I am the only one for you."

Elizabeth knew in her heart he was right. She knew her asking him to kiss her now would be something they would remember and then think of as being done out of grief. The first time she asked him to kiss her should be everything he had just described. She nodded her head. "I'm sorry, Daniel."

He brought his hand to her hair and began stroking it. "There is nothing to be sorry about, Love. I know you were trying to help me and I thank you for your heart. I just want it to mean so much more for you."

She nodded her head again. "I know. Thank you."

Holding her tightly, Daniel looked at his father. "Is he really sleeping, Lizzy?"

"The Bible says that those who have died have only fallen asleep and that we will see them one day. Just like I will my husband, David, we will see your father again. And we will all be happy again."

He stood up straighter. Her words sounded like the words that his father said to him when Gen passed. "How do you know that, Lizzy? How do you know we will see him again?"

She sniffled as she looked up at him. "Just like you say you love me and that you can't stand to be away from me, I know your dad is waiting for us." She took his hand and pressed it against her heart. "Because I feel it in my heart." She took one hand and closed his. Whispering, she said, "I wish I could make you see the faith in my heart, Daniel, but you have to feel it for yourself."

He opened his eyes now. He didn't move his hand. He could feel her heart beating beneath it. He looked down into her eyes. "I have faith in you, Lizzy."

"Don't… don't have faith in me, Daniel. I am not a good person. I'm only going to let you down. If you want to have faith in someone, have faith in God to see you through everything. He will do it if you ask Him."

He felt her heart beat faster. He couldn't tear his eyes away from her. "I want to pray, Lizzy." He took her hands in his. "I want to pray that God gives us the strength to handle my father's death and that He sees us through anything we need." He stepped closer to her and laid his forehead against hers, closing his eyes. "Dear Heavenly Father, we come to you saying that we love you."

Elizabeth opened her eyes but did not comment on Daniel saying he loved God. She closed them again and found herself moving closer to him.

"Help us, please, as You take my father home…" The prayer Daniel recited was beautiful. In her mind's eye she could see Daniel talking with God as she watched him.

She opened her eyes and looked into his, a tear sliding down her cheek. "That was beautiful, Daniel."

"I think He heard it, Lizzy." He sounded hopeful and happy. He was grinning.

"I know He did, Daniel." She smiled at him, noting he hadn't moved from her. "I know now is not the right time, but I think it will be soon. I am going to ask you to kiss me soon." She looked into his eyes and saw his grin get bigger.

"I am counting on it. And I will be ready."

The sound of the doorbell made them both jump. Daniel took Elizabeth's hand and shut the door behind them. He led her downstairs and let in the two paramedics. He led them to his father's room and watched as they checked him.

"I'm sorry, he's gone, sir," One of the paramedics said to him. Her voice was soft and kind.

"No, he's not." He pulled Lizzy to his side, sliding a hand around her waist. "He is visiting," he turned to Lizzy, "David and my mother, his wife. He is visiting Lizzy's mother and father and brother." He looked to the paramedic worker. She smiled at him.

"Do you believe, sir?" She sounded relieved.

He looked at Lizzy again, grinning at her again. "I am beginning to."

He knew he should be unhappy and that he should mourn, but he couldn't bring himself to—not when he knew his father was with Jesus. He gasped. "I know, Lizzy."

She felt him pull her to himself, laughing. He picked her up and held her. "What do you know, Daniel?"

He put her down and she searched his face.

"I know that my father is visiting with your parents. That he is with my mom and they are all together." He sounded sure. It was like he felt when he tried to learn some tough lines and then he just got them.

"How do you know that, Daniel?" She looked at him expectantly.

"Faith, Lizzy. Just like I have faith I can be the kind of man you need one day. That all of us here need you. Faith that with you, I can come to know the Lord better."

"I knew you could find it, Daniel." She hugged him. "I always knew you had it in you."

They let go of one another and turned to the paramedics. They had a hold of one another's hand, smiling. The paramedics looked happy. The female stepped up to Daniel and slid something off of her wrist. She handed it to him.

It was a thin leather bracelet with a small metal plaque in it. He looked to the woman as she smiled at him. "It is an ABC bracelet, sir." She moved closer to him as she saw Lizzy move from him. "See," she pointed at the plaque.

A is for admit. Admit to God that you are a sinner. Do you know what sin is, sir?" She saw him nod his head. "Good." She laughed. "Makes this a little easier. The next letter is B for Believe." She looked into his eyes. "Do you believe that Jesus is God's Son?" She squinted now, trying to gauge his answer to her.

"Yes. I have always believed that."

She smiled bigger. "Great. Now, the C is for Confess. This is the hard one." She winked at Lizzy. "This one means that you confess your faith in Jesus as your Savior and Lord. After that, you read His word and live your life for him." She shrugged her shoulders. "That's it."

"So if I admit that I sin, believe that Jesus is the Son of God, and confess my faith in Him, choosing to live for Him, what?" He looked to Lizzy and then to the woman. "What does that mean?"

"It means, sir, that today I will have gained a new brother. And that woman over there looking at you like you are everything to her, she gains a brother, too." She put her hand on his back and her eyes on the man in the bed. "And one day when you pass, sir, you will see your father. You will see all the people you have loved before."

He frowned and looked to Lizzy. "Not Gen, I won't see Gen, Lizzy."

She stepped up to him as she noticed the woman step over to the bed. Out of the corner of her eye, Lizzy saw the woman begin to help the man with Daniel's father. She turned Daniel from it.

You don't know that, Daniel. She may have accepted Him when she was a child. Look into your heart, Daniel. See if she is with John." She saw him close his eyes. "If you don't see her, Daniel, that's okay, because God knows if she is there." She laughed as he opened his eyes. "They may all be there hanging out and waiting on us." She winked. "And I for one would like to get to know the wife of the great Daniel Templeman."

"I know what the paramedic said, Lizzy, and I hear you speaking, but I am still not sure." He wanted this to be a decision he made.

"No pressure. Okay." She looked up at him as he looked into her eyes. She smiled at him and saw him smile back at her. The light was back in his eyes. She liked that light.

The sound of the paramedic clearing her throat came to their ears and they turned, holding hands.

"We are done with your father." She eyed the stretcher that held the man. "Would you like a moment before we leave?"

Daniel nodded his head and looked to his dad.

Elizabeth noted that the workers went to the door and bowed their heads, closing their eyes. She felt Daniel pulling her toward John's body.

He pulled Lizzy close to him as he let go of her hand. He could feel her body against his and it comforted him.

He found his knees failing as he laid his head on his father's chest. He cried, wrapping one arm around Lizzy's legs. After a while, his tears were spent and he pulled her to him. He buried his face in her long, blonde hair.

Elizabeth could feel the grief coming off the man holding on to her. Her heart ached for him. She moved closer to him and held him tightly. She heard him sniffle and pull back from her a little.

"I'm ready, Lizzy. They can take him now," he whispered to her, his voice raw from the crying.

Elizabeth looked to the paramedic workers and nodded her head. She pulled Daniel away from the stretcher and heard it roll out of the room.

The door closed behind them. She felt Daniel lay his forehead against hers. His eyes were closed. She waited. She saw him open them now.

"We have to tell the children, Lizzy. We have to let them know about Dad." He looked at her and didn't feel like Ironman. He felt like Superman in a cave full of kryptonite. He needed her and God to pull him through this.

"We will, Daniel, when you are ready." She kept looking into his eyes.

He took a deep breath and steadied himself. "I'm ready now." He took her hand and from a distance he heard the front door shut.

They walked down the stairs together and went to the back door. He opened it and called the children in. He saw Davey moving behind the other children and picked him up, carefully bringing the little boy close to him.

"How are you doing, Son?"

"I'm a little sore, Daniel, but God is good." Davey was holding his belly gingerly now. Daniel knew it still hurt and he was being so careful with him.

He sat him down in a chair close to him. Through it all, little Davey loved God. Maybe he could, too.

He sat next to Lizzy and took her hand under the table. He needed her strength right now.

"Everybody having fun outside?" He saw heads nod and look to one another. He knew they weren't sure what was happening. "I am glad you are all here for this." He took a deep breath and squeezed Lizzy's hand. "Your grandpa," he looked to his own children, "Reverend John," he looked to Lizzy's children, "went to be with the Lord today."

April and Lily gasped and held their mouths. Daniel knew Paul was sixteen, but guessed Lily was around thirteen and April was around eight. Ben, who he guessed at eleven, sat taller in the chair and glanced at Paul.

His son Tayler was between Lily's and Ben's ages. Olivia fell between Ben and April, and Raven between April and David. Their reaction to their grandfather's death was quiet.

Tayler's words surprised him. "You mean granddad is sleeping?"

Daniel looked to Lizzy as if to ask who had told him that. He saw her shrug her shoulders. "Where did you hear that, Son?"

Tayler looked sad but hopeful. "Grandfather, Dad. He always said in his sermons that those who have died have fallen asleep, but one day they will rise. They will have a new body and a new name but that we who believe will still know them."

"How will we know them, Son?" His children were on a completely different spiritual level than he.

"Because, Dad, those who believe, their souls will know the souls of other believers. So we will see him one day." He sounded confident. Daniel wondered if that was what he sounded like sometimes.

"Do all of you believe?" He looked around the table. Everyone nodded their head. "Then you will all see your granddad when you get to heaven."

He saw some of his children and Lizzy's children begin to cry, too. Daniel and Lizzy comforted them.

That night, most of the children weren't very hungry and the adults ate little. The kids all cleaned up and went to their rooms.

Lizzy sat on the couch, watching the black television screen. It was dark in the living room, but she was alright with that. This is where Daniel found her.

He had been looking all over for her after dinner. He sat down beside her on the couch, not touching her. “Lizzy?” He watched as she looked at the television. “Lizzy?” He reached for her hand and held it.

She turned to him, ready to help him. “What do you need, Daniel?” She felt lost, but helping him was a way to help herself.

“What are you thinking about, Lizzy?” He moved over to her and let go of her hand, laying her head on his shoulder. He heard her sigh.

“I think once everything is done with your father’s affairs, Daniel, that it will be time for me and the children to move on.”

“What?!” He was angry now, livid at the woman beside him. “I lose my father and now I have to lose you, too?!”

“Quiet down, Daniel.” Her eyes flew to the stairs, hoping he hadn’t disturbed the children.

“Don’t give me a ‘quiet down, Daniel.’ I’m not a child. Why do you want to leave?” He put his hands on his hips and glared down at her.

“I don’t want to leave you, Daniel.” She stood now. “I just think we need to move on soon.”

“Why?!” He didn’t understand her reasoning. His children liked her children and the two of them finally had something going in their lives.

She looked around the room. “Because this house, Daniel.” She looked back to him.

“Everywhere I look in this house, I see your father.”

She walked up to him. "He was so kind to us when other people just saw a widow and her five children. He took us in and loved us." A tear slipped down her cheek. "I know he is your dad, Daniel, but it feels like I have lost mine all over again."

"You're hurting, Lizzy." He stepped up to her and softened his voice. He cradled her face with his hand and she closed her eyes. "I want to comfort you, Lizzy. What can I do to comfort you?"

She shook her head. "Jesus is my Comforter, Daniel, and I lean on Him." She smiled. "But I love the feel of your hand on my face. It makes me want to...." She sniffled and felt a rolling tear down her face. She sobbed out loud.

Daniel brought her to himself. "Oh, Lizzy. My Lizzy." He laid his hand on her head and stroked her back. He whispered soothing words to her. When she had quieted, he said, "Let's tuck the children in and go to bed." He took her hand and led her to each of the children's rooms.

It had gotten late. As he watched Lizzy with all the children, he knew that he loved her. There was no doubt about it now.

The pain she had shown him earlier was replaced with joy as she tucked each of the children in bed. Together they prayed with all of them and kissed them good night.

They had tucked Davey in last and checked to make sure he had everything he needed. It was only when Elizabeth was sure David was alright that she told him good night.

Chapter Twenty-Five

Daniel led Lizzy to his room and shut the door. Walking over to his dresser, he pulled out his pajama bottoms and a T-shirt.

"Would you like to use the bath first?" He had turned to her and watched her.

Turning away from him, Elizabeth said, "I can't be in here with you, Daniel." She heard a soft sound on the bed and felt him behind her.

"Where would you go, Lizzy?" His voice was low and deep.

"To the couch, Daniel. I will sleep on the couch." She shivered at the sound of his voice.

He wasn't touching her, but it didn't matter. His voice was holding her captive.

"I mean when you leave me, my children. Where would you go?"

She shivered again. She honestly had no idea, only that she couldn't stay here. "I don't know. Probably do what we did before and have Davey pick. See where God wants us to go."

"Do you not like me, my children, and this house?"

"I see your dad everywhere in this house." She sighed. "When David and I picked out our house, he loved it. We spent months looking for a place. He said the one he picked out was home. I didn't care; my home was him. But when he died, my home died with him. I couldn't be in the house that he picked out. I could see him everywhere. So I became a wanderer."

"So you can't stay here because my dad is still here to you and it hurts."

"Yes, Daniel."

He turned her to face him. "You're going to sleep in the bed tonight, Lizzy, and I am going to sleep on the floor. We will leave the door open to listen for the children if they need us in the middle of the night." He turned from her, looking around. "Where is your bag?"

"In the laundry room. All of my things were dirty so I threw them in the washer when I got here." She shrugged. "They will probably need to be run again."

"Does that mean all of your gowns are…?" He looked off to the side. He saw her nod her head out of the corner of his eye. "I will go down and restart the washer. We will dry them in the morning."

He went over to another dresser and pulled out a long white gown with a matching robe.

"This was Gen's. You are about her size. This should do for the night."

"Daniel, I can't." She shook her head.

"Oh, pish-posh, I'll fetch your toothbrush and hairbrush while I am restarting your things. It will give you a chance to wash up and change." He laid the nightclothes in her hand and shut the door behind himself.

Lizzy looked at the items in her hand. She went into the bath and changed. As she finished, she heard a knocking on the door.

Daniel's voice came softly through the door. "Lizzy? I have your brushes."

She opened the door. "Thank you, Daniel."

She left the door open as she brushed her hair and then her teeth. Turning, she saw Daniel looking at her.

Daniel watched as Lizzy moved in the bath. She brushed her long, golden hair and then her teeth. The gown she was in was Gen's, but she was definitely Lizzy Seraphim. She truly did look like an angel as she moved through his bath. He couldn't take his eyes off of her.

Elizabeth looked at the gown and then to Daniel. She reached for the robe and slipped it on, tying it at the waist.

"Sorry." She felt her cheeks redden. "I guess I am getting too comfortable around you."

He smiled at her, looking into her eyes. "People go to museums every day, Lizzy. They go to appreciate the artwork. The lines, the color, the texture. You are living art. I could look at you all day."

Elizabeth blushed redder now. "Thank you, Daniel."

She turned sideways to move past him and stopped to look in his eyes. He was standing right next to her.

Daniel could feel the heat coming off of her body and smell her scent. There was a mix of Gen's and hers, but it was Lizzy's scent that he looked for and found. He inhaled it slowly, drawing it into him. He watched her, unmoving, beside him. He smirked.

"If you stand in the doorway of the bath, I shall have to go to the walk-in to change." He saw her look at the floor and bring her lower lip under her top teeth. "It would be a challenge to brush my teeth in there," he teased.

Elizabeth moved from him and to the bed. She gave him a shy smile.

"You look beautiful, Lizzy." He turned and shut the door to his bath.

She put a hand to her heart and felt it pounding in her chest. What was wrong with her?

She picked up the phone Daniel gave her, found the application for the Bible, and opened it. She knew where her reading was tonight. It was First Corinthians, chapter seven. She read the whole chapter, but it was verses eight and nine that grabbed her attention.

Elizabeth considered the words. She thought, when it came to Daniel, he was exercising a great amount of self-control. She didn't consider herself "burning with passion." So they must be fine.

She closed the application and bowed her head. She prayed tonight for Daniel, so many things for him. Next she prayed for his family and then hers. More prayers fell from her lips and she finished with an "Amen."

When she looked up, she realized she had been praying out loud and that, at some point,

Daniel had sat down beside her and prayed with her.

"Hello, Daniel." She smiled at him. "I didn't hear you come to bed." She stopped and closed her eyes. "The bed. I didn't hear you sit," she stopped, knowing she was foundering, "I didn't hear you sit down on the bed."

She stood up and picked up the phone.

"I was reading the Bible application on my phone, being as I am without mine tonight."

She knew she was rambling. "And I was praying so I didn't hear you."

Swiping the phone out of her hand, he heard her say, "Hey!"

He opened the application. "My, my, Lizzy."

She closed her robe more tightly around herself like a shield. He wasn't about to tell her that it only accentuated her curves when she did that. Nope, those words would never be uttered from his lips.

He looked down at the screen and then back to Lizzy. "Good reading tonight, then, Mrs. Seraphim." He read some more. "Oh, I love these verses:

Now to the unmarried and the widows I say: It is good for them to stay unmarried, as I do. But if they cannot control themselves, they should marry, for it is better to marry than to burn with passion."

"Sometimes I think the Bible is not for young eyes, Lizzy. Any thoughts on tonight's verses?"

He closed the application and handed her the phone, making sure his hand brushed hers. "N-n-no." She cleared her throat. "Um, not really, Daniel." Her hand where he had brushed her felt sensitive as she brought her hands around her chest and crossed her arms.

He made his pallet on the floor and sat down. The door was still shut and he was glad for that. He noticed that she had crossed her arms on her chest. He tried not noting how that made her look and instead looked at the door.

"None at all, huh?" She looked heavenly. "The door needs to be open, Lizzy."

She uncrossed her arms and her robe loosened a little on her body, giving it less of a shape. He thought both were bittersweet things to have happened to her.

She opened the door and turned off the light. A dim light from the street filtered through the window. She turned her eyes to Daniel as she lay down on the bed.

"Are you tired, Daniel?"

"Yes." He was tired of fighting how he felt for her. Tired of losing everyone he loved. He knew if she offered that, he would forget it all for her, but he knew she wouldn't offer.

He saw her reach out her hand and take his. He had purposefully lain close to the bed tonight. He wanted to see her fall asleep.

"Davey looks good, Lizzy. I wish I could have been there to take you both home. If I had known...."

"Don't think about it, Daniel. You had things to do. I handled Davey and the rest of the children."

She was sleepy, but she wanted to comfort Daniel with her words.

"You mean your children," he stopped, "not our children."

What she had said sounded like she could handle all the children, as in hers and his.

"No." She took off the robe and laid it on the end of the bed. She laid her head down and brought her body under the blankets. "I mean, when Deacon Wayne brought me back here and Paul told me about your father, I made sure they didn't know about him until you were ready to tell him. I made sure the hospital was called." She looked at him. "I handled the children." She paused. "David didn't make good money, Daniel. He didn't do mobile commercials or make movies, but he loved us and we made do with what we had. I learned to handle a lot, Daniel."

"I bet you are more fragile than you let on, Lizzy. You have learned to keep it all inside." He knew he had her because she was quiet. "How did you handle things at the hospital today?"

"I would hope graciously. I was representing you and I knew that if I did something wrong it would reflect badly on you. So I tried to do all the right things."

She saw him smile at her, the light back in his eyes. "Just like God. People who know me know I believe, see Him in me, and when they don't, I reflect a bad image of Him, which makes me sad." She shook her head. "So when people kept calling me the 'Future Mrs. Tensely,' I smiled and pretended like I was the happiest woman in the world. I took names and addresses and am going to mail out thank-you cards to all of them," she winked at him, "with a short scripture verse on them."

"You were perfect today, Lizzy. I think you have some acting abilities in you. When I kissed you and Davey on the cheek and said that I love you, you glowed under my words. It takes a true actress to play the part of a devoted and loving fiancé when you aren't." He smiled. "Yet."

Lizzy looked at Daniel. "Reflecting you, Daniel. I had to make them believe I loved you and that you were everything to me."

"Do you think you might love me one day, Lizzy? That I would be everything to you?"

He knew he sounded hopeful. He heard her sigh.

"I don't know, Daniel. Are you doing okay?"

"Yes, Lizzy," he squeezed her hand. "I am doing more than okay." Because you are here, he wanted to add but didn't. The light coming through the window made her hair glow and the white straps of her gown highlighted her face.

"Good night, Lizzy."

"Good night, Daniel." Elizabeth felt herself relax and fall asleep.

Chapter Twenty-Six

The next sound she heard was a whimper. She rolled over and saw little David sitting on the bed. He was looking at her sadly. Daniel was sitting behind Davey, his arms around him.

"Hey, Baby." She sat up and pulled him carefully into her arms. She leaned against the tall headboard and pulled up the cover. "What's wrong, Sweetie?"

She laid her head on his and looked to Daniel. He was watching the two of them.

"My belly hurts. Daniel gave me some medicine and he says it will help me feel better."

"I heard him whimpering so I went to take a look," he said quietly. "You looked so peaceful resting, I couldn't bring myself to wake you. When he said his belly hurt, I took him downstairs and read the discharge instructions lying on the kitchen counter. I found his medicine, measured it, and gave it to him." He looked to the little boy. "You'll feel better soon, Davey." He touched the little boy's face and saw him draw his little arm out to him.

Daniel looked at Lizzy. David was lying on her chest and to hug him meant laying himself close to her. She nodded her head and he felt the little boy pull him to them.

He laid his hand across Davey's waist and part of it fell on Lizzy's waist. The feel of the child in his arm, the scent of his mother, and the feeling of family washed over him and he had to blink back the tears in his eyes.

He tried to move and felt Davey's arm tighten on his neck. Daniel had tried to keep from touching

Lizzy, but Davey was forcing Daniel closer to him and her. Daniel gave up and laid his head on Davey's neck, moving next to Lizzy.

He heard Davey sigh and it was all over for Daniel. He felt sleep pull him under as he held mother and child closer to him.

"Daniel." He heard his name whispered. "Daniel." Lizzy was whispering his name. "Daniel, you need to move."

His head felt warm and was lying on something soft. He opened his eyes and realized where he was at. Davey had moved over in his sleep onto the bed and Daniel's head now rested on Lizzy's chest, her heartbeat thrumming in his ears.

He sat and moved away from her, reluctantly, if he was honest. He was getting the best sleep he had since Gen's death. He thought to apologize but thought it would be a lie, so he didn't.

"What time is it?" He moved over to the other side of the bed and lay down, pulling the covers to his chest.

"It's two-thirty a.m., Daniel." She watched him and saw his breathing even. "Daniel?" She whispered but saw Davey stir anyway. She carefully pulled her son to her and lay on her side, her back to Daniel.

She would pretend he was not there. She had slept in a bed alone or with one of her children for a couple of years now. She closed her eyes and went back to sleep.

Now she heard giggling. She opened her eyes and looked at the clock. It was 4:00 a.m. Rolling over, she saw Daniel and Davey sitting up on the bed, playing. They were talking quietly and laughing.

"Daniel?" The two of them looked at her and laughed together.

Daniel looked down at Lizzy. She looked sleepy and he knew she wasn't awake. "It's alright, Lizzy. Bit of a night owl myself."

He looked at Davey as Lizzy began to sit up. He pushed her shoulder back down carefully. "Side effect of the medication: may cause excitement in young children. Seems Davey shoots and scores on that one, don't you, Son?"

David looked to Daniel. "Daniel and I are playing, Mommy. You just go back to sleep."

Lizzy saw her son smile at her and she looked to Daniel. "You wear glasses?"

"Yes. Contacts during the day." He turned to Davey. "You mean to tell me your mum didn't know that about me?"

David nodded his head. "Oh, yeah, we have seen plenty of things with you in it that has you wearing glasses, Daniel. You were reading papers. Mommy said you were memorizing lines."

Lizzy blushed. She did know that. She liked him better with glasses than contacts, but she would never tell him that.

"Did she, now? I bet your mum knows a lot more about me than she is letting on." He winked at her and saw Davey nod. He looked back to Elizabeth. "Go ahead and go back to sleep, Lizzy. David and I are just dandy, aren't we, Son?" He saw Davey nod. "See?"

Daniel saw her try to stand. "What are you doing?"

"Fixing poor judgment, Daniel."

She felt him push her back down on the bed. "What do you mean?"

"We shouldn't be on the bed together, Daniel, especially in front of my youngest son."

Did he really not get that?

"So you are going to move to a cold floor off of a warm, soft bed?" He looked at Davey, shaking his head no. "Mommy can't do that, can she, Davey?"

"No, Daniel. You just lie down, Mommy, and go back to sleep. Daniel and I are having fun."

She saw Davey pout. "Alright, David, just this once."

She lay back down and felt Daniel pull the cover up over her. She hadn't realized it wasn't covering her. She must have been tired. "Thank you, Daniel."

"You're welcome." He smiled at her goofily but he knew she missed it. She was already asleep. He looked to Davey. "What else does Mommy know about me that I don't know she knows?"

"Oh, lots, Daniel." Davey laughed at Daniel. He proceeded to fill Daniel in on the things Lizzy knew about him.

Chapter Twenty-Seven

"Lizzy?" Daniel leaned over her on the bed. "Lizzy?"

Elizabeth heard Daniel calling her name. The body behind hers was warm so she moved back against it, thinking it was Davey. She heard a gasp and opened her eyes.

"Elizabeth Seraphim."

She moved off the bed now, noting Davey was on the other side of Daniel, asleep. She had moved next to Daniel's body. She blushed.

"You know when you do that, wearing that gown, it makes me think of the Garden of Eden." He reached above him and found the robe to the gown she had on. "I see now why Adam ate of the fruit Eve offered him."

He handed her the robe and saw her turn. When she turned around again, she had pulled the robe tight and cinched the belt. He looked into her eyes, but he could see more than that. "I bet it was very sweet."

Elizabeth blushed brighter. "I am sure you didn't wake me up to tell me a Bible story, Daniel. Your version of a Bible story."

"If you think that one was good, I have another." He moved away from Davey a little and sat up in the bed, looking at her.

Elizabeth shook her head. "I bet you do, Daniel."

He opened his eyes and looked to her, eager. "Do you wanna hear it?"

"No!" She saw Davey stir. "No, Daniel, I don't." Yes, you do, the voice in her head taunted her. Shut up! "When did Davey fall asleep?"

She moved over to his side of the bed and sat down on the floor. She brushed a piece of hair out of Davey's face.

"A few minutes before I woke you up. I know you like to read with the children early in the morning and today being Friday, my children have school."

"Do you think he will be okay here?" She looked to Daniel.

"I tell you what, let's do the Bible reading in here." He stood and began to make his way out the door.

"Where are you going?" She went to stand and saw him shake his head.

"I doubt he will wake soon, but if he does, he needs his mother beside him. Crawl back in bed and I will wake the children and have them meet in here."

"I can't do that, Daniel." She did stand now and begin to make her way over to him.

"Davey needs his mother, Lizzy. If a child doesn't have that…" He sighed. "I have seen my children go two years without a mother and I will not have Davey know what that is like. Not while you are here." He looked down at her. "Now go lie down by your son and I will bring the children in here." He turned and walked out of the room.

As Elizabeth lay back down, she thought about what Daniel said about children needing a mother and knew he was right. She had seen his children blossom in the short time she was in the house. She wished they never knew what that was like.

She pulled David next to her as her children began to trickle in with their Bibles. They saw the pallet on the floor and sat down around the room. Next, Daniel brought in his children and gave Elizabeth her Bible. She sat up and thanked him.

"Good morning, children. I thought we would do something different today. Today we are going to do favorite scriptures. If you don't know book, chapter, and number, we will all look them up together. Does anyone want to start?" She saw Daniel raise his hand. "Yes?"

"Ephesians five, verse thirty-one."

He snickered and saw all the children and her look it up. This was part of what he was reading yesterday in the car. He saw her look up to him and narrow her eyes. He knew he had her.

"I got it," Ben said, holding up his Bible. "*For this reason a man will leave his father and mother and be united to his wife, and the two will become one flesh.*" He looked proud as he finished reading and looked to his mother.

"Yes, thank you, Ben." She looked to Daniel and saw him draw his knees to his chest. He looked like one of her kids. "Can anyone tell me what this passage is about?" She saw Daniel raise his hand. "Yes, Daniel?"

"The writer talking about Christ and the church."

"Yes, Daniel. Thank you." She looked around. "I think Mr. Templeman knows more about the Bible than he lets on." She glared at him but couldn't help the smile on her face. She saw him raise his hand. "Yes, Daniel?" She almost cringed, wondering what verse he was thinking about now.

"I am not the only one in the room that knows more about something than they let on."

He looked at her pointedly. "Just this morning Davey filled me on my life history." He laughed. "I think Davey's mommy teaches more than just Bible to her children, eh, Lizzy?"

Elizabeth blushed and looked to her Bible. "Anyone else?" She could guess what Davey had told him. She saw him smile at her as he sat in the middle of the children. She would have to talk to her children about not giving away all her secrets.

The favorite scriptures part of their morning was fun end everyone laughed, having a good time. All too soon it was time for it to end.

"This is the best part of my day," she announced to everyone around her. "Let's pray," she said, bowing her head.

Daniel hadn't sat in on something like this in a long time. He liked the feel of unity and family.

"Lizzy, can I lead the prayer this morning?"

"Of course you can, Daniel." Elizabeth opened her eyes and looked at him.

Daniel got off of the floor and sat on the bed beside her. He bowed his head. He really didn't know what to say, so he said the first thing that came to his mind.

"Dear Heavenly Father, I know that my dad is with you this morning. I thank You for carrying him in Your arms to see his wife and our family members who are there with You. Please be with him. I pray today for my family," he squeezed Lizzy's hand, realizing he already thought of her as his family. "Be with them as we go through our day. We love you. Amen."

He picked up his head and looked to everyone around him, smiling. His children's mouths were hanging open. He saw Lizzy's children looking at him, too.

"That was amazing, Daniel. Thank you for leading us." She couldn't keep the awe out of her voice. Daniel's prayer had been sweet.

"You're very welcome, Lizzy." He turned to his children. "I know today will be a little different and in light of what happened yesterday, is everyone alright to go to school?"

They all nodded their heads 'yes.' He was amazed. His children looked sad, but they were willing to move through their day. Lizzy's were sad, too, but she didn't look as unhappy as his children.

As he watched, Lizzy's children began talking with his and leading them out of his room. They each had begun a conversation with them about his children's favorite things. He was amazed that her children would help his.

Elizabeth watched as Daniel turned to her, his brown hair messy, his glasses on his nose, and Bible beside him. His face was soft and he smiled as he looked at her.

"I have to take care of my father's arrangements today, Lizzy." He swallowed. "I know what he wanted, we had discussed it. But," he felt his heart twist, "I don't know…" He felt the tears run down his face and looked to the bed.

Elizabeth moved over and put her arms around him. She felt arms move around her. She touched his hair and leaned her face into his neck. She felt him pull her into his lap and begin to rock her. He was crying so softly that it made her heart hurt.

"I know, Daniel. I know." She held him for a few more minutes and he pulled back from her. He looked into her eyes.

"I can be the man you need, Lizzy. It's going to take time. Will you wait for me?" He looked at the bed. "I don't know if I will accept Him, though. I want to be honest with you." He saw her nod her head. "But I know scripture, so if the children ask I will probably know where what they are talking about is. But I still don't know what to do with God."

Elizabeth nodded her head. "I know, Daniel." She laid her hand on the side of his head. "Yes, I will wait for you to make a decision about God." She dropped her hand and saw him look at it. He had frowned.

"I don't know if I love you," she said. She saw him look up. "I want to be honest with you about that. You need me to be honest with you." She smiled at him as her top teeth covered her lower lip. "I like that you led the prayer this morning. It reminded me of what my husband and I used to do in the mornings with the children. He was always so much better with scripture than I was."

"I wish I could have known him, Lizzy. Doctor Reynolds said he was a great man. I am beginning to know that is true." He swallowed as he looked at his Lizzy.

"I love him, Daniel." She smiled and looked down. For the first time she realized where she was. She tried moving from him.

He tightened his hold on Lizzy as she started to move. "I like the feel of you in my arms, Lizzy. I like the smell of my bed when you are in it." He saw her blush. "I know I probably shouldn't tell you that, but it's true. If I had my way, you would always be where you are right now."

Elizabeth nodded her head. She couldn't move her eyes from him. Her body wasn't responding to her unspoken request to move, either.

"Pray for me, Lizzy. I prayed for the children and you, but I need you to pray for me, Love. Pray that I have the strength to get through this and be brought closer to God and not pushed from Him because of this." He pulled her to him and felt her arms come around him. "I need this, Lizzy."

He closed his eyes, holding his breath, waiting for her prayer to bring him the comfort he could always find from her talking to God for him.

Elizabeth closed her eyes and turned her face toward Daniel's neck. She breathed in the scent of Daniel Templeman. Her heart ached for his loss.

"Dear God, we love you. We thank You for everything that You have given us and everything You have taken from us. It is in times like these that we draw comfort from You. Please lift Daniel in Your arms. Please draw him so close to You that he has no doubt You are there. Help him to live according to Your will. Give him the words to speak. Thank You, Lord, for everything. Amen."

She knew she should lift her face from him but didn't want to. He was holding on to her tightly as if he never wanted to let her go. She could feel his breath on her neck, warm and comforting. She knew the measure of his breathing, she realized, and it was hypnotic. She felt herself relax a little.

Daniel didn't want to let the woman in his arms go. She brought comfort and hope to his life. How was he supposed to let go of someone so special? Elizabeth Seraphim encouraged him spiritually and helped him to find peace in all that was happening in his life.

"Daniel?" She felt his hold on her tighten. "Daniel, I have to make the children breakfast before they leave for school." He pulled back from her and smiled a crooked smile at her. She asked, "Do you feel better?" She laid her hand on the side of his face again.

"Yes, Love, thank you." He wanted to kiss her again. Instead he put her on the bed and stood. He went to the door as she rose.

"Why don't you stay here with Davey, just in case he wakes up? I'm sure I can manage some toast and juice with the children this morning."

He smiled at her as she sat on his bed with little Davey lying beside her. He wouldn't tell her that her hair was tangled and that the gown she had on hugged her curves like a second skin.

He wouldn't tell her that her outward beauty was nothing compared to what was in her heart.

"You are a beautiful woman, Lizzy. I'm not talking about how you look right now, but how you love others unconditionally. You have a faith I am beginning to understand and I thank God He has put you in my life."

He smirked, looking at her. One day she would be his. He turned on his heel and descended the stairs.

Chapter Twenty-Eight

Elizabeth lay down and pulled her son to her. Davey was soft and warm. It was so thoughtful of Daniel to stay awake with her son this morning.

She knew that Daniel was doing well with everything that was happening around him. Thanking God, she smoothed back her son's hair and kissed him.

She closed her eyes as she thought of all that had happened to her. Six days ago she had been walking in the rain with no idea where she was going. Now she was lying in Daniel Templeman's bed curled up next to her son, waiting on the man to make a decision about whether or not he could make God the Lord of his life. In such a short time, so much had happened.

With the level of emotional intimacy that she and Daniel had developed, she began to ask herself questions. Because of the intensity of her feelings, could she only be friends with Daniel if he decided not to love God and live for him? She didn't know the answer to that. She knew that time and separation would ease the transition from the closeness they now shared to a good friendship. But her heart rebelled at the thought of leaving Daniel Templeman. Never seeing him again, she knew would devastate her.

She had tried so hard yesterday to represent him when she lied, please forgive me Lord, I know it was wrong, to so many people, but to deny that she was engaged to Danny Tensley would have made him look like a liar and she wouldn't hurt him like that. Nope, better to ask forgiveness than to make Daniel look bad.

She didn't really like all of the attention she got. People liked her not for who she was but for whom she knew. And they didn't even know the real Daniel Templeman. They only knew Danny Tensley, the actor.

She had only seen that side of him once, yesterday at the nurses' station when he had used his clout to remove the male nurse who had grabbed her. She didn't know if she could like that guy. He seemed to dazzle and charm his way into getting what he wanted.

Of course, Director Reynolds had given Danny everything he wanted. Bow to the celebrity and give him anything. She found herself nodding her head. No, Danny Tensley was not the man for her.

But Daniel Templeman. She sighed. He was a good man who was devoted to his family. He loved them. That guy she could learn to love under the right circumstances.

It seemed her heart was holding itself back from loving him, though. She knew why and so did he. She felt the emotion in her heart and knew if he ever did make God the ruler of his life, that dam would break and the love for him that was being held back would come pouring out.

She blushed and brought her lower lip under her top teeth. She knew she could love him but wouldn't allow it to happen right now.

But she could. Oh, yes, she could. She sighed again.

David moved on the bed and Elizabeth saw him looking at her. “Hey, buddy. How are you feeling?”

“I’m hungry, Mommy.” His little voice was small and he sounded tired.

“Do you want to sleep a little more or eat some breakfast?” She looked into his blue eyes. God had given him her eye color.

“Breakfast, Mommy,” he said, smiling back at her.

She stood and pulled on her robe again, tying it loosely. She picked him up and took him downstairs. “Then let’s find something to eat.”

As she moved around the corner to the kitchen, she saw the children and Daniel laughing as they ate breakfast. She heard Daniel asking the children about their plans for the day. She wondered what her own children thought now as they sat at the table with Daniel. They knew him as Danny for so long from television and movies, but she wondered how they saw him.

Making her way into the kitchen, she caught Daniel’s eye and he smiled. He looked to David then and smiled at the little boy.

“Good morning, Davey.” He stood and made his way over to the tyke. He held out his hands and Davey moved into his arms. Taking him to the table, Daniel put Davey in his lap when he sat down. “How are you this morning?” He looked to the little boy. He made sure David sat at his eye level so they could see one another better.

“Hungry, Daniel.” He peered at the table and winced a little as he moved.

Daniel removed a piece of toast on his plate and handed it to Davey. "Your belly still hurting, Son?"

David nodded his head. "Yes. But only if I try to move a lot." He bent his little head and closed his eyes. Everyone at the table stopped and looked at the little boy as he prayed. Opening his eyes, he took a bite of his toast.

Daniel looked to Elizabeth. "I gave Davey the medicine around one this morning. The bottle says he can have another dose in six hours." He looked at the clock, noting it was about 7:00 a.m. "He could have another dose anytime." He looked to Davey. "Does your belly hurt very badly, Davey?" The little boy nodded his head.

Elizabeth measured the medicine and moved over to them. "Here, you go, Sweetie." She saw him close his little mouth and turn his head to Daniel.

"Can Daniel give it to me, Mommy?"

Elizabeth looked to Daniel and saw him nod his head. She handed Daniel the spoon of medicine. "I suppose so."

She witnessed Daniel become Detective Russell Baker.

"Alright, this little boy has a belly ache. I say we can clear this up snippety-snap." Everyone at the table laughed except Lizzy. "How about we take this elixir, my boy, and it will clear up the pain right as rain." He tipped the spoon into Davey's mouth and saw him swallow all of it. "Case solved."

Daniel glanced at Lizzy. "Thank you, my good man," he looked her over and saw her blush. "Ooh, may have to change that line." He looked her in the eyes. "You are definitely not a man, Lizzy." His voice dropped as she blushed redder. He looked to the children. "Do you all know the story of Adam and Eve?" He heard Lizzy gasp.

"Daniel!" She looked to the floor. He had to bring that up now?

"What, Lizzy?" He knew he sounded innocent like his father did when he was up to no good. He felt a stab of pain, but looking to Lizzy helped his heart to feel a little better. "It's a good story." He looked to the children again. "Eve had a very tempting fruit and Adam ate of it."

He smiled at Lizzy. "Well, that's the short of it."

Elizabeth turned to the sink. She had to get herself under control!

"But that was wrong of Adam to do, Daniel," Paul piped up. Paul had seen what happened between his mom and Daniel. Despite what the rest of them were hearing, he knew Daniel wasn't talking about the Bible story.

Daniel looked at Paul. He was surprised Lizzy's son had picked up on that. "You're right, Paul. It was wrong of Adam to eat of the forbidden fruit. He shouldn't have done it." He had been looking around as he spoke. Now he only looked at Paul. "Not all men are like Adam, Paul. The good ones don't eat of the fruit just because it is offered to them." He looked at the boy pointedly.

Lizzy's son had a good head on his shoulders. But even the best of teenagers went wrong.

He wanted Paul to go in the right direction, and to know that Daniel wasn't going to take advantage of Lizzy.

Paul nodded his head. He knew what Daniel was saying to him. He looked to his mom and saw her turn back around, eyes on Daniel. He would bet his mom liked Daniel. A lot.

He looked to his siblings now. He stood, as did his brother and sisters. "We probably should get things cleaned up, guys."

"And you should head to the stairs and get ready for school." Daniel had looked at his own children and saw them leave the table.

"I would like to take Davey, Daniel." He saw Paul reach out his hands for his brother.

"May I get him ready for the day, Mom?"

"That's fine, Son." She saw Paul pick up David carefully and bring him to his chest. She asked, "Do you want to lie down, Baby, or try to do some work with the kids?"

David smiled brightly. "I want to work with the kids, Mommy."

"Alright," she turned to Paul. "I have the outfit for him in the washer…"

Daniel cleared his throat and looked at Paul. He stood from the table. "I put the things in the dryer when I came down. They should be dry by now. I'll get them for him and today we'll stop by the B&B and pick up a few things for all of you." Daniel went to get the things from the dryer and came back with them. He handed Davey his outfit, smiling at the little boy. "There you go, Davey, clean as a whistle. Your belly feeling a little better?"

David nodded his head at the man. "Yes, Daniel. Thank you." With that, Paul turned and carried his little brother up the stairs.

Except for Elizabeth and Daniel, the kitchen was empty now. She turned and made a cup of tea. Turning back around, she saw he had moved closer to her and leaned back against the counter.

"How does your day look, Daniel? Do you need me to do anything for you?"

He shook his head. "I have an appearance today for the mobile company I am hired for. I worked the few commercials and they have a luncheon this afternoon I have to attend for them.

Danny Tensley is the star guest in attendance. The car should be here around ten."

"Ooh, a car," she took a sip of her tea and sat it on the counter. "Danny Tensley has a car?"

He moved closer to her, almost an unconscious effort. "Yes, my agent insists I have one everywhere I go. They have several in their fleet, so it's not always the same one. Shows Danny Tensley is important but reachable to his fans."

"Important and reachable." She winked at him. "I bet his fans love him being reachable."

He drew his arms around her waist. "I have always wanted to be an actor. My whole life, this is what I wanted. When I met Genessa, she became what I wanted, too."

"And what Danny Tensley wants, Danny Tensley gets." She knew the routine, she had seen it at the hospital.

He laughed. "Not always. Trust me," he said cryptically.

"Well, Danny Tensely seems to be the charmer and pretty sure he will get what he wants when he wants it. I don't know if I could like him. But Daniel Templeman, that guy is pretty special. I like him."

"You could love him, Lizzy." He spoke honestly as he looked into her eyes.

"Maybe. One day." She looked down at her hands. "So, luncheon for the famous Danny Tensley." She looked back to him, softening her voice. "When would you like to take care of your father's arrangements, Daniel?"

"I know Davey just got out of the hospital, Lizzy, but I was wondering if you would go to the funeral home with me after the luncheon. The children can look after themselves for a few hours while we talk with them." He sounded hopeful that she would go with him. He found he needed her there with him.

"Yes, Daniel." She laid her head on his chest and felt the tears well in her eyes. "I would be honored to help you with your father's arrangements." She sniffed back her tears and looked to him. "I loved him, too, and if there is anything I can do to help you with your father, I will."

She smiled at him, feeling the tears well in her eyes again. She had hoped it wouldn't happen, but it did. Daniel moved his hands to her face and smiled at her. He could feel the love she had for his father. She respected John very much.

"I would have you beside me all the rest of my life, Lizzy. Until then, to have you offer to help me with my dad makes me happier than you will ever know."

Paul and the rest of the children moved into the kitchen now. A small area had been set up for their school supplies.

Elizabeth moved out of Daniel's arms and over to her children. "How is the school work going?"

She looked her kids over, waiting to see if there were any questions.

"Good, Mom. I am checking Lily's work, Lily is checking Ben's, and Ben is checking April's work. We are going to have Davey," he looked to his younger brother, "color and listen to us read while we do our work." He tickled his younger brother's ear and heard him laugh.

"What are you doing today, Mom?"

Elizabeth looked around. The house wasn't really hers and she didn't know anything about it. She looked to Daniel.

Daniel saw Lizzy's eyes as she looked to him. She looked out of place and unsure. "You can do anything you want here, Lizzy. Or nothing at all. It's up to you. Dad," he caught his breath and then continued, "kept the house straightened. I had someone come in once a week on Saturday to do the major stuff, though. He or I would take the children out for the day."

Elizabeth smiled. "Probably see what you have been doing the last few days, Paul. See if there is anything you need help with. Help the children with their work, too, play with David."

Daniel took her hand. "But first we need to dress for the day."

He led her up the stairs and to his room, shutting the door behind them. He went over to his dresser and began to pick out his things.

"Daniel?" She saw him look to her. "If I am going to be staying here with my children for a bit, I'm going to need a room of my own."

She looked around. She knew all six bedrooms in the house were full. Paul and Ben had a guest room, Lily and April shared the other guest room, Tayler had his own room, Olivia and Raven shared a room, Daniel had his own room, and so had John.

"Or I could just sleep on the couch." She shrugged. "I could take the kids and myself back to the B&B."

Daniel knew his face turned red from the anger he didn't let out when she mentioned leaving his house. He counted to ten and then spoke quietly.

"I know we can't sleep in my room, Lizzy. That it paints a picture for the children that you don't want." He saw her nod her head. "But I can take the couch or," he took a deep breath and continued, "keep sleeping on the floor with the door open."

"This isn't my home, Daniel, this is yours. Yours and your children's. As sweet as it was for you to invite David here for a visit, we can't stay." She saw him draw himself up. "No. I can take the couch tonight and then tomorrow we will go back to the B&B." She turned now and started to make her way over to her bag.

"Lizzy?" He moved up to her but didn't touch her. "Lizzy?" He saw her turn. "What if I made a space for you in this house? Would you stay then?"

She shook her head, moving up to him. “No, Daniel. Somehow, someway, it would get out that we were sharing a space and that would start a whole lot of gossip for you. I don’t want to do anything to hurt your name.”

“It’s my name. I should be the one to worry about it.” He looked down to her. She was talking about leaving him and he didn’t want that to happen.

He was right, of course, but she just couldn’t do it. “The B&B is close, Daniel. I can still help you with your father’s arrangements.” She saw him shake his head. For her to leave him now felt wrong. “What?”

“What if I don’t want you to go?” He moved up to her, his hands on her shoulders. “What if I want you to stay? We can redo my father’s,” he stopped and he felt her bring her arms around him. He held her, too. “We can move the rooms anyway you want them, Lizzy. Just stay.”

Elizabeth shook her head. “I can’t stay here, Daniel. Tonight will be our last night and then we will go back to the B&B.” She moved out of his arms.

“Is that your final decision?” He knew his voice sounded distant.

Elizabeth closed her eyes. “Yes.” *No, no, no*, her mind railed at her.

“Alright.” He turned back to his dresser. He heard her make her way to the bath and shut the door. He slammed his dresser and sat down on his bed. The covers still held the shape of Lizzy and her son from where they had rested in his bed.

He brought the pillow to his nose and could smell her hair, her scent. Why of all things did she have to smell like fresh berries?

He still remembered the feel of his mum in his arms. She was warm and soft. He felt protected and loved. It was the same feeling that he had with Lizzy. No, she wasn't his mum but he knew that in his heart he loved her. Lizzy taking her family and leaving him would break his heart.

The sound of the bath door opening startled him and he turned to see Lizzy dressed in a purple top with matching capris. Her feet were bare and he saw the shape of her toes. He looked to her face.

Her hair was still damp and he could feel the air as she moved through the room.

Blackberries? Blueberries? What was that?!

Elizabeth moved to the doorway now and she saw him turn. "If it's alright, I would like to walk the kids to school for you."

He reached over onto his dresser drawer and pulled out a set of keys. "This was my spare to dad's car and to mine. Keep them in case you need them to go somewhere while I'm gone." He looked at the clock. It was 8:00 A.M. "If you would like to accompany me, we can take my children together."

"Yes, Daniel, I would love to." She nodded her head. Smiling at him, she shut the door behind her as she left the room.

Elizabeth wanted to stay with Daniel. If he asked her again, she would stay. But she knew she couldn't. She knew when all was said and done with John Templeman's funeral and Daniel looked okay, she would take her children and leave.

She made her way to the kitchen and stood in the doorway. Her children already had their books open and were studying. Daniel's children were sitting by them. They were asking questions and her children were having fun answering them.

"They look like a brothers and sisters, don't they, Lizzy?"

The sound of Daniel's voice behind her made her jump. Not like when Ronald grabbed her, though. Goosebumps popped up on her skin and she stifled a shiver. She chose not to answer him. She knew he was right.

"Alright, Tayler, Olivia, and Raven, to the car." He looked to Elizabeth and then to Paul. "Your mother said she would ride with me to the school to drop off my children." He saw Paul nod his head. "We will be stopping by the B&B for some things. If any of you children need anything, let your mother know." He smiled at her and turned to head out to the car.

"We're staying another night, Mom?" Ben was in awe. "At Danny Tensley's house." He looked around himself.

Elizabeth furrowed her brows at him. "No, Benjamin, we are staying this last night at Daniel Templeman's house and going home tomorrow morning. He says a cleaning crew comes in the morning, so that will be the perfect time for us to head back to the B&B."

She saw three of the five faces drop. Paul and Lily were ready to leave at any time, she knew. It was Ben, April, and David who didn't want to leave.

"Anyone have anything they want me to get while I am there?"

Paul shook his head no. Lily did, too. Ben dropped his head and shook it, and April looked mad but didn't say anything. It was David who voiced his opinion.

"But Daniel's my best friend, Mommy, and so is Raven. Do we have to go?" His little blue eyes implored her. David looked like he was going to cry.

"This isn't our home, David. We don't belong here. Our place for now is at the B&B. If we get tired of being there, we'll go someplace else."

"But I don't want to be someplace else, Mommy, I want to be with Daniel!" He was adamant about what he wanted.

She softened her voice, saying, "I know, David," me too, "but Daniel has to get back to his life and so do we."

"Can't Daniel's life and our life be the same? Can't we live here, Mommy so we don't have to move anymore?"

"No, baby, we can't live here." She knew her voice was sad. She also knew there was no way for her youngest child to understand. "Now, if no one needs anything from the B&B, I won't stop. We will wash our things from last night and hang them out to dry this morning. We can wear them tonight and wash tonight what we have on today." She looked all of her children over and saw them nod their heads. "Alright, Daniel and I will be back soon. I love you all."

"I love you, Mom, all of her children said, finding their way back to their work.

Elizabeth proceeded to the garage and soon the car was moving down the road. She turned to the kids. "So what is everybody doing today?"

"David and I are going to play when I get home," Raven said, smiling. "I like David."

"That sounds like fun." She looked over to Olivia. "What about you?"

"Lily, April, and I are going to play dress-up. I have a lot of things in my closet. Lily is going to be the queen and April and I are going to be princesses. Raven is going to be a princess, too." She nudged her younger sister, who smiled at Elizabeth.

"Sounds like after school you are all going to have fun." She saw the school now. "Did your," she paused clearing her throat, "did he ever pray for you when he dropped you off at school?" She saw them nod their heads. "Then I would like too as well, if that's okay."

She looked to Daniel. He was looking at the road, and he nodded his head.

"Alright." She closed her eyes and bowed her head. "Thank you, Father, for these children and this school…" She continued the prayer and finished with, "Amen."

She watched the kids as they opened their doors and ran out. "See you after school." She heard the car doors close and looked to Daniel.

Chapter Twenty-Nine

Daniel did a U-turn but he wasn't heading to his home or the B&B. He was taking Lizzy somewhere else. Somewhere he hadn't been in a while.

The door to the building opened and Elizabeth heard a bell as the door shut. The front windows of the space had pictures of different places in them. She wondered what they were doing at a travel agency.

She saw Daniel walk up to the counter and heard Daniel speaking softly. He looked angry, resolute.

He placed his hand on her back as they were shown into a room and she saw pictures of different places all over the room. She sat and so did Daniel.

The older gentlemen at the computer turned and smiled. "Daniel Templeman," he leaned over the desk and shook Daniel's hand. He smiled at Elizabeth. "And who, may I ask, is this?"

"Lizzy Seraphim." His voice was short, clipped. "Do you still have that packet of information?"

"Yes." The man went to the cabinet and pulled out a folder. He brought it to the desk and sat it down. "Everything is still in there, Mr. Templeman. Are you planning on doing it?" He looked to the woman and then to Daniel. He saw his client looking at Elizabeth. "Perhaps you two would care to discuss this?" He stood. "Just open the door when you two are finished." He shut the door behind him as he walked out of the room.

Daniel handed the packet to Elizabeth. "Open it."

Elizabeth looked at the packet in her hands. It had no marking on it. "What's inside of it?"

"Open it and see." He looked at the packet and then to her.

Elizabeth carefully opened the packet. Inside, neat and orderly, were passports, birth certificates, and everything else the Templeman family needed to leave the country. Also in the folder was a smaller folder about a different country.

"Scotland?"

"I'm not from England, Lizzy."

"I know that, Daniel. I can hear it when you speak sometimes. You have gotten very good at affecting the English accent, but I know you are not English." She looked confused.

"I had my agent get all of this together and keep it updated so that one day I could take my family back to my country."

He stood now and moved around. "This was Gen's place, not mine." His heavy Scottish brogue came through his words. Elizabeth's mind was hearing his words in clear English.

"I only wanted to be in England because this is where Genessa wanted to be." He looked around. "She's not here anymore, Lizzy, and neither is my dad." He looked sad.

"I am going to send his body back home. The children and I will follow. We aren't coming back. I am going to have the children pack some things to take with them, but when we leave, that house won't be ours anymore."

He rifled through the folder and found a picture, handing it to her. "This is the house I have in Scotland. It has ten bedrooms in it, Lizzy. Ten."

"Sounds like you and the children will be well prepared for company then, Daniel." She went to hand him the picture back.

He took it from her hand and sat it on the desk. He picked her up out of the chair and brought her to himself.

"That is a room for everyone, with an extra one." He picked up the picture and looked at it. "I went with my dad and picked out the house two years ago, Lizzy." He looked at her. "It was supposed to be an anniversary gift to Gen." He frowned. "I never got a chance to give it to her."

He chuckled as he looked at the picture. "Dad actually picked out the house. He said I had to prepare for rain. In case Gen and I had more children, I supposed. I know now why I had to have that house, Lizzy." He looked at her. "It was for you, me, and all the children."

Ten rooms. All together with her family and Daniel's family, there were ten people. She gasped. But how did that leave one room empty?

"I can't live with you, Daniel. I can't do it." She shook her head, stepping back toward the door.

He stepped toward his Lizzy and took her hands. He looked down into her blue eyes. "I want to say 'as you wish' in the morning to you, Lizzy. I want to say 'as you wish'" in the afternoon. And when I lie down at night, I want to say 'as you wish to you as we pray and fall asleep together."

He looked deeper into her eyes, bringing his face close to hers. “I wanted to do this better. I wanted it to be traditional and make it look spontaneous. Now it’s all wrong!”

She shook her head, trying to pull her hands from his. “Then don’t do it. If it’s the wrong time, don’t do it, Daniel.”

“It’s the right time, Lizzy. Now is the right time. But I wanted it to be better, for you. I wanted to have a ring and be down on one knee.”

Elizabeth shook her head frantically now. She could hear her heart pounding in her ears.

“It doesn’t feel like the right time for me, Daniel.”

“Marry me, Lizzy.” He saw her shake her head again. “Marry me and make me the happiest man alive.” He put his forehead against hers and closed his eyes. “You said you would kiss me, Lizzy. Do it now. It would be perfect.”

She heard her pulse racing in her ears. She wanted to say yes. She even opened her mouth to say it. “No, Daniel, I can’t.”

She was probably the first woman in the history of forever to tell the man who she admired from afar for so long, who professed to love her, and asked her to marry him, “no.” She saw his eyes fall and he stepped back from her, closing himself off again. She wanted to cry out at the injustice of it.

He turned and stomped around the small space. He was on the other side of the room from her.

“And I know why, don’t I?! Because I don’t have God in my life. Because I haven’t asked Him into my heart! That's why, it isn't Lizzy?" He stalked up to her and saw her draw herself up.

She nodded her head. "I can't, Daniel."

"You could. God would let you marry me, Lizzy." He took her shoulders. He nodded his head. "Oh, yes, He would let you marry me. You could teach me to love Him by loving you. I could learn," he took her hand and placed it over his heart, "to love Him by loving you. I would do that for you, Lizzy."

His heart was beating wildly in his chest. She could feel it.

"Then you would be doing it for the wrong reason, Daniel."

"Why?!" He exploded at her and saw her jump. "Why is loving Him for you the wrong reason, Lizzy?"

"Because you should love God for who He is and not who someone else is, Daniel. People followed Jesus," she stepped toward him but saw him step back, "but they didn't love Him because He was God. They loved Him because of His kindness and love He displayed. They loved Him because they knew He cared about them. They loved Him because somehow they knew who He was but that wasn't important to them. They knew somehow that He was special, that He would die for them. He would keep them safe."

She looked up at him. "You should love Him because you want to. Because you can't breathe without Him in your life. Because facing the day without Him is incomprehensible. Because He, even above me, above your children, is what you need."

He looked down at her. He had just lost his father. He knew that losing his children would be beyond hard. "How can I learn to love someone above my children, above you? How do I learn to lean on Him to protect me and to not want to go any day without Him?"

Daniel's eyes were piercing her now. She made her way over to the chair she had been seated in.

"My mother went first, I leaned on David and God and they both got me through her death. My father was next, such a short time from my mother. Again I leaned on God and David.

Next was my brother. He went just a few weeks after my father. Again, God and David."

She felt a tear slide down her cheek. She was silent, trying not to cry harder. She needed to make Daniel understand.

"When David," she sobbed, "I had just God. No… no one else." She shook her head. "I have learned to lean on Him more and more." She stood straight up and she saw him flinch. She walked up to him. "He became everything, EVERTYHING to me. He became my children's father, my friend, my confidant, my father and my mother and my brother and my husband."

"He took everything from you but your children so you could learn that He is everything to you? That doesn't sound like the God I would want to know."

"No. He didn't take anything from me, Daniel, he gave me everything. Yes, really bad things happened in my life but He was there to see me through the things that happened."

She took his hand. "I believe...." she looked down to their intertwined fingers, "that everything happens for a reason. That the death of those I love happened for a purpose. Railing at God won't change it. Turning my back on Him won't bring them back. But leaning on Him got me through those times, Daniel."

She squinted her eyes at him. "I firmly believe if David hadn't known God and introduced me to Him, I would be a completely different person today, Daniel. One that Danny Tensley or Daniel Templeman wouldn't want to be around." She thought for a moment. "Is that what you want? Do you want me to sacrifice who I am to marry you and start a life with you only to have you "try God" and find out you don't like Him? That this 'relationship not religion' stuff isn't for you, so you go on your merry way doing whatever you want to fit in with your peers?"

She stepped back from him. "Because I can't do it. I won't do it. No matter how much I want to say yes to you, no matter how much I want to marry you, to be your wife, because," she took a deep breath, "because I do love you, I won't be that person." She dropped her eyes, a tear slipping down her cheek, and hunched her shoulders.

Daniel walked up to her and held her in his arms. She was right. She was always right. He shouldn't love God because she did, he should do it for him. He didn't want her to marry him because they wanted to. He wanted her to marry him after he found God, when he knew that God was who he wanted. But what was he supposed to do with the woman in his arms? The woman who said she loved him too. Where were they supposed to go from here?

Elizabeth looked up to Daniel. "I think you should do it, Daniel. If your house is not where you want to be, not because Gen was there or your father lived there, but because you want to go home, you should go home. Do it and don't look back."

She smiled at him. "Start a new life with your children. Your career will still be your career. People will still love Danny Tensley because he will charm and give them what they want from him."

She touched his face. "But if Daniel Templeman wants to take his children back to his heritage, do it."

He felt tears well in his eyes and half smiled. He pulled her to him and held her tightly. "I love you, Elizabeth Seraphim. Come with me. Me and my children. Come with us and be with us when we go. I need you."

He held his breath. She was the air that he breathed, his reason for waking. But somehow, some way, he knew that wasn't enough.

"I don't know, Daniel." She stepped back from his arms. "When you and the children leave, I don't know if I will go with you. I'll probably pull out the map in my bag and have David pick where we go next. We have to go where the Lord wants us to." She sat down in the chair, looking at her hands. The room was quiet and somewhere Elizabeth heard a clock ticking.

Daniel watched the woman sitting in the chair. He knew he loved her and he knew why they couldn't be together. In his heart he felt he wanted—needed—to ask for her to help him to God but he didn't. Instead he went to the door and opened it. He went back to the chair and sat down.

As the agent came into the room, Daniel took Lizzy's hand. He loved her convictions, her entire being—mind and soul. He wanted to touch her and if holding her hand was the only thing he could touch, he would do it.

The agent looked at the couple in front of him. He watched them for a moment. Something intense had happened while he was out of the room; he could feel it. The couple in front of him looked good together. He noticed a slight shift in the two of them as they moved closer together. He picked up the papers from the folder on his desk, now scattered, and organized them.

"So, Mr. Templeman, what would you like me to do with these?" He put them back in the folder neatly.

"Get them ready, Hunter." He squeezed Lizzy's hand. "My dad died and I will be shipping his body home. The children and I will follow."

Hunter looked to Elizabeth and then back to Daniel. "Are there any more papers that you would like to include?"

Daniel shook his head and frowned. "No."

Hunter saw a look of sadness cross the Lizzy's face. "Alright. Just let me know when you would like to have these ready and you can pick them up. Will there be anything else?"

Daniel shook his head and stood, tugging Lizzy up with him. "No," he reached over and shook the other man's hand. "Thank you."

The entire car ride back to his house was silent. He had to hold Lizzy's hand, so their hands rested between them. He knew there was a countdown now. A countdown to losing the one thing in his life that he needed.

He opened her car door and he escorted her into the house. He saw her sit at the big table with Davey and talk quietly with him. She also answered a few questions from the other children.

He made his way upstairs and got ready for the luncheon. He looked forward to it now. He could be Danny Tensley for a while. Not a care in the world, happy and carefree. He could play the part, but he knew that his heart would be at this house, sitting at his kitchen table with five more wonderful children he had come to care for.

Daniel shut his door, fell to his knees, and closed his eyes. He felt tears slide down his face. "I love her. I want her in my life." He knew he should have started with "Dear Heavenly Father," but he couldn't. He had to tell God how he felt and didn't feel the need to pretty it up with words. "Can't we be together? I just want her with me and my children." He stopped.

He probably shouldn't tell the Creator of the universe what he wanted but should ask what God wanted for him. "Help me today, Lord, do what you want me to do. Guide me and protect me. Thank you for what you have given me," he thought of Lizzy and her children, "and for…" he swallowed, this was hard, "for what you have taken away. I know you will help me. Amen."

He stood, feeling better now. He made his way down the stairs, his heart a little lighter. It was a few minutes until nine.

Marching into the kitchen, he walked straight to Lizzy. He saw all of the children look at him. He tugged her up out of her seat and over to the back door.

Standing at it, he took her hands in one of his and brought himself to her. He smiled down at her. He saw her long, blonde hair catch the light of the sun and shine. Her eyes shone, too, with the love he now knew was there for him. He felt her move closer to him. He ran his hand down her hair and smiled at her.

"I have to leave in a few minutes, but I wanted to let you know I talked with God. I told Him I wanted you and your children. I asked Him if I could have you. I listened but didn't hear anything. I just want you to know that I think I am about ready, Lizzy."

He noticed her gasp. "At the travel agency, I just knew that I wanted God to rule my life. But I can't make that decision yet. I'm almost ready. Wait for me?" He knew his voice sounded hopeful, but he knew they loved one another now.

Elizabeth looked to Daniel. "Yes, Daniel. I will wait for you." She smiled. "I'm glad you talked with God. I know He heard you and He loves you."

She began to hear her heart pounding. She knew she wanted to kiss him but that now was not the right time. It seemed it was always the wrong time.

"I need to check if the car is here. Will you be here when I get back from this event?" He looked to the children. He didn't want this to be the last time he saw them, especially Davey. He loved that little boy.

Elizabeth pulled him to her. "We'll be here when you come back. I promise." She pushed him away from her and laughed.

Taking his hand, she led him toward the front door and looked out the window. "Looks like your car is here, Mr. Templeman." She turned back to him. Opening the door beside her, she winked at him. "Time to give the world what they want."

"Not the whole world, Lizzy. Not you and the kids. For you, I am yours, I am Daniel." He stepped up to her and took her hands. "I will always be yours." He bent down and kissed her cheek, turning toward the door. "I will be back after the luncheon."

He turned and shut the door. The taste on his lips was fresh berries. He smiled. He wanted the taste of her skin on his lips all day.

He looked out to the car. The sight was a most welcome one to his eyes. "Roger!"

Roger stood at the car and watched as Daniel walked toward him. There was a spring in his step and he positively glowed. He felt Daniel hug him tightly.

Daniel stepped back from Roger. This man was his driver but he was also his friend. "I'm sorry, Roger, for what I said to you. I was insensitive and wrong. You were so right. I am in love with Lizzy."

He sighed as he sat in the car. Roger started it now and they moved down the road. "I am trying to hold on to her, but I can't, not without God in my life. I know that. I know we can't be together without Him being more important than either one of us, but I can't do it yet."

He shook himself. He knew something was holding him back but he didn't know what it was. "We have read the Bible and prayed." He laughed. "I even found a Bible app and installed it on my phone. I've been reading it, too." He blushed and looked at the man. "We have even prayed together and she taught me how to talk with God." He seemed proud of himself.

He sighed. "I was wrong to tell you not to tell me how I should love her. And I always want you to drive me. I have requested that you be my personal driver from now on to functions I have to attend. Can you forgive me, Roger?"

"Back in Scotland I am a Laird. Have my own place, but I stay because Danny Tensley needs someone to handle his arrogant self. And because Daniel needs a friend. I am glad God has placed this woman Lizzy in your life. I thank Him she is teaching you about the Lord. I prayed that He would find someone to help you with your soul, too, and help you find your way to Him. It sounds like you have that in your Lizzy."

Roger was happy for Daniel. He had noticed something different in the other man as soon as he walked out the front door.

"I'm moving to Scotland, Roger. My father," he paused, wishing and then imagining Lizzy was holding his hand and smiled, "died yesterday," he looked to Roger. "The kids still went to school and I still have work. I know he is with the Lord and I have a peace about that. So with God and Lizzy, I can move through all of this." He smiled wider now, remembering the look of her hair in the sunlight, her smile.

"I swear you are positively glowing, Daniel." He glanced at his client.

Roger signaled and pulled into a deserted lot. He didn't know what he was doing, only that he needed to do this. He got out of the car and saw Daniel step out.

"This isn't the luncheon, Roger."

"I wasn't always a man of God." He had seen the bracelet on Daniel's wrist. He held it up now. "I grew up in another faith. I know what these letters mean."

"You saw that?" He looked at the ABC bracelet. He thought he had pushed it up far enough to hide it. The bracelet must have slipped.

"A is for Admit." He looked to Daniel. "Be is for Believe. C is for Confess. Has someone told you what that means?"

"Yes." He remembered what the paramedic said to him.

"Then this will make my job easier." He looked into Daniel's eyes. "Do you admit that Jesus is God's Son?"

"Yes." Daniel felt tears well in his eyes.

"Do you believe that He is the Son of God?"

Daniel felt the tears fall and humility settled into his heart. His voice broke and tears continued to fall from his face. "Yes."

"Do you confess, now, your faith in Jesus as your Savior and Lord, Daniel?" He looked deeply into the crying man's eyes. "Don't lie. God knows. He sees what's in your heart."

Daniel felt Roger staring at him. He felt his knees give and more tears fall from his eyes.

He pulled his arms around his chest and rocked himself.

"Yes! Yes! I believe, Roger. Yes!"

"Then welcome to the family, Daniel." Roger got down on his knees and hugged the other man. He knew that what Daniel had said was real and true. "I got a new brother." He pushed the other man back from him. "Welcome to the family of God, brother." He cried with Daniel and hugged him.

Pulling back now, he helped Daniel to his feet and patted his shoulders. They walked back over to the car, got into it, and continued on their way.

Daniel pulled out his phone to text Lizzy. He felt free! His soul felt loved and a great peace about everything: his wife's death, the loss of his mother and father—all of it felt lifted from him. He needed to tell Lizzy.

Opening the text window, he looked up. Roger had a big grin on his face. He looked so happy.

Daniel looked down at his phone again. It had timed out. He turned it back on.

"Roger, I…" His eyes swung forward and widened.

At that point things seemed to move in slow motion but happen very quickly. He saw a lorry directly in front of their car. Both were moving at a good clip and he knew they were going to collide. He braced himself as he prayed, "Protect us, Lord." He closed his eyes.

Chapter Thirty

Elizabeth was sitting at the table when the house phone rang. She debated whether or not she should answer it. She decided not to. Instead she heard the answering machine click.

"Elizabeth Seraphim, this is Doctor Reynolds from Mercy Hospital. I am going to give you my personal number at the end of this message. Call me as soon as you get this. It's about Daniel, Lizzy. There's been an accident."

Elizabeth went to the phone and picked it up. The message clicked as she did. She replayed the message and wrote down Doctor Reynolds' number. She dialed it and waited as it rang.

"Hello."

"Doctor Reynolds, it's Elizabeth Seraphim. Daniel? What happened to Daniel?" She was shaking. All of her children walked over to her and hugged her.

"Is there any way you can come to Mercy right now, Elizabeth?"

"Yes." She picked up the keys Daniel had given her this morning.

"Come when you can, Lizzy."

"I'm on my way, Doctor Reynolds." She hung up the phone. "It's Daniel. He's been in an accident. We need to pray."

She gathered her children and fell to the floor. "Dear Heavenly Father, I come to you in Jesus' name. Please be with Daniel," she remembered she saw a man outside the car, "and his driver. Keep them safe in Your hands. And if You want to take him home with his father," a tear slipped down her cheek, "if You do, please help us with that. We love You and thank You. Amen."

She looked up to her children. "I have to go to Mercy Hospital. The same hospital Davey was in."

She stood and strode to her bag. She handed Paul her mobile from the States. "I will text you when I know something. Call me only if there is an emergency." She looked to the garage door.

"I will be back as soon as I can."

She ran for the door and went to John's car. She slid inside it and started the drive to the hospital. Driving on the opposite side of the road seemed strange, but she managed.

She prayed the entire way there and the trip seemed to take forever. She knew it was because she was in a hurry and because she was so stressed. She didn't want God to take Daniel from her. She didn't want to lose anyone else she loved.

It wasn't fair! She banged on the steering wheel. She didn't want to lose Daniel. He was close, so close to accepting Jesus. "Don't take him yet, please. Not yet."

She slid into the parking space of the A&E section and slammed the door behind her. The chirping sound of the door lock followed as she ran through the doors.

The nurse at the station blinked at her a couple of times as she approached her.

"Daniel! Daniel Templeman! I need to see him!"

She started bouncing on her heels, impatiently waiting for the nurse to answer.

"Name?" She looked bored as she stared at a computer screen.

"Daniel Templeman!" Didn't she just tell her that?!

"Your name, ma'am." Her voice was dry and her reply rote. She had done this before.

Elizabeth moved up to her. "I want to see Daniel Templeman." She glared at the woman as the woman's eyes got bigger. "You can either tell me where he is or I can find him myself."

"I can't give you any information on a patient unless you are a family member." This was a rote answer, too.

Elizabeth put her hands on the desk. The nurse just sat, staring at Elizabeth.

"Then get me Doctor Reynolds." Elizabeth opened her mouth and drew in a deep breath.

"DOCTOR REYNOLDS! DOCTOR REYNOLDS! DOCTOR REYNOLDS!"

The nurse behind the desk came around it now and put her hands on Elizabeth. Elizabeth tried to shake the nurse's hands off of her.

"Stop! I just want to see Daniel…"

"Nurse Drew? What are you doing to Elizabeth? Let go of Elizabeth this instant!"

Doctor Reynolds had heard Elizabeth Seraphim yelling his name and had run toward her voice.

The nurse seemed to realize what she was doing and let go of Elizabeth. "She was screaming like a banshee. I had to restrain her."

"We'll talk later, Nurse Drew." He took Lizzy's hand and began to lead her away from the woman.

"But she isn't relation to the patient, Doctor. She can't go back there."

Doctor Reynolds turned to Nurse Drew. He heard her gasp. "Elizabeth Seraphim can go anywhere in this hospital she chooses, Nurse Drew. Do you understand that?"

Nurse Drew nodded her head. "But rules…"

"Hang the rules. Elizabeth is coming with me." He pulled Elizabeth in front of him and began leading her.

She felt tears fall from her face. "Where is Daniel? I have to see Daniel, please." She stopped as Doctor Reynolds did.

"Elizabeth, look at me."

They were standing in front of a shut door. She felt him take her shoulders.

She said, "Daniel..."

"Elizabeth." He saw her eyes swing toward him. "Focus on me, Elizabeth." He waited until she did. "Elizabeth, Daniel has been in an accident." He looked toward the room and then back to her. "He…"

"Is he in that room?" She looked toward the door and then back to Doctor Reynolds.

"Yes, Elizabeth, but…" He felt her tear out of his arms and open the door. He heard her gasp.

Elizabeth ran into the room and straight into Daniel's arms. He had been sitting up on the bed, waiting to be released. Doctor Reynolds didn't want him driving home so Daniel had given him his home number.

He heard the door open and Lizzy stood there for a moment. He saw shock register on her face as she looked at him and then she knocked him over on the bed as she hugged him tightly.

He could feel her body trembling. His arms came around her and he held onto her. She was half lying on him now, crying loudly. He could feel her relief as she held him.

She stopped crying after a few moments and shifted a little, still lying on part of him.

"Daniel." She looked him over. He didn't seem to have a cut or a bruise on him.

"I'm alright, Lizzy. I'm fine." He held her around the waist now.

"Doctor Reynolds said you were in an accident. What happened?!" She knew she was panicking but couldn't seem to calm herself down.

"Roger and I were talking on the way to the luncheon. I looked up and, honestly, Lizzy, right in front of my car was a lorry. I mean right in front of it." His hug got tighter. "It was right in front of the windshield of the car."

She clutched at him. "Daniel, what happened?"

"I swear, on the grill of that lorry, Lizzy, was Jesus. I could see Him. He had on these long flowing white robes and His hair was blowing. He held the lorry back from hitting the car. Roger didn't even have time to stop the car, it was so close to us. Somehow, the car and lorry stopped just a few feet from each other. I saw the skid marks, Lizzy. The lorry stopped in five feet. The car in just a few inches."

"What?!" Lizzy's mind couldn't comprehend it. "But that's impossible, Daniel." Not that she didn't believe him, but if what he said was true, it would be a miracle.

He pulled out his phone and handed it to her. "Look at the pictures I took, Lizzy."

She took it from him and saw the first picture. The lorry was right in front of the car. Neither one of them were touching but they were very close. She swiped the screen and saw the next few photos. When they ended, she handed him back the phone. "That was a miracle, Daniel."

"No, Lizzy, it was Jesus." He put her in his lap now. She turned to face him. "Roger and I were talking on the way to the luncheon. I told him what all had happened. He pulled off into the parking lot and prayed with me, Lizzy." He looked down into her eyes. "I did it. I just knew it was time." He felt the joy fill his heart as he looked at her. "It was time I came home. Roger prayed with me, Lizzy." He brought her to him and cried. "I found God! He was right there waiting for me the whole time. I didn't know it, but He waited and I found him." He pulled back, looking at the shock on her face for the second time today. I have a new brother, lots of them, and sisters, too."

Elizabeth held her breath. Daniel had accepted the Lord. He was exactly where she needed him to be so they could be together.

"Lizzy?" He saw her eyes widen and could literally feel the gears in her mind turning. "Elizabeth?" He looked into her eyes, smiling.

"I want to kiss you now, Daniel. It's the right time." She didn't move despite the fact that she was telling herself to. "I want to give you all of me now. I want to do that, my love."

She held her breath. Would he still want her now that he had just begun his journey with the Lord?

"Do you remember what I told you, Lizzy?" He moved closer to her as she moved closer to him. He saw her shake her head. "I said I would wait for you. I would wait for you to need to kiss me. Then I would kiss you like you need to be kissed."

He looked down at her lips. He already knew what they tasted like. He felt his mouth water. Her pupils were dilated again. "Know this, Elizabeth Seraphim," he noticed her breathing quicken, "when you kiss me, you should be ready. I am going to kiss you until I know every corner, every recess of that mouth. Because I intend to do that as often as I can for the rest of my life." He tore his eyes from her lips. "When you kiss me, it will be for forever."

Elizabeth couldn't tear her eyes from his mouth and when she did it was his warm brown eyes that had her heart racing. She nodded her head. She took his hand in hers and held it between them.

"With God, Daniel, it will be."

She leaned toward him and just before their lips met, he pulled back. She looked into his eyes.

"Say it now, Lizzy, before you kiss me. Say it, so when I taste the fresh-picked berries that are your lips, I'll know it."

Elizabeth looked at him. "I'll say it, Daniel. I don't know what you want me to say, but I will." She looked from his eyes to his lips again. "I'll say anything you want me to."

He clutched her hand. “Say you’ll marry me. Say you’ll be my wife.”

Elizabeth felt her toes curling in her shoes. Every nerve in her body was screaming at her to kiss him.

“Yes.” She felt him breathe a sigh of relief. Peppermint. He smelled like peppermint, cool and sweet. “I’ll marry you, Daniel Templeman.” She moved her mouth toward him again.

“What God has joined together, let no man put asunder.” Daniel remembered that verse as he watched her lips come closer to his.

“Kiss me, Daniel.” She drew in a deep breath.

“As you wish, Lizzy,” he said as his lips met Elizabeth Seraphim’s.

He pulled her closer to him. Neither of them heard the door opening and closing. Neither of them saw Doctor Reynolds quietly witnessing their first kiss as a couple. He bowed his head and thanked God for Daniel Templeman and Elizabeth Seraphim. He waited quietly and patiently. And when they pulled back from one another he cleared his throat and laughed as the couple on the bed jumped.

He saw Elizabeth move off it and stand on the floor by Daniel. Daniel slipped an arm around Lizzy’s waist and looked at her with love in his eyes.

“Before you both leave I need to give you my address.” He saw them turn their heads toward him questioningly. Daniel looked so proud to be holding Elizabeth in his arms. Elizabeth blushed. “I expect a wedding invitation." He looked to Elizabeth as her eyes met his. He walked up to her.

"I know that your husband would be proud of this man. If you would like to have someone walk you down the aisle to begin your new life," he nodded over to Daniel, "I would be proud to be the one to do it."

Elizabeth let go of Daniel and hugged him. "Thank you, Doctor Reynolds."

"Call me Gabriel," Doctor Reynolds said, laughing. "My wife does."

Chapter Thirty-One

Elizabeth Templeman looked up from the long table in her and Daniel's home in Scotland. She loved this place and the table at which her children sat was full. John would have loved to sit at the table and watch over the children as they lived their lives.

The Templeman household had packed and the few things the Seraphim family had were moved alongside them. Daniel and Elizabeth had gone to the travel agency and added more papers to Daniel's folder. Then both the Templeman family and the Seraphim family had made their way to Scotland.

John's funeral had been one of rejoicing! The congregation had come together and celebrated John Templeman's life and legacy. Daniel was the first to speak in remembrance of his father. He had asked Lizzy and her family to sit with his as they were now engaged and soon they would be one family legally, not just in their hearts. Deacon Wayne made the trip and gave an excellent oration on his pastor's life and what he meant to him. Those who wanted spoke of John as well.

Daniel and Lizzy's wedding had been a small one. They had married at the church John had pastored before they left Scotland. Gabriel walked Elizabeth down the aisle and gave her to Daniel. A small party afterward completed the affair and Gabriel introduced Mr. and Mrs. Daniel Templeman to the crowd.

Once the media had caught wind of Danny Tensley and Elizabeth Seraphim's engagement, congratulations had been received for them from all over the world. Gifts were given to them and the house filled with beautiful things. They kept the ones they could use and the rest of the items were donated to various organizations that would distribute the items to those who needed them. The entire family sat down to write thank-you cards to everyone who gave them something.

Elizabeth heard the front door shut. The children had all just gotten settled with their schoolwork and Elizabeth had sat down to pray with them before they started.

Looking to the door, she saw her husband and another man standing in the doorway. The man beside her husband smiled at her. But it was her husband who drew her gaze. The combination of his handsome smile and unruly hair was devastating.

She stood and carefully made her way to them. She was almost eight months pregnant now. Her first year of marriage to Daniel was a little bumpy. Being the wife of Danny Tensley was rougher than she imagined, but the nursery next door to their room was stocked with furniture and items all given to them by his fans and companies vying for Danny's name and face. She didn't mind as long as she had him beside her.

Daniel stood now, watching his wife waddle over to him. She was still beautiful, but the fact that she was carrying his child made her glow. Her beauty, he knew, did not come from what she looked like but what he knew was in her heart.

"Lizzy, I would like you to meet Roger Blain." He turned to Roger. "Roger, this is my wife, Lizzy Templeman."

He had wanted them to meet for so long and now they did.

Elizabeth walked over to Roger. He was a big man, but she already liked him.

"Thank you for leading my husband to the Lord, Roger."

"Thank you for showing him the Lord, Mrs. Templeman." He knew she was an answer to a prayer. He liked the woman in front of him.

"Do you have time for a cup before you two leave?" She gestured toward the stove.

Roger looked at his watch. "No, ma'am, I'm sorry, but Mr. Tensley has to be at his first shoot by 10 a.m."

"Elizabeth, Roger. My name is Elizabeth." She winked at her husband. "But my husband calls me, Lizzy." She laid her hand on his arm. "Thank you for driving my husband. I know he treasures your friendship."

Roger looked with admiration to Daniel. "He's my brother in Christ, Elizabeth. I love him like such." He gestured toward her stomach. "Your wee bairn, when is it due?"

"A couple more months." She smiled at him and then at Daniel. "Which reminds me, husband." She walked up to him. "If the famous Mr. Tensley can be unreachable about three-fifteen this afternoon, Daniel will get a chance to make a visit with his wife to see Gabriel this afternoon."

Daniel pulled Lizzy into his arms. He smiled a charming smile at her. "Daniel is always reachable, Mrs. Templeman." He eyed her stomach and then looked into her blue eyes. "That is how our child got where he is. Have you talked with Gabriel this morning?"

"Yes, he says to be prepared for a surprise today. He says he was looking at the sonogram pictures and saw something." Daniel frowned. She smiled knowingly at him. "Oh, it's good. Very good. He already told me. He is also waiting on an answer about being a Godfather."

"What did he say, Lizzy?" He smiled down at her.

"Nope. Can't tell you everything, Daniel. It would ruin the surprise." She shook her head, bringing her lower lip under her top teeth as he pouted.

"Roger has asked about being our child's Godfather."

She put her arms around his neck. "I think Roger would make a wonderful Godfather."

She looked to the man and saw him blush.

"What about Gabriel?"

Elizabeth looked to Daniel, smiling. "Oh, he can be a Godfather, too."

"Do you mean our son is going to have two Godfathers?"

Elizabeth shook her head. She still watched him, waiting for him to understand what she was saying. She saw the realization slowly dawn on his face.

"Two." He looked to Roger and then to her stomach. He looked to her now. "We're going to have twins?" He was going to be a father to two more children. He saw Lizzy nod her head and picked her up carefully. "I'm so happy!"

"So am I, husband." She looked to the clock. It was 9 a.m. "Your shoot is in an hour." She let go of him and took his hand. Next she took Roger's hand. "Before you two leave, can I pray for your day?" She saw Roger take her husband's hand. She bowed her head and heard Daniel begin the prayer.

"Dear Heavenly Father, we love you and praise Your holy name…" When he finished the prayer he looked to his wife. She had stepped up to him and tilted her head as she looked at him.

"Will you kiss me before you start your day, husband?"

He put his arms around her waist and drew her to him. Looking into her eyes, he brought his face closer to her.

"As you wish."

THE END

Made in the USA
Las Vegas, NV
03 July 2021